Addicted to Hate

"Silence can be so loud!"

Addicted to Hate

- A Novel -

Lucia Mann

Grassroots Publishing Group

GRASSROOTS PUBLISHING GROUP™
3184 Bernie Dr.
Oceanside, CA 92056

10 9 8 7 6 5 4 3 2
First Edition 2018

Printed in the United States of America

ISBN: 978-0-9975677-2-4
Library of Congress Control Number: 2018954200

Cover & book design by CenterPointe Media
www.CenterPointeMedia.com

Dedication

THESE PAGES ARE DEDICATED TO VICTIMS OF HATE CRIMES.
MAY WE MEET OUR BAD SEEDS IN HEAVEN AND
REPAIR THEM BEFORE THEY, EVER AGAIN,
CAN RECYCLE THEIR VICIOUSNESS.

ACKNOWLEDGMENTS

This is a fictional retelling inspired by actual events. It reflects a recollection over time, a haunting glimpse into hateful, resentful human hearts running like nonstop trains.

To protect certain victims of abuse from being victimized again, names and characteristics have been masked; some events have been compressed, and certain dialogue has been recreated so that the "he" or "she" is not identifiable.

My gratitude to my friend, supporter, editor, and publisher, Nesta Aharoni, and to the teenager who sent me the text, "I wish you were my *mother!*"

Thank you to Matthew and Joan Greenblatt of CenterPointe-Media for bringing life to the front and back covers and interior pages.

Thank you to my many friends and colleagues who had no clue until now that I was harboring and hiding deep, raw agony. They arrived on my doorstep with tender love, warm hugs, and cold beer!

To my loving husband, thank you from the bottom of my heart for being there for me constantly and consistently for twenty-five years, regardless …

To SW, you have proved to be the greatest friend ever.

Finally, I thank myself for turning regressive shame into mounting courage, something I could not have contemplated if it were not for the spiritual wisdom of a shaman on the island of Haida Gwaii, British Columbia. This ninety-year-old spiritual man opened my eyes to the link between my plane of existence and the higher plane. His ancient wisdom resonated with me and gave me my wake-up call, my rebirth. *Shaman Nana'eek-chechowa's* eye-opening foretelling can be found at the end of this book.

TABLE OF CONTENTS

FOREWORD

Some facts in this story are derived from a unique memory system (contextual information system) in my brain called "episodic memory." A conclusive DNA analysis indicates that my storage and retention system is genetic. Episodic memory means I can relive sights, sounds, aromas, and their accompanying feelings (phenomenology); in other words, I can retrieve past experiences effortlessly. I can travel back in time mentally and recapture specific events, times, and places vividly ... who, what, when, where.

Have I been blessed or cursed?

Both!

LUCIA MANN

Note to the Reader

For those who are not familiar with my work or my background and experience with human ownership—slavery—the four books in my *African Freedom Series* hold the answers to your questions and fill in the gaps in this, my latest writing.

Rented Silence
The Sicilian Veil of Shame
Africa's Unfinished Symphony
A Veil of Blood Hangs over Africa

> **Please note** that the first page of each chapter contains a relevant quote. All quotes without written attribution were written and contributed by the author, Lucia Mann. This was done to avoid repetition throughout the text.

PROLOGUE

"So vile a sin is a hate-filled heart."

W hat are the chances a human being can survive being the target of umpteen hate crimes and other atrocities without suffering a mental breakdown? Is it a million to one?

Madeline Clark is one of those survivors. From her first birthday to her eightieth, she endured unspeakable human and civil rights violations: abandonment at birth, racial discrimination, childhood physical and sexual abuse, physical torture and body mutilation, adult sexual and domestic abuse, wrongful imprisonment, and, finally, the topic of this book, *parent and disabled senior abuse*.

This is her story.

CHAPTER ONE

"To lose a child is to lose a piece of yourself."
—DR. BURTON GREBIN

It's December 1968. Silver, sequin stars wink in a winter sky. They frolic around the pale glow radiating from the moon, which is shrouding the three-story, red-brick medical facility that has treated patients through two world wars. A new featherweight is about to break through the timeworn walls of Croydon General Hospital in Great Britain.

A wafer-thin, scantily-clad teenage girl wearing inappropriate clothing for this bone-chilling season enters through the hospital's automatic door. An unfashionably baggy, yellow-flowered skirt hangs just below her bare knees, and the long sleeves of her flimsy blouse protrude out from under a Mexican poncho that has seen better days, as have her brown, slip-on shoes. Her inappropriate apparel raises eyebrows from the waiting emergency room crowd. Maddie rubs her cold hands over the cranked-up oil heater, then, in a combing gesture, runs her fingers through her midnight-black hair, which hangs limply below her bony shoulders. She looks around, finds a seat, and ignores the sign that reads "REPORT HERE. PLEASE HAVE YOUR NHS CARD READY." Maddie sits down and crosses her legs. The elderly man beside her gives her a nudge. "You have to go to the nurse up there," he points, "or you'll be waiting a long time."

"Thank you," says Maddie. She rises from her chair, sweating profusely and feeling dizzy. She is in intense pain and has trouble breathing. She stands on her wobbly legs and begins to sway toward the reception desk. Suddenly, her vision goes black, as if someone is pressing chloroform to her face, and *thud*, she collapses unconscious on the floor, a pool of blood widening around her body.

"Probably a drug overdose," comes a remark from an elderly man.

"There's a lot of that going on," the orderly returns.

When Maddie opens her dazzling wolf eyes—a rare amber-copper hue—she doesn't remember a thing, not even hitting the waiting room floor. She is lying in a blindingly bright room, which is not helping her reach a comfortable level of consciousness. Through her confusion and a splitting headache, she notices a dark-featured man standing by her side. In almost a murmur, he says, "Hello. I'm Dr. Prajit Barazani. How are you feeling?"

What an oxymoronic question! Look at me!

"What is your name, and how old are you, young lady?"

She babbles unintelligibly for a few seconds before responding. "My name is Madeline Clark, and I turned seventeen today."

"Well, happy birthday, and I'm sorry it won't be as celebratory as you would wish. The tests we performed to diagnose your condition eliminate gastroenteritis, menstrual issues, and endometriosis.

Cut to the chase, Maddie's eyes beseeched him.

"It is an ectopic pregnancy ..."

Maddie's quizzical, focused expression is begging for further explanation.

"You have a fetus, a baby, growing outside the uterus. It is well into six weeks ..."

Maddie's eyelids snap shut. *It's not possible! There must be a mistake!*

"Madeline, do you understand what I'm telling you?" Prajit asks in a subdued voice.

With her upper lashes cemented to her bottom eyelid, Maddie bobs her head confirmatively. "Yes. I know what an *ectopic* pregnancy is."

The sixty-year-old doctor couldn't help but stare at his patient's tightly closed eyes. She was a mystery. How many girls her age knew medical terminology? And when and why had her tubes been tied? What is troubling the seasoned gynecologist most is that the surgery had been botched, undoubtedly, because a fetus is maturing in one of Maddie's mangled fallopian tubes.

Dr. Barazani touches Maddie's arm, and she opens her eyes. "Maybe can you tell me about your tubes being tied ..."

Prajit's question is swept away, like marshmallow clouds in a cosmic twister. Maddie's emotional numbness, confusion, and painful cramping unite to shut down the rational part of her brain. Every nerve in her body seems to be dying. She feels a spinning, spacey sensation, as if her physical form is departing to a sweeter world. She stares blankly at the doctor.

Knocked off mental balance, she curls into a ball and fights to regain a grip on reality. *Breathe. Take deep slow breaths.*

Maddie's fragility is as frantic and exhausted as a hamster tumbling on an exercise wheel. After what feels like forever, her natural common sense prevails. Yes, she is young, but not naïve. She does not want to be treated like an ignorant child. She draws a sharp, obstinate breath and fixes a dogged glare on the doctor. "I want a *second* opinion."

Obviously this girl, speaking with a trace of foreign accent, is mature beyond her years. "I want a second opinion" was delivered with an attitude approaching pushiness. But Maddie's feistiness is short-lived; she will soon be returning to a dark chapter in her life.

Prajit reaches for his patient's right hand and squeezes it firmly. "Maddie, we don't have time to redo all the earlier testing, even though it is your right. Given your age, I don't think you have grasped your situation. You can bleed to death. I must operate immediately." Prajit notes her vacant stare and responds by raising his voice authoritatively. "You *will* die if I don't help you *now!*"

Maddie's spirits dampen, and her body begins to shake. She knuckles under. "Okay. Do what you have to do." *How can he assume with certainty that the diagnosis is 100 percent correct? Is he guessing? Doctors are error prone, like the rest of us imperfect humans.*

Has Maddie's medical practitioner placed her in "a Petri dish" of misdiagnosis? Do doctors ever get it wrong? Absolutely!

Maddie's pain-blurred eyes follow Prajit as he makes his way out of the curtained vestibule. She hears his voice instructing, "Get hold of her husband. He must sign the underage consent form. Meanwhile, prep her for surgery."

Later Prajit will discuss other visible medical issues with Maddie. First, she is a bag-of-bones, so thin that she triggered the nurses' tongues to wag. Maddie is dreadfully underweight, 85 pounds. This might be normal for a younger girl, but not one her age. Also, he notices neck bruises and bad teeth, which appear gray and eroded, probably from a poor diet. A non-medical concern also begs explanation: Why had she come in dressed for a summer's day, exposing herself to the harsh winter elements?

"Do you have your NHS card with you? And can I please have your home phone number so I can contact your husband?"

"I'll have my card shortly," Maddie replied. "It's coming in the mail." Uncomfortable with bending the truth, Maddie avoids making eye contact with the doctor. She hopes her dishonesty does not prompt her cheeks to redden, as it always does when she tells a "white" lie. Lately, though, lying had become her norm. Maybe the frequency of her untruths would restrain her cheeks. A medical insurance form offering free care will never be "coming in the mail" for Maddie. And, if she had filled one out, it would have raised more than official eyebrows. It would have read something like this:

```
LEGAL NAME:  Unknown.
DATE OF BIRTH: Unknown, no birth record.
COUNTRY OF BIRTH: None.
PARENTS' NAMES: Unknown. Applicant is
     an orphan.
DATE OF ENTRY: She's illegal, smuggled
     out of Europe.
STATUS: Married in April of this year,
     but that's not legal either.
```

Maddie *had* begged her thirty-seven-year-old partner, David Blakely, to drive her to the hospital. He had responded with a wintery cold glare and ridicule. "Why should I do that. I'm not the one who's sick! You know where the hospital is. The walk will do you good."

"David, it's freezing cold, and I don't have a winter coat!"

With a mocking, threatening expression, he said, "You're a big girl. The cold won't kill you, but I will if you don't get out of my face!"

Thinking ahead, Maddie asked, "What if they refuse to treat me because I don't have an insurance card?"

With a jutting chin, he grimaced. "Just say the card is coming in the mail, and you'll give them the number as soon as it arrives. If push comes to shove, tell them to send the bloody hospital bill by mail."

"Please, David, come with me," Maddie pleaded, even though she really wanted to say, "You're the best pathological liar I have ever seen. You can get away with it, but I can't. My cheeks will blush to the heavens!"

David's top lip curled up. "No. Now bugger off," he barked. "I'm watching football."

"Can I have some money for a taxi?"

"No! Do I look like the Bank of England?"

Today is Maddie's birthday, December 2, 1968, and it will remain uncelebrated by David's indifference. If Maddie were to arrange her misfortunes in chronological order, her ill-fated meeting with this narcissist would be at the top the list.

An unhappy birthday girl walks from the apartment she shares with David and his mother, Jean, toward the hospital. She trudges on ice-white sidewalks for two hours in debilitating pain.

Holding a piece of paper with David's phone number on it, the nurse leaves Maddie's side. Maddie is confident that the hospital's request for a signature will result in a no-show. If, by some miracle, the heartless David turns up, he would face a big dilemma. Maddie has, unthinkingly, given her *real* age—not "twenty-one," as David had instructed her.

In spring of this year David had deliberately misrepresented Maddie's age and given a false date of birth on their marriage license application. The lawful age for legal documents was twenty-one. At the time, the teenager thought twenty-one was so *old!*

While the pre-surgery sedation is making Maddie sleepy, she is not mentally water-logged. She feels salty tears spilling onto her prominent cheekbones, the unwilling victims of her insufficient weight since childhood. Thoughts of her past send her back to one of many dark chapters in her young life.

Maddie inherited a photographic memory. She sighs deeply as her mind's video recorder activates. Could she ever forget the cruelty of being incarcerated and tortured within the grim, secluded walls of the holy convent for crimes committed not by her but by her father?

In high resolution, unspeakable events take shape.

Click. Click. Click.

It was 1951 ... Good Sisters' Convent ... the British Commonwealth of South Africa.

Maddie was nine years old. She was being held against her will in a place earmarked for *colored* children and run by malignant *white* women of the Church.

When Maddie was five, she was ethnically stereotyped by the ruling British government. Her Caucasian British-born father raped her olive-skinned Sicilian immigrant mother, who was, by British racial definition, colored and the lowest notch on the totem pole of humanity. Maddie's mixed blood would not "allow" her admittance to a "whites-only" orphanage. But being classified "colored" was the least of her victimization. It was intended that she be locked away forever so she could never reveal the abuses she endured in the home of a British aristocrat ... beginning at age five.

Maddie gulps a full pail of sadness and pulls the warm hospital blanket over her head. The memory of her childhood is unspeakable, but never forgettable. What she was about to relive would send even strong, healthy people to the psyche ward.

The past rewinds.

Click. Click. Click.

Early that fateful morning in Cape Town, South Africa, a pale-green hospital gown hung from Maddie's drooping shoulders. She looked like the animated misfit Dopey in *Snow White and the Seven Dwarfs*. *Whoosh, whoosh, whoosh* was the only sound heard as her gown lapped the cold tile floor. Like Dopey, the child wearing the ill-fitting frock was silent. To survive this cold-hearted fortress,

Maddie had become an "elective" mute. Acting deaf and dumb, she withdrew into soundless solitude, the safest place to be in an institution that showed no mercy to discarded *colored* children. That day there would be no kind, loving Snow White to protect Maddie from what she was being forced to undergo. And she felt it. She couldn't quell the feeling that something horrible was about to happen to her. Maddie became a sitting duck, an easy target for dark human behaviors.

The skin-and-bones nine-year-old—with sunken cheeks and a closely shorn head dotted with bald patches from a haircut hatchet job—walked barefoot down a long, marbled corridor. She was flanked on either side by Sisters Aurelia and Mary-Jean. Her naked toes recoiled from the cold, hard floor tiles.

Maddie was ushered into a brightly lit room, where the air was cold in contrast to the heat of the overcooked summer sun. Maddie shivered from head to toe. Her teeth chattered as her eyes scanned the unfamiliar setting. She saw a man, arms at his sides, arrayed in a protective medical uniform: scrubs, disposable shoe covers, mask, surgical cap, latex gloves, and eye shield. And he was *black*. The only black men she had seen there so far were the garden workers employed by the convent. Maddie recognized the white woman standing quietly to one side, a stethoscope draped around her neck. In front of Mother Superior was a shiny metal table on wheels. Stainless steel instruments glinted ominously under the fluorescent lights. Maddie wanted to cry out. *Is something bad going to happen to me?*

In a trance of terror, silence wrapped wings around the child.

Without a word, Mother Superior hoisted the waif onto the narrow operating table and applied straps to keep her tightly positioned. A dismissive wave of her hand sent the flanking nuns packing. Now Maddie was left with only the black man and one nun.

Maddie's hot, panicked breath penetrated the icy walls of the torture chamber. She was too terrified to detect the life support equipment or other emergency resuscitative devices. But she did recall her fears spilling silently from her eyes. *What is this room? Why am I here? What are they going to do to me? Are they going to kill me? I'm so scared. I'm so scared.*

Click. Click. Click.

The anesthesia mask was placed on Maddie's face. Fear took a stranglehold as she tried to fight the drug. But oblivion had the upper hand and engulfed her.

In the twilight world of anesthesia, Maddie envisioned millions of Matabele army ants, which she recognized from her days in the African bush. They were trooping down her throat and heading toward her female parts. She imagined the queen ant guarding her eggs. She could not have foreseen that her eggs were being murdered at the command of her biological father.

Maddie breaks free from the disturbing memories and grabs hold of her 1968 mind. She tells herself, *Fear is your worst enemy. Don't let it devour you.* Maddie momentarily nurses herself with self-pity. Then reality forces her to face the truth—the early tubectomy had been botched. She fiercely clutches her hospital gown as a cascade of emotions assails her.

Maddie's face takes on a waxen pallor. Her eyes are dull, in stark contrast to the twinkling Christmas ornaments decorating the plastic tree outside her cubicle. Maddie trembles uncontrollably before she speaks. "I have to tell him. I have to tell him."

She presses the push-button room alert. When a nurse arrives, Maddie does not recognize her own voice. It sounds frantic and childlike. "Please, ask Doctor Barazani to come and see me. There is something he needs to know before the surgery."

"I'll try to reach him, but he is probably already prepping for your surgery."

Minutes later Prajit pushes back the curtain, sits down on Maddie's bed, and looks into his patient's eyes. "It will have to be quick, Maddie."

Her voice trembles slightly. "There is something you should know before you cut me open."

"Is it important? Time is of the essence."

"Yes, Doctor. It is very important."

Prajit sat down on a chair near the bed.

"When I was nine years old ..."

Prajit's knitted eyebrows communicate his sorrow. Her woeful story is unimaginable, incredulous. *It must have been paralyzing for her to retell it.* His strong, comforting arms reach out and cradle the sobbing girl. She feels his tears mingling with hers. He detaches himself hurriedly when he sees a nurse heading their way. He remembers what he learned in medical school: In order to best apply their technical expertise, doctors must remain emotionally detached. Prajit ignores this medical wisdom and says in a soft, soothing voice, "I'm so sorry, Maddie. Your secrets are safe with me. I'll always be here for you."

Maddie gazes at the middle-aged doctor with newfound respect, but she can't resist thinking: *Why do so many people apologize for so many things? "I'm sorry" is overused and often doesn't relate directly to the person it is intended for.* If this "I'm sorry" had come from the black *butcher,* she would have socked him in the jaw.

"And there's something else …"

What could be worse? Prajit thinks.

"Don't worry. I will sort this insurance stuff out," he says. Her candor about no insurance is important, but not as crucial as *time,* which is running out for his death row patient.

Prajit picks up the phone and reaches the Chief of Staff, the hospital administrator responsible for all hospital activities. Prajit's words are rushed: emergency trauma, botched surgical procedure, no medical coverage; no husband in person or on the phone to vouch for payment, no relatives, no family at all, and at death's door. The response is clear and concerned: "Oh, my goodness. Go ahead. We will worry ourselves about all the rest later. Please keep me updated on the girl's progress."

Prajit hands Maddie the "permission" form, and she scribbles an illegible signature … because she can neither read nor sign her name! However, in a brief time she *has* become proficient in English, "the *rug-rag* of all languages," as she once described it.

At seventeen, Maddie's reading, writing, and spelling skills were nonexistent. However, when she *did* reach the age of maturity, twenty-one, she achieved the maximum score possible, 162, on the Mensa (FSIQ) intelligence test. Her high IQ and remarkable linguistic skills did not go unnoticed. In the early 1970s she was "recruited" by Security Service, Section 5, the antiterrorist squad, and having undergone the intense training required, she signed the Oath of Loyalty to Her Majesty Queen Elizabeth 2. Under the Official Secrets Act, Maddie kept this career a secret from her children for the rest of her life. On her initial recruitment, she was cautioned that it was a crime, risk of imprisonment, to disclose her clandestine work. Even so, one day she would be accused by an individual in Scotland of being a "spy," a British traitor!

The fallopian tube that had been keeping Maddie's "miracle" baby warm now enters Ancestral Heaven. She, however, enters Limbo, a place where she never knows a baby's love. Never holds her own baby in her arms. Never feels the warmth of her child snuggled against her breast. Never knows the caress of her baby's fingertips. Never hears an endearing voice directing "mama," "mummy," "mum," or "mom" to her. It appears Maddie will never experience the invisible umbilical cord that binds a mother and her child forever.

Maddie longed for a baby of her own and, surprisingly, she kept that hope alive. *Don't you dare give up,* her optimism smiled. *What if the remaining tube beats the odds and carries a wiggly sperm to your uterus? There is nothing wrong with that domain, as far as I know.*

Maddie's hope sunk like a weight to the bottom of the ocean when the imaging of the remaining tube showed it, too, was beyond salvation: "thickened tubal wall ... septa ... mural nodules ... suspected tumors ... inadequate blood flow." Gallows humor helped turn her mood around. A reluctant grin tugged at her lips. Did her fallopian tube resemble a Vienna schnitzel pounded to death? Wryly, she envisioned spikes of mangled flesh protruding like pimples. Suddenly, a healthy dose of gravity overwhelmed her silly respite. *Why wasn't this deadened piece of flesh removed when I underwent the ectopic removal?* Prajit gave her the answer: "I ended the surgery quickly because of massive hemorrhaging. You were losing too much blood. It was a close call, Maddie."

This can't be happening. I'm in someone else's nightmare!

Maddie would have scoffed if someone told her the will to die is stronger than the will to live because Maddie had always believed all life was precious. And she still did … for now. But this attitude would be tested and would later become a debatable perspective in her life.

At midnight three liters of rare AB negative blood save Maddie's life. She spends ten days in the ICU … alone.

Where is David?

Maddie will discover soon that *love*, to David Blakely, is nothing more than *ownership*.

But she is not entirely forsaken in Croydon General Hospital.

She is "adopted" by some compassionate souls. The day and night nursing staff becomes her family. They bring her fish-and-chip takeout, fresh fruit, flowers, and magazines. Dr. Barazani's wife sends a cold-weather wardrobe, some belated birthday gifts, and Christmas surprises concealed in festive bags. Maddie revels in the attention, something she has not had for a long time. However, she declines the invitation for grief counseling. She convinces herself that she has passed through the emotional pain of losing her child.

But she was wrong!

The loss of *this* baby, whom she privately named "Sky," haunted Maddie to her core for rest of her life. And things yet unknown to her—a "Petri dish" of misdiagnoses and unexplained medical impossibilities and anomalies—are headed her way. She will one day ponder: *Why are medical practitioners so often wrong? What is lacking in their basic training? Is the Hippocratic Oath now the "Hypocritical" Oath? Why doesn't Jesus care about unfortunate mothers who give birth to demons? After all, he had a Mother!*

Miracles *do* happen!

The ocean would spit Maddie's dashed *hopes* right back at her … in the form of healthy, wiggly sperm. They would swim up her mangled Vienna schnitzel six times! But only three of her "miracle" children will survive.

Today Maddie defines her "miracles" as *Reincarnated Bad Seeds!*

Her three living children would forever pierce her decent heart with shards of grief and drams of poison.

After her discharge from Croydon hospital, Maddie walks back to "Kinloch Gardens," her mother-in-law's apartment, clutching bags of clothes and assorted gifts in both hands. She happily dwells on the kindness she received during her ten-day hospitalization. Before she left, a nurse offered, "Maddie, I get off in an hour. I can drive you home. It's not good to walk in this nasty weather."

"It is kind of you to offer, but the walk will do me good. I need to focus on healing."

The nurse shrugged. "I wish you well, Maddie. Here's my telephone number if you ever need someone to talk to."

Exhausted, Maddie finally arrives at the dismal concrete building that has been her home for nine months. She climbs the stairs and, after catching her breath, clatters the door knocker on apartment 24. She had never been given a house key, and, judging from the control freaks who lived inside, she probably never would.

David, unsmiling, greets his wife as if she had merely stepped out for a breather. "So you're back at last. Good. Mum's out and I'm hungry," he demands with steel-cold words. "Make me something to eat."

What goes around comes around.

David and others she knew of his ilk eventually got their comeuppance. Protective medical clothing did not shield Maddie's convent butcher. He faced his music at age seventy, when he was arrested and held accountable for his diabolical crime against Maddie. He was sentenced to death. And David Blakely got what was coming to him. He was shot to death. His executioner, a sniper, pumped seven bullets into his body. Other lowlife individuals who had badly "abused" Maddie did not get off scot free either.

Revenge is mine, sayeth Madeline.

CHAPTER TWO

"Some dream of becoming rich or famous;
Maddie dreamed of being a mother."

Two months later, in the early months of 1969, Maddie suffered familiar painful spasms and abdominal cramping. *It's not that time of the month,* she reminded herself. She hadn't had a period since her ectopic surgery in December of last year. Was she one of the few teenagers who did not suffer this monthly curse? She did not even consider the idea of being pregnant again.

After her post-surgery checkup, Dr. Barazani diagnosed *amenorrhea*, absent menstruation in a woman of reproductive age.

Trying to be jovial, Maddie thanked her lucky stars her condition did not result in masculine characteristics: excess body hair, a deep voice, and the over-developed muscles of a weight lifter. It was bad enough that she only weighed 101 pounds, which was an improvement over her earlier eighty-five. She wasn't anorexic. She was malnourished, having grown up hungry her entire childhood. Starvation also explained her poor dental health. Several molars, both upper and lower, were missing. In addition, she had immature white blood cells (myeloblasts) in her bone marrow, a hereditary leukemic disorder. Nasty *gremlins* had been trying to end her life for as long as she could remember. Even more so during her pregnancies.

Maddie made her way to the hospital alone, yet again. This time, the ultrasound left little doubt—miracle baby number two!

The rapid, prenatal heartbeat, 140 beats, sounded like thunderous horse hoofs galloping through the examination room. Maddie's expression was unreadable to the sonographer, whose smile was as warm as the weather. "Congratulations. Is this your first baby?"

Had she read Maddie's medical history, she would have subdued her naturally cheerful nature.

Thubalep, thubalep, thubalep.

Hoof beats pounded Maddie's head. Her stomach felt like it held undigested rock. "This can't be real!" she blurted as she snatched the hand-held device from the practitioner and ran it over the skin of her belly.

Thubalep, thubalep, thubalep.

Maddie's thoughts raced with the hoof beats. *Has the Universe Magician deity that the African witch doctor told me about taken pity on me? Or, as a master illusionist, is he playing a dirty trick—now you have it, now you don't.* She was troubled by how she was going to tell her husband. He hadn't taken the ectopic news well.

Click, click, click.

"You are a bloody lair!" he had exploded. "You told me you have been fixed … couldn't have kids!"

David had made no effort, the first time or now, to step foot into the medical facility to be by her side, and he still hadn't applied for her medical papers. When the topic of papers came up after the surgery, he had been agitated. "Medical coverage is out the question. Do you want our unlawful marriage to be *investigated*? Let's put it this way: It won't be *me* who will be deported! You should be grateful I've been kind enough to take you in, you worthless piece of shit!"

So vile a sin—cruel, verbal insults, and other versions of savage abuse.

Maddie wanted to walk out for a pint of milk and never return, but that would never happen. She was at David's mercy in a foreign country. She yearned to be Debora from the *Book of Judges*, a fighter, not a coward. But how could she fight back? The odds were stacked high against her. It was in her best interest not to respond to David's ugliness.

Maddie withdrew into silence, a submissive response she had grown comfortable with.

Had she been exposed to playwright August Wilson's positive message, she may have been influenced to feel differently about herself: "Confront the dark parts of yourself, and work to banish them with illumination and forgiveness. Your willingness to wrestle with your demons will cause your angels to sing."

Low self-esteem affected Maddie's self-worth ... profoundly. She convinced herself she was inferior, amounted to nothing, had no potential. These erroneous conclusions had taken their toll. Her previous intention not to cling to negative energy had vanished.

A gelatinous lubricant was slopped across Maddie's abdomen. The horse hoofs now sounded like someone chewing on crunchy biscuits. Her thoughts paced the room. *Maybe David would have a change of heart—be over the moon.* Hell, no! David Blakely was a cold-blooded man, nothing like the soft-spoken person she first met, who could charm the birds out of the trees. He certainly had pulled the wool over her eyes in Europe last year.

"Come into my parlor," said the spider to the fly.

CHAPTER THREE

"The oldest and strongest emotion of mankind is fear, and the oldest and strongest kind of fear is fear of the unknown."
—H.P. LOVECROFT

A "dehumanized" sixteen-year-old was dumped like trash in Milan, Italy, in early March 1968. It was the only country willing to accept Maddie. Why was she kicked out of her country of birth, South Africa?

Racism!

After Britain withdrew from the Commonwealth, the New Republic's apartheid ruling classified the bronze-skinned teenager as an undesirable, illegal resident, and colored, to boot! Not human by any consideration! The white immigration official issued her exit visa saying, "This deportation order is final, missy. No coming back, *kaffir!*" His ethnic slur hadn't fazed her. She had been called worse.

"Am I clear?" he ended.

This abominable trait, addiction to hate, followed Maddie for the rest of her life.

Can hatred be avenged? Yes.

Just two days into her exile, Maddie was dumped again, this

time by her South African escort, an Afrikaans woman paid by the British consulate in Cape Town to take care of the teenager until further arrangements could be made. Roland Harcourt, a British ambassador, had befriended Maddie in South Africa after her escape from the convent, but he had been powerless to stop the deportation order. Maddie's callous escort decided her newfound love affair was more rewarding than babysitting a displaced person. She not only deserted Maddie and left her to her fate, but she also took the substantial wad of cash that had been provided by the ambassador for food and lodging.

When Maddie and her escort arrived in Milan, they found a cheap hostel favored by backpackers. They planned to stay there until further instruction came from Roland. He told them it would take him about seven to ten days to put a permanent plan together.

The next day Maddie woke to find the adjacent bed empty. A folded note was lying on top of her pillow. Maddie turned to face a traveler four beds down, who was packing her bags. "Could you, please, read this for me?" she asked handing over the correspondence. The young woman from Wales stared at Maddie quizzically.

Maddie, eyes downcast, said, "I can't read."

Alwyn unfolded the letter and read: "Forgive me, Maddie, but I have a life too. I can't tell you how happy I am to have found the love of my life. Good luck. I mean it."

Maddie's English was not yet refined, but she got the drift. She had been thrown to the wolves, cast out by selfishness.

Alwyn shook her head. The "Dear John" message was as plain as day. Her kind heart reached out to the stunned teenager, whose eyes were stretched wide in surprise. "Are you going to be all right? Is there someone I can call for you?"

Crying is the language of the heart, but Maddie, devastated, chose to smother her tears with a glib reply. "I'll be okay. I have a contact. Thank you."

"I'm sorry. I wish I could do more for you, but I'm returning home to Wales after three months away ..." The traveler's words trailed off. Maddie bent down to check under her bed. To her horror, her small suitcase was gone. "Oh, no!" she cried. "Where is it?"

"What's the matter?" Alwyn asked.

"My bag is gone," Maddie answered. "Now I have no clothes, no hairbrush, or toiletries. Only this nightgown and the shoes I'm wearing."

"I'll ask the proprietor to call the police," Alwyn said in a concerned voice.

Maddie grabbed her arm firmly. "No. Please, don't do that."

The look on Maddie's face said "I'm hiding something," and it sent a silent Alwyn back to her spot. She reopened her backpack and pulled out a flowery hippie skirt, top, and poncho. She approached Maddie, who was lying face down on the bed. Alwyn touched the girl's shoulder and said, "Here," as she handed over the bundle of clothes. "I hope they fit." It was a daft question being that Alwyn was over six-feet and Maddie, five-foot-five.

"Thank you, kind lady."

"I'm sorry, Maddie," Alwyn apologized, "but I don't have any money to give you. I've just enough to see me home."

"It's okay," Maddie replied tonelessly.

Alwyn hugged Maddie. "I'd better get a move on, or I'll miss my train. With all my heart, I wish you well," she finished.

Maddie never forgot Alwyn's kindness, and would one day seek her out by placing an advert in the Welsh newspapers: "Looking for a friend, Alwyn, whom I met in Milan at a backpackers' hostel in March 1968. Please contact."

What are the odds of finding this particular Alwyn when "Alwyn" was such a common Welsh name? One million to one?

Maddie was the lucky *one*!

Maddie folded the elastic waistband of Alwyn's skirt several times. She slipped on the poncho and left the hostel.

Adrenalin flowed through her veins as powerfully as salmon returning to their spawning ground. She traipsed up and down the busy streets in search of her so-called protector. Finally, intimidated by the darkness of night, she stopped her search. Maddie really didn't give a hoot about the woman's reasons for leaving her, but she did care about the money intended for her keep. Maddie became concerned about how she was going to take care of herself. Crushed, she returned to the hostel, walked through the front door, and was stopped by the owner. "Good evening, Miss. Will you be staying another night?" He peeked over her shoulder. "Is your friend coming?"

Maddie shrugged.

"She's only paid for two nights."

"She's gone," Maddie said with dejection. "I have no money."

"I'm sorry. No money, no bed." He was a sensitive man, but he ran a business, not a charity. He worked hard to provide a living for himself and his wife. If he had given in to every sob story he heard, he would be broke. He watched the unfortunate girl leave his premises and prayed for God to protect her.

Scared half to death, Maddie walked along the bustling streets, joining other sidewalk strollers going about their business. Eventually, she connected with various homeless folks, all ages, and slept and begged on Milan's Via del Boschetto, an affluent part of town. The homeless welcomed her, asked no questions; however, Maddie, a stray waif, continued to experience the same unpleasantness of the past, being treated as if she were subhuman. But pondering would have to wait. Getting something to eat took precedence.

I'm so hungry I could eat a horse and then go for the rider! At this point, the seriousness of her situation had not yet crossed her mind. Homeless women were easy targets for sexual assault. She had no knowledge of human traffickers prowling the "begging" street. And she was unaware that she could be arrested as a vagrant. The rich were quick to report vagrants in their neighborhoods. Would that become the "lost" teenager's concern? No. She would have gladly spent time in a jail cell rather than on the streets in the cold.

Maddie found a solitary spot under a bright street lamp, where she sat down on the bitterly cold sidewalk. She crossed her legs and echoed the Italian plea for survival she had heard the others recite:

"*Avete qualche cambiamento* (Have you any change)?" Her question was answered not with change but with people turning their backs and averting their eyes. A string of obscenities, gestures, and leers were also common, and a string of pitiless jibes:

"Get a life, girl. I have my own life to worry about."

"No time to take in strays."

"If you want money, work for it."

"I'll be happy to show you where the red-light district is."

One elderly woman, wearing a warm mink coat and expensive jewelry, crossed herself saying, "Pray to God, child. He will save you."

Yeah, right! thought Maddie. She was long done with falling to her knees to beseech higher powers. When she was little, her pleas were ignored.

An elderly man with small, round eyes gleaming lecherously asked if she was a virgin. "If so, come with me. I'll pay you well."

"Get lost, old man," she hollered.

Just after midnight, the streets began to empty of people, and Maddie's faith in humanity flew out the window as she totaled her lira. There was hardly enough to buy a decent meal. A warm drink would have to suffice. With cold, blue hands, she hugged herself against the night air. She found her way to the all-night café she had visited with her missing escort.

Maddie selected a booth where the café's warm electric heat could soothe her cold, tired, and hungry body. She was eager for a hot beverage.

"Caffé, perfavore," she said to the smiling waitress.

"Do you want a specialty coffee or black?"

Maddie reached into her skirt pocket, pulled out her crinkled money, and handed it to the waitress. Expressionless, the woman counted the notes. "I'm sorry ..." Evidently, specialties from this part of town—lattes, mochas, espressos, and cappuccinos—could not be savored on Maddie's budget.

A mug of bergamot tea hit the spot; so did the free white-chocolate-tipped biscotti that Maddie wolfed down. She was so touched by the server's gesture, she wanted to cry.

Has humanity been resurrected? Yes, for the time being.

Maddie hugged the waitress and walked back to the begging street. Not a soul was in sight. She crouched in the shadows of a deserted office building. Her spot was void of sound, but she couldn't sleep. The frosty temperatures and a grumbling stomach kept her awake. Her situation was unfathomable. Three days ago, before she arrived here, she was in a country drenched in blazing hot sun. Now she was exposed to what felt like Arctic frigidity. How she was going to beat the bitter cold and gnawing hunger so she could get some sleep was beyond her. She recalled a conversation she had earlier with another homeless soul. "There's a dumpster over there," she said as she motioned ahead in the direction of a large, metal container. "You'll be surprised how much good clothing is thrown away by the rich folks. It's my favorite store," she laughed.

It took some effort to climb into the dumpster, but Maddie was happy that she did. She found a fleece-lined, waterproof raincoat in good condition and, to her delight, a large unopened packet of almond-flavored biscuits.

The twenty-four treats were devoured in one sitting!

At daybreak Maddie awoke with the rays of a weak sun. Before returning to the begging street, she peed behind some dense shrubbery and splashed her face in water from a nearby fountain. From this moment on, living in the now, getting money to survive, was all she could think about. Finally, what appeared to be a good Samaritan came along. Maddie had no conception of a world other than the one she had known in South Africa. She was inexperienced in the ways of the modern world and lived behind a veil of ignorance. A spell was being cast by the hypnotizing, seductive voice of a soft-spoken older man. Until now, she had known only brutal, inhumane, hateful masters who had "murdered' her innocence. Fate had dealt with her harshly. Was she to experience yet another blow? Doubt attacked her on this inhospitable walkway.

David Blakely was thirty-six years old, and no Adonis. Slightly shorter than Maddie, he was a pudgy fellow carrying one too many pints of beer under his belt. His appearance was paired with the smell of stale beer and tobacco. He was a heavy drinker and a chain smoker. His stained, crooked teeth were the color of toffee. He wore thick, horn-rimmed eyeglasses with milk-bottle lenses. He had wispy, auburn hair, balding at the crown. In contrast, Maddie was pretty. But the ugly girl she perceived inside longed to belong to anyone who would have her. She believed no one would ever want her because she came weighted down with a mountain of baggage—no money, no parents in her life, no siblings, no friends, and no country to call home. Worse, she had no legal identity. That only came to those with birth registrations. Her immigrant mother had abandoned her when she was a newborn. She was simply known as Madeline Clark, the name given to her by the orphanage.

From birth to present day, Maddie had stared into unthinkable adversity. Had misfortune come calling again? Definitely!

Peering over a generous portion of spaghetti and meatballs, the grateful teenager didn't see an ugly toad. Instead, she imagined a knight in shining armor. She gathered from his conversation that he was wealthy and had had everything handed to him on a silver platter. Being desperate to belong, never to be "lost" or hungry again, her judgment clouded. Had this financially secure man been sent by an invisible hand to save her? Had the hostel owner's prayer been answered? Hell, no! Blame mental fragility, youthful naivety, stupidity, whatever, but Maddie's logic was overruled by her need. The ill-perceived notion that this stranger held the keys to her freedom was irrational. Nevertheless, she let her guard down. She poured her heart out—retelling her life's trials. "I really don't blame anyone," Maddie said. "I am not really motherless or fatherless. I'm the daughter of Mother Earth and Father Sky, but I believe they, too, may have abandoned me."

David's jaw dropped. Was this for real, not the product of a vivid imagination designed to snatch a sugar daddy? How is this possible? There were thousands of displaced persons after the war. Why had she not received the same humane treatment, been given a new identity? It puzzled him that she was born in a country ruled by the British Empire. Didn't that make her a British subject? Didn't she have rights to a British passport, rather than a deportation visa? In a split second, David's compassion shifted to a review of his numerous failed relationships, most of them ruined by interfering family members. Could it be he found his perfect match—an orphan who couldn't say "boo" to a ghost?

A self-assured smile creased David's mouth as he reached for Maddie's hand. "I'm sorry for what you have gone through, lovie. The tough times are over, though. I'm here. I will take care of you. And, by the way, I don't give a damn if you can't have children. I *hate* kids. It will be just you and me in a castle, my castle, which is awaiting its queen."

Just because something sounds great, doesn't mean it is, thought Maddie.

But she felt elated, her mind spinning like a top with gullibility. She did not give a second thought to her own warning. And so, like a doe, unaware of the danger lurking in the forest, she turned her trust over to this Samaritan—a big mistake!

A happy, smiling Maddie, with David at her side, entered the five-star Intercontinental Hotel. The clerk at the front desk couldn't take his eyes of the smaller of the two, whom he thought was a boy who resembled a Dickens character: the Artful Dodger in *Oliver Twist*. The oversized Mackintosh, much too large for the scrawny *boy*, extended to *his* heels. The clerk couldn't see what lurked under Maddie's outerwear. Alwyn's donated clothes were magnets for dirt flecks that Maddie had accumulated while wandering the streets. The dust-encrusted "bunnies" clung to her flesh like lice.

In a plummy Sherlock Homes voice, David addressed the hotel clerk. "I'd like your best room for one night, please." Maddie's eyebrows knotted confusingly. This upper-class accent was nothing like his earlier voice pattern.

"Certainly, sir," the clerk replied. "May I see some identification, please?" His suspicions caused him to subtly observe the gentleman's companion. *Definitely not blood related.* The boy was as dark as night, and the man looked like a green alien. The youngster's hands were black, dirty, and grubby, as if he had spent time in a coal mine.

David handed his UK passport to the clerk, who promptly asked, "What about the young man's passport? Is he your son?"

David shot him the evil eye and, in a hostile tone, retorted, "*She* doesn't have one. I'm paying the bill so why does it matter?"

The registrar's expression was stoic. "I'm, sorry, sir. Hotel rules are for *all* guests," he stated factually.

Maddie read the man's mind: *What's this fellow trying to pull? But … neither male nor female hookers need passports to service Johns! I hope she takes a bath first!*

A generous wad of lira soon changed hotel rules. Door access was handed over, and no registration card was presented. David grabbed hold of Maddie's hand and led her to the elevator. Neither David nor Maddie uttered a word as the elevator lifted them to the sixth floor. Maddie foolishly convinced herself that everything was going to be okay.

On entering the hotel suite, Maddie's face froze. She blinked. Had she just stepped into a palace fit for a queen?

The two-bedroom suite with a private balcony was massive, offering enough room for a party of tired travelers. Luxurious touches pleased the eyes: yellow and teal accent walls, queen-size beds decorated with more pillows than Maddie had ever seen, a separate living room with a large television, a walk-in shower and ensuite jacuzzi. The room was booked for one night, but Maddie wanted to live there forever. It was her first experience with how others, who could afford such luxuries, lived.

But ... it would be her last taste of how others lived for a long time to come.

Maddie relaxed into hot, foaming bath water. Suddenly, out of the blue, she felt a queasiness so intense her breathing stalled. Apprehension bubbled like jacuzzi jets. *Why did this stranger bring me here?* He had not looked embarrassed when he presented his dirt-ridden companion, resembling a twelve-year-old boy, at the desk. *Oh my God, he's a pimp. He is going to sell me to a human trafficker.* Many young girls had disappeared from the orphanage. It was only afterward that Maddie learned of their fate. *He's going rape me! What's the matter with me? I'm a pathetic idiot. Why didn't I see this coming? How could I fall for his lies? I've never trusted anyone, so why did I trust him? I can't get something for nothing.*

Maddie had to make her escape, but how? She grabbed the soft bathrobe hanging from the door and cloaked her trembling body. Gingerly, she exited the room. David was nowhere to been seen. *What now?* Before she had time to deliberate further, the sound of the front door opening sent her flying backwards into the bathroom. She locked the door and held her breath.

In a gentle, flowing rhythm, David spoke to the locked door. "Knock, knock. It's only me—not the big bad wolf. When you're done, I have a surprise for you."

Maddie couldn't spend the night in the bathroom!

David stood in front of her clutching numerous shopping bags. He wore a cheesy smile. "I went to the shop in the foyer. The sales assistant was extremely helpful, so I hope they fit."

The designer nightgown, mid-length purple corduroy skirt, matching top, warm stockings, cotton panties, and flat shoes could have been made to measure. Maddie's puzzled thoughts ran riot: *How did he know my shoe size? Or even my clothing size? How did he know not to buy a bra? Did he notice I am flat-chested?* Maddie referred to her tiny breasts as baby fried eggs. *How did he know my favorite color is purple?*

Maddie regretted she had had doubts. She flung her arms around David and kissed him on his cheek. "You are so kind. I love them!" She fingered the silky fabric of the nightgown. She had never felt anything so soft. She gushed, "I will feel like a queen in this."

"You are a queen …. my queen."

"*Step into my parlor...*"

"And you are my king," she cooed back.

"Are you hungry? I could order room service," he said handing Maddie the hotel menu. Her illiteracy crashed into her happiness. *Should I tell him? No, no. Not yet!*

"I'm not hungry," she replied faintly. "I'm still stuffed from the earlier meal." Her honest reply concealed her shame and embarrassment.

"Do you want to watch television then?"

"*Yes*, please." Maddie hoped she didn't sound too enthusiastic, but this would be her first encounter with this modern device. South African television would be introduced nine years later.

With her legs tucked under her body, Maddie sat mesmerized,

even though the three channels were all in Italian. Halfway through a documentary on Australian wombats, a big yawn hinted she needed sleep.

Maddie slept alone in a bed with sheets so fresh and soft that they really did make her feel like a queen. Where was her king?

After depleting the bar fridge of its alcohol contents, David had passed out on the sofa where they had been watching TV.

Maddie awoke to sunshine streaming through lace drapes.

How great it was to feel alive!

CHAPTER FOUR

"Expressing doubt is how we begin a
journey to discover truths."
—KILROY OLSTER

Maddie's confusion—*I don't know what to feel anymore*—carried her back to the backpacker's hostel. She couldn't grasp her new situation. David had brought her lovely clothes. She had slept for the night in her own bed—he had not once tried to mess with her. And he had promised her the world. He had told her she would go with him to England to start a happy new life. That all changed over breakfast.

"I'm leaving today, going home."

His singular statement elicited a frantic response. "What do you mean? I thought you were taking me with you."

"No. You must stay here until I can make proper arrangements for your travel."

"I don't understand?"

"Ah, come on Maddie. You can't be that dumb! You have no legal paperwork to prove who you are. Your exit visa from South Africa doesn't cut it. What would you have me say to the Passport Officer?

I found an orphan on the street. Please let her in."

"I don't know what you should say," she responded in a defeated tone. "You promised to rescue me."

For the first time Maddie heard David's tone change from gentle and soft to indifference. "Do I look like a bloody saint?" he said curtly. "I need time to organize stuff."

"How much more time?" Maddie asked anxiously.

"About five days," David responded. "You must go back to the hostel and stay there until I return for you."

An hour later Maddie handed the surprised hostel owner David's cash for a five-night stay. At night she slept with her belongings under her pillow. During the day she took the plastic shopping bag with her when she ventured out of the hostel to sightsee. She had five days, so why not?

During her days Maddie hopped onto a yellow-and-orange 1920's tram to take in the Milan's centuries-old symbolic monuments. She didn't get the chance to view Leonardo da Vinci's inspirational *Last Supper* because the ticket price was well beyond what her dwindling budget would allow. But she was able to window shop at the Galleria Vittorio arcade, which displayed Prada, Louis Vuitton, Armani, Versace, and other hot-off-the-catwalk clothing. However, it was the magnificent glass and the iron dome of the Galleria that impressed her the most, not the luxury designer goods. She neither wanted nor dreamed of owning such outrageously priced, upscale fashions.

Each day at dusk she scurried back to the hostel, having already dined at a local cafe that provided decent food at reasonable prices. It was her only meal of the day.

While money was disappearing, her trepidation was heightening.

Five days had passed. No sign of David. The little cash she had left wouldn't cover another hostel night or warm meal.

One week passed. She was officially homeless again. How was she going to survive the second time around? Hoping for a miracle, she revisited the "begging" street. What other choice did she have? Pray to God? That wasn't going to happen. But a big "maybe" dealt her an optimistic hand. Of course, he had forgotten the hostel address and would come to this familiar spot to find her.

As evening approached, leaving Maddie with little in handouts, fear, anger, vulnerability, and homelessness became her brutal reality—*my good Samaritan is a cold-hearted fraud.* In her thinking, David had used her for his sick, warped entertainment. But why had he gone to such lengths to pay for food, clothing, hotel accommodation, and extra money? It didn't make sense. In time, the answers *would* reveal themselves.

Pitch-black midnight enveloped Maddie on the empty sidewalk. She burst into tears. *Should I find a church, ask for food and shelter?* Hell, no! That wasn't going to happen. She would rather sleep in a lion's den than turn to …

Click, click, click.

Maddie's camera automatically recaptured one of many sadistic scenes that had victimized her while she was "interned" at a convent. During morning prayers, five-and-half-year-old Maddie wet herself. The pooling urine found its way to Sister Mary-Jean's shoes. "You disgusting child," she raged, as she grabbed Maddie by the hair and dragged her up the narrow aisle separating rows of pews.

Outside, God's *helper* removed her wet shoe and beat Maddie's head and face with it. Maddie was injured so badly she couldn't see out of her swollen eyes for days.

Frantically, Maddie shut off her memory bank. She had no intention of rolling over and dying, not here, not now. Panhandling to prevent starvation and sleeping and washing in the park's bathrooms were her survival. But by mid-March her chances of enduring looked bleak.

The daily downpour, the wettest season on record, forced Maddie to take cover under shielded entranceways and wait for someone to notice her and throw her money, or hand her a half-filled cup of coffee or a half-eaten sandwich. It was under these circumstances that Maddie first began to contemplate suicide. *How can emptiness feel so heavy? How long can I last on these uncaring, inhospitable streets? And who the hell would care? After all, aren't I subhuman?*

Finally, a genuine Samaritan came along; in fact, two of them.

"In the name of Allah!" the religious man uttered. "This is where you ended up."

Maddie looked up at a man with Moorish features, the hostel owner. Unable to control her emotions, she sobbed.

"Come, girl," the man said, extending his hand. "You are coming with me."

Ammon Nasser, a curator at the Cairo Museum, and his British-born wife, Edrice, an anthropologist, had fled Cairo, Egypt, during the 1952 anti-British riots sixteen years ago. They chose "neutral" Italy for their new beginning. Unable to find work in their respective fields, they set about turning a rundown building into a twelve-bed dorm for budget travelers, often offering at additional cost their homemade authentic food. Over the years, they had an array of visitors, including the "saving" types.

Maddie needed saving.

She entered Ammon's modest quarters behind the hostel. Edrice was standing at the stove stirring something in a large pan. Their eyes met. Edrice gaped at her husband's wet companion, and they exchanged words in Arabic. While they were talking, Maddie spotted a framed picture on a colorful wall. The mysterious eyes of Queen Nefertiti, known for her elegant beauty, were mesmerizing. Preoccupied, Maddie didn't notice Edrice's dark-brown eyes clouding over with tears. She rushed over to the disheveled girl and gave her a bear hug. Maddie clung to the woman's plump body, certain she was an angel.

Maddie sat on a rickety chair pulled up to the couple's Retro-style chrome dining table. She retold some of her misfortunes, omitting the most graphic events, as best she could in a mixture of English and Italian. Eventually she would learn to speak Arabic, Italian, and even the Sicilian dialect fluently.

Both Ammon and Edrice shook their heads. Catholic-slanting Milan was not the place to be abandoned, unless you were a *believer*. After so many years here, they were still not "accepted" because they were Muslims. Maddie wasn't knowledgeable about Allah, but she was well acquainted with this country's theology. Her camera flashed, walking her back through a storm of memories accumulated by a girl who, like many others, had been judged by the color of her skin and her faith.

Click, click, click.

"You were born a *kaffir* and will die a *kaffir*," Sister Mary-Jean insulted. "You will always be inferior to whites!" Little Maddie imagined Satan with horns and pitchfork standing behind the nun and egging her on. "One thing is sure. You'll not bring any more little *kaffirs* into the world."

Maddie was convinced she had been doomed from birth by the color of her skin.

Bitter bile rose at the back of Maddie's throat, but she tried to sound lighthearted. "Mr. Nasser, I would rather believe in a cosmic green creature with three legs and googly eyes than the Christian God who never gave me a fair shot, who rejected me and subjected me to torture."

Ammon grinned. "Don't worry, girl. The one true God, Allah, all-powerful and all-knowing creator, is watching over you now. He sent me to find you. Later I will read his healing teachings from the *Quran*."

Whew! I got out of that one. I won't have shame written on my face.

Edrice wanted to have her say. "You can stay here as long as you like. You can work for us. We have a mountain of laundry each day. We have sweeping, tiding up the dormitory, cleaning the dirt travelers carry in when they do not remove their footwear. We can pay you cash."

Maddie's heavy heart floated. She felt relieved. "I'm overwhelmed with your generosity. Yes, I will work for you, but just for food and lodging. You don't have to pay me money."

Ammon laughed, "Don't be silly, girl. Do we look like slave keepers?"

After a long soak in a claw-foot tub, Maddie put on the outfit Alwyn donated to her. When she was angry at David, she had thrown his clothing gifts into the communal dumpster.

"Tomorrow we will go through the storage locker and find a wardrobe for you," Edrice said. "It's amazing how much stuff gets left here."

With her damp hair tied behind her head in a controlled bun, Maddie joined her gracious hosts for their evening meal—falafel—a deep-fried mixture of herbs and beans placed atop a bed of aromatic rice. Before Maddie, with a growling stomach, could dive in and attack the food, Ammon lifted his hands into the air and chanted, "Bismillaahir rah'maanir rah'eem ..."

Maddie gathered it was a prayer. *Could you please hurry up?*

Maddie wasn't prepared for the next step. "I have asked Allah to bless this meal and bless you. Now, after you wash your hands, we will eat the food He has put on our table."

But I've just had a bath!

Maddie did what Ammon asked and then lunged into the food, the finest she had ever tasted. She was happy, but tired. Because she nearly fell asleep at the table, she was excused from her host's reading of the Quran.

That night Maddie slept in a narrow bed with clean sheets, a large jacquard bedspread, and a down pillow, all of which lulled her into an exhausted, dreamworld sleep.

Click, click, click.

A thirteen-year-old desert dweller dressed in a thobe, a black full-length tunic woven from goat's hair, stepped out of a tent made from of the same type of hair. The dwelling was divided into two parts—the men's apartment and the women's. But in *this* desert abode there were no men. They had been taken captive, enslaved in Egypt to work in rock quarries.

Lela, her mother, and two sisters were exiles from the Kingdom of Judah, forced to live in the Western Desert, west of the river Nile. It was an unforgiving, desolate wasteland.

Lela stepped back into the tent to help her mother prepare food. The hearth used for warmth as well as cooking was bellowing away. At her mother's feet lay a dead baby goat.

"Daughter, skin the animal and chop it into pieces." Then she ordered Lela's sixteen-year-old sister: "Go to the watering hole. I need more water." She cared not if the water contained sewage from visiting camels or appeared brackish in color. Water was life, regardless.

One day, unexpectedly and surprisingly, Lela's father appeared holding the hand of a young boy wearing a dark blue turban. The pair had escaped slavery. Both were plagued with festering eye infections, ugly skin eruptions, punishing coughs, and intense back pain, all from prolonged hammering of rocks to build statues. They had worked from daybreak to sundown.

The eight-year-old Fellahin Arab, Hassam el Din, and Lela became inseparable.

In stifling hot weather, Hassam el Din accompanied Lela as she herded goats, hoping to find native vegetation not yet wiped out by severe drought. He told her that his mother had died a few months earlier, been decapitated trying to prevent the slavers from taking him away, as his father had been. They spoke about their different beliefs. He was a Muslim, she a Jew.

"Who cares … there is only one God," she said, taking a swig from her goat-skin water pouch. She nearly chocked on its contents when Hassam announced, "I'm going to marry you one day."

Lela's dark eyes glistened with amusement as she scolded, "You are crazy, little man. I'm much older than you, and even if you were of age, our families won't allow it. My marriage will probably be to some old goat, like my firstborn sister. I must obey my father. Arranged marriages are our custom, and you are not a Jew."

Hassam took a swig of water from the pouch and giggled. "Do you want to marry an old goat or the most handsome boy in the land?"

Lela playfully slapped him on the shoulder. They walked back toward the camp holding hands and singing a cheerful song. Abruptly, Lela dropped his hand, as if she had been bitten by a scorpion. Her father was approaching them. Had he seen them hugging and holding hands?

When Lela's father, Chaim, caught up to them, he grabbed Hassam's hand and said, "Come with me, boy. I have no choice but to take you back to the rock quarry."

Two sets of bewildered eyes glared at Chaim. Sighing deeply, he explained. He could have his freedom if he brought the boy back, but if he did not obey the order, he and his family would be killed.

Hassam froze under Chaim's strong grip. "But you said you would take care of me, old man, and I believed you. Now you want to send me back to the cruel slave masters?"

Chaim's head lowered. "Child, I can't protect you anymore. I have family to take care of."

Hassam's cries of alarm pierced the hot, suffocating air. The sound was heart-rending. Lela couldn't muzzle herself, even though it was disrespectful to address any man without permission. "Father, this is madness. Please don't do this. We can move camp to where no one will find us."

"I wish it were that simple," Chaim sighed. "You go back to the goats, and I will get back to what I must do."

Lela clenched her mouth in anger, but there was nothing she could do to stop the madness. When her father and Hassam were out of her sight, she dropped her head between her knees and prayed, "Hear O Israel, the Lord our God. Bring giants to kill the slave masters and save my Hassam, the only person I truly love …" As quickly as the flick of a finger, the skies turned dark and a thunderstorm threatened. Heavy rain began to fall on the parched land. Lela lifted her drenched head to the Heavens. "You heard me …"

Bang!

The sound of the table lamp hitting the floor jerked Maddie awake. She rubbed her eyes, which felt heavy and dust-encrusted. How can emptiness feel so heavy?

Many people do not remember their dreams, but Maddie was the exception. She had her "gift," and this specific dream reoccurred for years.

Would the interpretation finally be revealed? Yes.

CHAPTER FIVE

"Nothing is as painful to the human mind
as a great and or sudden change."

The gloomy weather continued into the next day, but it didn't dampen the spirit of Maddie's happy heart. She cheerfully collected dirty linen from the hostel dormitory. As she loaded the washing machine, she hummed a classical tune, synchronizing with the music streaming from a walnut-veneered transistor radio Edrice loaned her. Maddie's taste in music wasn't that of a typical teenager. She thought the kids her age—who went ape for the Beatles, Rock 'n' Roll, Sonny and Cher, and other pop artists, all imported like Coca-Cola into every home—were insane. However, she did like a couple of female singers from that time. Nancy Sinatra's *These Boots Are Made for Walking* always propelled her to boogie around the room.

Maddie was happy. She loved working for Ammon and Edrice and enjoyed interacting with the world travelers. Many handed her loose change that would not be accepted at their next port of call. Maddie, working as a housemaid, had amassed the equivalent of

$20 U.S., a fortune to her, after working for such a brief time. It was her intention to save up and buy something nice for her new family.

Classical guitarist Joaquín Rodrigo's *Concierto de Aranjuez* was being drowned out by the noisy old washing machine, and so was the knocking on the door. Maddie jumped out of her skin when Ammon touched her shoulder. "Oh, I'm sorry. Did I scare you?"

"You sure did."

"Maddie you have a visitor waiting in the kitchen."

"Who is it?" Maddie asked, scratching her head. She couldn't imagine who it could be. David had been long forgotten.

"He didn't give me his name. Just said he was a friend and wished to speak with you."

The penny didn't drop until she came face to face with David. "I've been looking all over Milan for you," he said, reaching out to hug her. Maddie stepped backwards. "What do you want?"

"Lovie, I've come to take you to my castle, as I promised."

Maddie bristled. Why shouldn't she feel outrage? He had abandoned her, just like the others before him. "You're too late! My castle is here with my new family, Ammon and Edrice," she said, turning around to look for them. They had quietly slipped away.

"Look, Maddie, I've said I'm sorry.

That tired old phrase again.

"It took a lot more planning than I anticipated, and I forked out a lot of money to help you," he explained in a whiny voice. "But everything is in place now. So get your things and let's go. We have a ferry to catch. You are going to love England, and once we are settled there, I'm going to marry you and give you my name. You will never be nameless or homeless again. And I'm hoping, given time, you will come to love me as I do you."

Deception oozed from David's sweating face. Only Maddie didn't see it. She was wearing blinders. Other factors began to run rampant through her brain: *Sooner than later, my illegal status will come to the attention of the Italian authorities. How long can I impose on the generosity and protection of my hosts? Will I put them in jeopardy? Could their Landed Immigrant Status be revoked? Could they be prosecuted for paying me under the table?* Her indecisiveness triggered her response. "I can't bring trouble to these kind people. I can't let this happen."

"What did you say?" David asked.

"I will go with you," she said softly.

Had Maddie been brainwashed to obey and readily embrace change? No. She was terrified.

Three days before the end of this dismal March, after tearful goodbyes, Maddie left her happy home, her music, and her savings.

Unable to write, she drew a smiley face on a piece of paper and placed it on top of her piggy bank, a golden Sphinx coffee container. Maddie treasured this gift from Edrice, and leaving it behind brought a lump to her throat. As she exited the building, she never looked back. She was afraid she would burst out crying.

The odd-looking couple walked arm in arm past the hostel and down a side street. The driver of a dark-green Morris-Commercial J-type vehicle—a "band van" used for touring musicians—was waiting for them. Bob, his face flushed with impatience, stuck his head out of the window and yelled, "Get a bloody move on! I've been waiting for hours." That was BS because the conversation in Ammon's home had taken barely thirty minutes.

While Bob and David took seats up front, Maddie settled onto a single back seat surrounded by tall Marshall amplifiers, and various other musicians' gear, and cigarette butts. She was clueless about the journey of 1,525 miles, twenty-six hours, that would take her to the *promised* castle. She knew it would not be a holiday drive, but driving in March was better than driving in high summer, because there were fewer traffic holdups. Her van would only slow down for toll booths, rest stops, gas stations, and restroom breaks. David had explained that even though the train would be faster, driving had fewer risks at the border crossings.

To de-stress after the first leg of the journey, the passengers alighted, stretched their legs, and used the gas station bathroom. A pizza and cola lunch, served at the Paranoia Café, fortified their spirits. To Maddie's delight, David handed her an elegant gift box of Bacio dark chocolate with hazelnuts. She tasted a piece of heaven in her mouth.

But hell was right around the corner!

Just after midnight, Bob pulled into a slummy motel that rented rooms by the hour. It was a far cry from the Intercontinental Hotel. Their one room was tiny and cramped: one double bed, no bedside table or lamp, worn carpet, tattered couch, electrical outlets with wires hanging out, and duct tape on the doorknob. Maddie's brow furrowed. She couldn't understand this shoddy choice. She had the impression David had more money than he could spend in a lifetime.

She shared the unhygienic double bed, fully clothed, with David. Bob curled up on the couch. The fetid smell of the bedding kept Maddie awake, as did the sound of sexual escapades passing through the paper-thin walls, and the loud snoring that bellowed from the other two occupants of her room.

At daybreak Maddie awoke to discover she was alone. She dove out of the disgusting bed, looked around the room, and panicked. *Did they leave without me? Why would David do that? Had he changed his mind?* She gave a sigh of relief when David arrived, holding take-out coffees and cheese-and-egg breakfast buns. "I thought you had left me!" she cried.

"Why would I do that, silly one!" he laughed.

Maddie smiled.

"Eat your breakfast. We have to get going."

After a quick wash at the stained bathroom sink, Maddie gladly left a room she never wanted to see again. When she joined the cigarette puffing men outside, David offered her one. "Ugh! It smells like dung!" It was a marihuana joint.

Maddie refused this substance, offered to her many times over the years, until, later in her life, nicotine took precedence as a habit.

"What a glorious sunny day," she said gleefully. Though there was still a frosty nip in the air, her heart was singing.

"It won't be long now," David promised.

Maddie noticed that the rear door of the van was wide open. Sitting unstably on the tailgate was a huge speaker cabinet. Its back panel had been pulled off and its inner parts removed, leaving only the mounted loudspeakers. When David ordered her to get in the cabinet, Maddie's face revealed her terror. "You have to get into this cabinet amp. We are not far from the border crossing, and you can't be seen."

Maddie's body stiffened. "How will I breathe?"

"Holes have been drilled into the sides. You will have plenty of air."

"I just can't! I'm claustrophobic!" Maddie's camera went into overdrive.

Click, click, click.

"You have been a bad little girl," Mother Superior scolded. "You must be punished for stealing food that is not yours."

The child's screams, coming from a locked cupboard under a stairway, were ignored. When little Maddie was let out twenty-four hours later, she couldn't stand up straight. She had barely had enough room to squat. From that terrifying day to this day, Maddie had dreaded crowded escalators, windowless rooms, unlit rooms, and even tight-necked clothing. Being placed into the back of this cabinet petrified her. "I can't do this. I will die!"

"Don't be frightened, lovie. You'll be okay. As soon as we get across the border, I will let you out."

Maddie's racing heart delivered 300-watts of output. She was released thirty minutes later, aching and sweat soaked, in France. Relieved to be out of her confinement, she inhaled as if her first breath would be her last.

Maddie traveled in comfort on the front passenger seat until they arrived at the Calais ferry crossing checkpoint. There, parked down a secluded back alley, she was again bundled into her transport cabinet. The ninety-minute, twenty-one-mile sailing to Dover, England, proved to be the nightmare of all nightmares for claustrophobics. The English Channel, a narrow passage separating England from France, was hit by a sudden storm. Fierce winds lashed viciously at the P & O vessel, tossing it from side to side. Sea water ebbed and flowed through the vehicle bay, and the majestic, chalky White Cliffs of Dover, were cloaked in dense fog. The contents of Maddie's sour stomach splashed onto her only set of clothes, Alwyn's gift. When David had asked where his gifts were, she struggled to keep her reddening cheeks from giving her away. "They were stolen at the hostel."

"Bunch of bloody thieves is gypsy travelers!" he huffed. "Anyway, you won't need castoffs from now on. I'll buy you beautiful clothes when we get home."

There was no turning back now. Trapped like a panicked animal in a bait trap, Maddie's suntanned face turned pea green, and her breathing became as raspy as a carpenter's tool. Was David thinking about her? Hell, no! He spent his time drinking and smoking at the bar with Bob.

Thank heavens! The green van passed through British Customs without a problem and parked down a back-country lane. The ensnared creature was finally freed, but not from the overpowering odor of vomit.

Bob pinched his nostrils. "Jesus, girl, you stink!" he shrieked as he turned to David. "I'm not driving with her in my van, not smelling like that!"

"Okay, okay. Calm down."

At a nearby petrol station restroom, Maddie removed her soiled clothing and discarded them in a trash bin. She sighed.

Again, her clothing bore a resemblance to Dopey's. She wore David's extra-large T-shirt, his pants, and a thin hand-knit cardigan that sagged down to her shoes.

She had no underwear to augment her humorous outfit; her

urine-stained panties had joined her other discarded garments.

Sitting on the back seat staring out a window, Maddie caught a glimpse of the medieval fortress, Dover Castle. "David, look. I hope our castle is nicer than that bleak, cold structure. David laughed like a madman, a term not far from the truth!

An exhausted Dopey slept soundly for the remainder of the journey. When the vehicle came to a halt, she opened her eyes and stared at a concrete jungle, a low-income housing complex. "David, what is this place?" she asked.

"Your new home," he laughed.

"What do you mean my new home? It doesn't look like a fancy castle to me."

"Like it or not, this *is* your new home," he snapped." F'ing get used to it!"

Maddie's eyes flashed in alarm. "But …"

"Shut up! Follow me," he ordered.

In a sullen mood, Maddie trailed behind David's bulky frame up two fights of concrete stairs until they came to door 24. In a stern voice he said, "Wait here."

An invisible lightning bolt fused Maddie curious tongue to the roof of her mouth. She watched David take a key out of his pants pocket and let himself into the unit. She leaned against the balcony railing and rubbed her hands together, warming them against the biting wind assailing her inadequately clothed body. Puffs of exhaled breath curled around stupefied thoughts. *Oh, my God, he's a human trafficker! Is this where he is going to make a deal? Run, run, run …* Fear froze Maddie's body and mind, and the ice sculpture was not going to melt anytime soon.

Time ticked by. Suddenly she spotted a person of medium height heading towards her, a fur-hooded parka obscuring his face. Ian Blakely stared at her outlandish attire and thought, *Blimey! What's going on?*

"What are you doing here, miss?" he asked in a strong London accent. "You'll catch your death of cold with no coat."

Stiff with fear and chill, Maddie's head remained downcast.

"Are you waiting for someone?"

Her finger, inflamed from the cold, pointed to the door. Ian's white eyebrows puckered. He turned his back on Maddie and walked through door 24. He passed the kitchen and walked into the adjoining living room. There he was inundated with tobacco smoke, thicker than diesel fumes, which coiled like ghostly fingers from floor to the ceiling. Ian, who did not smoke, felt thousands of chemicals assail his nostrils. He coughed and spluttered. "For God's sake, open a window," he moaned to the two heavy smokers. Ian glared at his estranged wife, her blue eyes bugging out behind thick, horn-rimmed glasses. Her chubby face the color of the red scarf draped around her neck.

Ian turned his attention to his son, who was sitting on a rocking chair wearing eyewear identical to his mother's.

"Hello, David."

"Hi, Dad," David replied with a hint of emotion.

"What the bloody hell is going on here? There is a frostbitten girl outside ..."

Jean cut him off. "Ask you brain-dead son why there's a female outside."

"Well?"

"Dad, like I've already told Mum, I met her in Italy. I've brought here because I'm in love and want to marry her."

Ian's taut expression mocked his son. They had been at logger-heads since David dropped out of high school to play in a band. His out-of-work adult son had been tied to Jean's purse strings for a long time. She had enabled him—paid for music lessons; bought him an expensive guitar, clothes, and jewelry; and given him money. Mommy's boy had gotten everything he ever wanted. Now her generous handouts were about to end.

"What were you thinking, you bloody numbskull? You're still living with your mother. You can't take care of yourself, let alone another person!"

"That's exactly what I told him," piped up Jean. "I'll not have the bitch staying in my home. I don't care if she freezes to death."

Ian's eyes dilated and glared at his ex and his son.

Jean's and David's eyes were set like a deer's in headlights. They both remained silent.

The sixty-year-old father turned on his heels, walked outside, took Maddie by her cold hand, and led her into the flat.

When Maddie entered the two-bedroom home, Jean jumped to her feet as if confronted by a monster. "Bloody Hell!" she shrilled. "What is that *thing*? A tramp? Is *it* human? Does *it* speak English?"

Maddie sensed instinctively that she was being brutally insulted and feared physical attack from this territorial lioness defending her offspring. Jean's predatory roar continued. "Marry her? Are you stark raving mad, David? Whatever possessed you to bring a good-for-nothing piece of shit into to my home?"

Nothing he could say or do could quiet the lioness's tongue. She was well practiced in the art of reducing others to within an inch of the ground. "Get her out of here!" Jean shrilled. "Throw her back into the rubbish where she belongs, or I'll kick you out too!"

Maddie stared at the bloated, pulsating vein in Jean's neck. She thought it would burst.

"How can you be so cruel?" Ian retorted. "She's barely out of diapers!"

"My point!" the fifty-two-year-old Jean said in a soprano voice. The wildcat's lips pulled back to reveal crooked teeth set in a small mouth. "So you think I'm being cruel?" Look who's talking! You walked out on me and David, your only son. That is *real* cruelty."

Maddie heaved a sigh of relief. This nasty, snaggletooth lioness couldn't bite a flea let alone devour her. However, the teenager was smart enough to deduce that this ranting and raving was not going to end in her favor.

Ian shook his head in disgust. Thinking back, he wished he had never hooked up with the "sly fox" from his workplace. Back then she was his boss's secretary, and he was a lowly parts manager. He never intended to pay her any attention. She wasn't his type. He preferred blondes, tall and slim. She was short, dumpy, and brunette.

At a staff Christmas party, thirty-six years ago, Jean set her sights on the physically appealing Ian. The unattractive woman flirted with him brazenly. Her seductive ploy—eye contact, hair flicking, lips licking, and touching—finally snared her inebriated coworker. "Your place or mine?" she asked shamelessly.

Their next move left little to the imagination: a car parked in a dark, secluded spot; steamy Vauxhall Velox windows; and rocking on the back seat. The next day at work, a sheepish Ian deliberately avoided Jean the best he could. The troubled Ian didn't apply "To err is human" to himself. Instead, he beat himself up for his lack of self-control. A stupid mistake, getting physically intimate with a woman he had no intention of "being" with. But Jean, completely smitten, wasn't going to take *no* for an answer. She bombarded Ian with love notes, gifts, and a final shocker. "I'm pregnant," she announced during a lunch break.

Their marriage had been far from mutual affection. Rather, it had been a marriage of convenience.

Following a "quickie" civil ceremony, Ian worked long hours to support his stay-at-home wife and their son. But Jean soon bored of her "workaholic" partner. Ian had learned from a workmate that Jean had cheated on him repeatedly throughout their marriage. Her infidelity with his best friend, James, was his breaking point.

The morning after David's sixteenth birthday, Ian packed his belongings and walked away from his loveless, adulterous marriage. Citing adultery, he was granted a divorce a year later. Of course, David took his "Hell hath no fury ..." mother's side. Ian tried hard to remain in his son's life after the divorce, but Jean's poisonous propaganda triumphed.

David had refused to have anything to do with his father, until now.

The drama reenacted in number 24 was far from over. A sneer crossed Ian's mouth. He knew her threat to kick David out would *never* take place.

When Jean learned she couldn't have more children due to a pelvic inflammatory disease, she started showing classic signs of possession and obsession toward David. He became the center of her universe. She even suffered separation anxiety when he left home to attend school. She did not welcome the idea of her son growing up.

Mother and son became codependent. Jean carried her son financially, morally, and emotionally. Her psychological makeup and her controlling nature contributed to the development of an unstable adult. Ian had no doubt that his son had become a carbon-copy of Jean.

Since dropping out of high school, David had showed no interest in girls, hobbies, or ideas of his own. But he did have a passion for music. When Jean bought him an electric Stratocaster bass guitar and paid for private lessons, he was content. It wasn't long before he met other musicians and joined an unremarkable local band. His dating and his flings never lasted more than a couple of days. Meanwhile, he began distancing himself from his mother by taking trips abroad with money "milked" from her pockets. Jean's anxiety attacks intensified.

Ian continued to brood. His residence was only three blocks away. It was the only low-income housing available at the time of their breakup. His job as parts manager at Vauxhall Motors paid minimum wage.

Until now, the divorced couple had kept a healthy distance from each other.

Jean had called him earlier this morning pleading in a sweet, manipulative voice. "You know I wouldn't bother you if it wasn't urgent. Please, I need a big favor. Sadie is very sick. I need to take her to the emergency veterinary clinic, and my car won't bloody start."

Ian knew her well. When she needed something done for her or David, she was as sweet as apple pie, but when alimony payments were one day late, she was the beast from hell.

"Okay. I'll get dressed and pick you and Sadie up."

The Blue Point Siamese cat was a gift, sixteen years ago, from soft-hearted Ian to Jean when her parents died suddenly in a car accident. Even though Ian still helped his ex, there wasn't a cat's chance in hell he would consider rekindling their relationship. He knew no other man had moved into her home and taken his place. Had she reformed? Hell, no!

Ian had not remarried, either, but he had a lady friend, Anne, whom he dated on and off. It was not Jean, but his love of felines—he owned three striped Tabbies rescued from the RSPA—that brought him to his ex's apartment this day. But now that he was here, his thinking changed. Veterinary care for the aged cat was no longer his priority. He turned his compassion, instead, to the bedraggled girl standing rooted to one spot with tears streaming down her thin face. "Don't cry," he said, patting her shoulder. "I'll sort this out."

Ian reached into his wallet and pulled out a wad of bills. As he placed them on the glass coffee table he pleaded, "Please, back off, Jean. Let her stay here with David until I can find them another accommodation."

Jean rolled her eyes and twisted her lips into an evil posture. If a face ever meant looks can kill, Ian saw it then. "For *one* week," she snapped, "and I mean it, Ian, or I will call the police and have them both thrown out." Next, she turned on her son, who was twiddling his thumbs mechanically. "Go on, thank your father. I was going to kick you out on your arse. Something I should have done years ago.

And for the week you will be here, there are going to be rules in *my* home for that *thing*. Okay?"

David nodded.

Maddie went numb. Her thoughts became as dead as her eyes. Standing as still as a marble statue, she was relieved when Ian and Jean left, taking the poor cat with them. Being an indoor animal, Sadie had grown old, outliving the outdoor cats. But she never again returned to the apartment. She died at the clinic from feline hypertrophic cardiomyopathy, heart disease. Of course, Jean blamed Maddie. If she hadn't turned up, her beloved feline could have been saved more quickly. David's mother would have gladly beaten Maddie to death with a whip.

Maddie, the stray waif, was not going to see a hostile-free environment for some time to come.

With his parents out of the house, David stood up and hugged the rigid statue. "Everything is going to be okay, lovie," he said holding her hand. He led her upstairs to his bedroom. "You can stay here with me until Dad finds us a place of our own."

With her bladder ready to burst, Maddie rushed to the bathroom adjoining David's bedroom, then climbed into his unmade bed. She pulled the patchwork bedspread over her head, overcome with inconsolable sadness. She was trapped in a world of her making because she had believed David. Maddie hugged the tattered panda she had retrieved from the Italian dumpster and berated herself for not listening to her inner voice back in Italy: *If it's too good to be true* ..."

CHAPTER SIX

*"You took away my worth, my intimacy, my time,
but you will never silence the voice inside me."*

In March of 1968, the morning after the histrionics in Jean's Kinloch Gardens apartment, Maddie awoke alone. She tried to keep her sinking feelings in check, but they were having none of it: *Not again! Where is he? Please, don't let me be dumped all over again, left at the mercy of the old lioness!*

Maddie glanced at the wind-up alarm clock on the bedside table. *Oh, my goodness! It's nearly noon!* Surprised, Maddie tried to comprehend the late hour. Had David merely let her sleep off her exhaustion from the long trip? Or had he slipped something into the cup of tea he gave her the night before? It had tasted bitter, but she had been so thirsty, she swallowed it without a second thought.

The last thing she remembered hearing was a moaning grunt.

Maddie got out of bed and started toward the door. Then she felt it—a gooey liquid with an acrid odor—and saw it—spots of drying blood adhering to her female parts. She stifled a fiendish, nightmare scream. But it was clear—David had taken advantage of her. She had been sexually assaulted! Should she confront him? No. That would be suicide given her circumstances. Even if she ran away, where would she go in this foreign land?

Before going into the bathroom, Maddie leaned over the stair railing listening for sounds. An eerie silence danced around her like ectoplasm. Where were David and his mother? Had they gone out together? At that moment, she couldn't have cared less. She just wanted to clean herself of the "crime."

No matter how hard she tried to wash the awful "deed" from her body, it remained embedded in her mind like a craggy piece of glass.

After leaving the bathroom, she stealthily found her way to the only other bedroom on the upper floor. It wasn't curiosity that led her there; it was the pressing need to find underwear.

Jean's bedroom was a mess: bed unmade, dirty laundry on the floor, makeup strewn over the dresser, and closet doors wide open. After opening a couple of dresser draws, Maddie found Jean's stash of undergarments. They were unflattering, to say the least, but Maddie was in no position to be choosy.

Dressed in the only set of clothing she possessed—David's T-shirt, the baggy cardigan, and Jean's pink tent-size knickers—she went downstairs. Not a soul was in sight, thank goodness. The kitchen was just as messy as Jean's bedroom: dirty dishes stacked high in the enamel sink, used tea cups cluttering the counter, and brown-and-cream squares of linoleum that looked like they had not been cleaned in years. Hunger-pains lead her to the refrigerator. That too hadn't seen a washcloth in some time. The moldy food contents made Maddie cringe. She found a packet of unopened Marie biscuits, poured herself a glass of water from the tap, and headed back upstairs. No sooner had a biscuit crumbled in her mouth, than she heard voices. Maddie quickly hid the "removed-without-permission" biscuits under a pillow.

A heavy-footed David mounted the stairs, opened his bedroom door, and put several shopping bags down. "Good. You're awake. I let you sleep in because you were dead to the world when I left to go shopping with Mum." He leaned forward to give Maddie a kiss. She recoiled in disgust, but she knew it was not in her interest to confront him, to speak her mind about the nonconsensual sex. Her inner voice commanded her to pretend nothing was wrong.

"Here," David said. "I bought you some clothes, makeup, and guess what? Look."

One item at a time, Maddie, eyes wide, laid outfits on the bed that were anything but modest. Though the material was of high quality, the ostentatious wardrobe looked like items a prostitute would wear: two *very* short slip dresses—one lime green and one crimson red—with revealing cleavage that left nothing to the imagination. Maddie had no breasts to set off these exotic outfits, but even if she had, she would never have chosen such slutty clothes. Drawing unwanted attention to her legs, breasts, or other parts was not in this shy girl's makeup. To accompany the sleaziness of the outfits, David bought her a slate-blue chinchilla jacket. Maddie cringed. She was fanatical about cruelty to furry friends, a hard-core animal lover, and she abhorred fur coats that fed human vanity. She was never going to wear something so brutal on her back, or so she thought! The skimpy underwear in a variety of bright colors was the last indignity.

"Go on, lovie, try them on," David said with a lecherous grin.

When Maddie objected saying she did not want to be mistaken for a "lady of the night," David snarled and approached her menacingly. "You should be down on your knees thanking me for these clothes. If it wasn't for me, you'd be dead, or you would still be speaking native!"

Glumly, Maddie put on the outfits, all two sizes too large, and modeled them. A slutty-looking, red-faced Dopey walked the fashion runway of their confined bedroom.

David announced his intentions. "Lie on the bed. You are going to enjoy this," he said, unzipping his pants.

Maddie died by pieces. Her eyes—dark-rimmed, wounded, haunted, and tragic—spoke volumes: *He can never rape and despoil what's in my head. I have a witness ... my camera!*

CHAPTER SEVEN

"I'm not what happened to me. I am
what I choose to become."
—CARL JUNG

A week dragged on with no sign of Ian, her defender. Had he developed cold feet? Maddie yearned to take control of her life, to escape from an abode where depraved persons dwelled. David and his mother were each holding her captive, enslaved, differently. She was living a life like the inhumane one she had left behind in South Africa. Sometimes her captors went out, but if they were home, they sat in the living room watching TV, eating snacks, and smoking. Maddie shared no such indulgences. She had become an unpaid slave.

From morning to night Maddie worked on chores: dusting, mopping, scrubbing, polishing, washing, ironing, and preparing countless cups of tea. "Do this" and "Do that" were thrown out endlessly. And nothing Maddie did was to Jean's satisfaction.

"You are a useless piece of shit! Can't you even clean a bathroom properly?"

Maddie was trapped indoors, not *allowed* to venture outside the confines of the grizzly apartment unless accompanied by David or the mangy lioness. Occasionally they let her stand in the sun on the balcony, if it suited them. Her hard and heavy life continued unrelentingly.

One evening all hell broke loose.

Tucked in bed after a grueling day, Maddie heard shouting loud enough to split the floorboards beneath her bed. She couldn't hear every word, but instinct told her it was bad. Then, as quickly as it had started, it died down. Maddie didn't give the commotion another thought. Fatigue weighted her weary eyes.

The next morning she was woken by a loud knocking at the front door. David was not in bed. Before she gathered her thoughts, the bedroom door flew open, and there stood two uniformed officers, one male and one female. "Madeline Clark, you are to get dressed and come with us," the female officer ordered in a clipped tone.

Numb with shock, Maddie wanted to ask why, but her comfort zone—silence—nudged her to button up.

With her cheeks flushed red with embarrassment, Maddie turned her back to the officers as she soundlessly dressed.

Maddie saw Jean at the bottom of the stairs flashing a plastic smile through creased lips. "Good riddance," she gloated. "I hate you. You took my son from me!"

Where was David? Probably hiding under a rock, Maddie mused. Her fearful expression melted to a resigned look as she was escorted from the flat in handcuffs. As they descended the building's stairwell, curious faces peered from behind window coverings at the young girl wearing a fur coat at the beginning of spring. Maddie didn't have many clothing choices and was certainly not going to wear the slutty outfits that David had given her. So it was either the "Dopey" outfit—David's extra-large T-shirt and cardigan—or Jean's holey nightgown.

Walking toward the paddy wagon, Maddie took a deep breath and wondered if she would ever again smell air filled with intoxicating plant perfumes—fresh cut grass, citrus blossoms, and pink jasmine. The scents presented a heavenly delight to seasonal "nesters."

Shame clung to Maddie like thick fog on a spring morning.

The forty-five-minute drive to the immigration facility for illegals who have overstayed was made in silence until the kind female officer broke the spell. "Here, dear," she said handing over a bottle of water. "I don't suppose you've had anything to eat or drink yet today."

The drive continued in silence.

Maddie gaped at the barbed-wired fencing surrounding the facility. With her escorts at her side, she waited at the admission reception desk, where she got more than stares. Someone in the back of the room was tittering at Maddie's appearance: a luxury fur jacket hanging from her boney shoulders, and the baggy nightwear, and a rat's nest of uncombed red hair that hadn't seen shampoo in a while.

"What's your full name, date of birth, country of origin, and occupation? And where is your passport?" the male officer asked with a poker face.

"Sex-trade worker," a comic voice whispered from behind the desk officer.

"My name is Madeline Clark. That's the name the nuns gave me.

I don't know when I was really born, but Mother Superior told me it was December 2, 1951. I was born in South Africa. And I don't have a passport ..." The sniggering got louder but soon ended when the officer turned and glared at the crude culprit and shook his head. This callousness was a first, even for an officer near retirement who received many unorthodox answers to the mandatory questions!

Maddie was marched to another room where she was photographed, fingerprinted, and allowed to use the bathroom before being steered to a shared cell. She was the sole occupant of a cell designed to house six, and she was grateful for the time alone. She needed to get control of her racing thoughts. As she sat on a foam mattress covered in institutional plastic, elbows resting on her knees, claustrophobic fears heightened her breathing and heartrate. She began to sob. *What did I do so wrong to deserve a nonstop train carrying nothing but suffering?*

Maddie's reality was stark. The South African government would *never* allow her to return. She was undocumented there also. 'You can't come back, missy,' the government official had told her.

The bad luck stacking up against her was staggering. She had been thrown to the wolves repeatedly. Was this latest indignity the icing on the cake? Far from it!

Maddie spread her hands over her tear-stained face trying to stop the claustrophobia jangling every nerve in her body. *Help! Get me out of here, or I'll go mad!*

Time rolled by.

Maddie sprang to her feet at noon when the cell flap clang open and she saw a hand push something through. "Lunch," said a flat voice.

The plastic, sectional tray held unexpected cuisine: a slice of roast chicken topped with a spoonful of gravy, mashed potatoes, marrowfat peas, two slices of buttered bread, a small carton of homogenized milk, and a banana. The aromas tickled her taste buds, but Maddie's stomach was so knotted, the food probably wouldn't stay down. She returned the meal uneaten. "You will wish you had eaten," the voice outside the cell door said. "You'll not get this at suppertime, only bread and tea."

Forced into this circumstance, Maddie couldn't tell if it was day or night, but a yawn hinted it was time to lie down. Her fur coat served as a pillow, but the ceiling light and her flow of tears kept sleep at bay.

After many agonizing hours, Maddie accepted her fate. There is no manual for this: "*How to Survive Hatred.*" And it wasn't hope that got her through this darkest hour.

"Wake up Maddie. You're being released," the guard announced casually. "You won't be getting an airline ticket like the rest."

Half awake, Maddie frowned. *Really?*

One hour later she was released from detention. Waiting for her at the exit gate were David, his father, and an unknown face. Maddie had seen neither hide nor hair of her "champion," Ian, since the day he promised to help her. And David's *promise* to give her a good life was a sick joke.

Maddie gave Ian a hug but did not offer the same to David. Instead, she felt like slapping him, and hard. Her bitterness faded when the third man—tall, wearing a black suit, white shirt, black tie, and bowler hat—stepped forward and introduced himself. "Miss Clark, my name is Edward Jones. I'm from the Home Office. I'm here at the request of Roland Harcourt, our British Ambassador in Kenya. He asked me to investigate your detention, which I have. But your case is extremely complicated. It will take time to officially fix your continued stay in the United Kingdom. But I can assure you, you will not be deported back to South Africa."

Maddie thought, *Ha, you old fart! I could have told you that myself! And how did Roland know I was in jail?* She had had no contact with the Consulate since she was dumped in Italy. But, deciding to ignore that thought, she was happy to be out of confinement. When David told her she would not be returning to number 24, she was over the moon. She never wanted to see number 24—or the wild cat, Jean—again.

Maddie, mentally exhausted but happy, was going to reside at Ian's home until matters were resolved, and the official promised to keep in touch with updates on the progress of her legal status.

Maddie was out of detention, but she was not free.

On the drive to Ian's home, David, with a long face, explained he had no idea his mother had called immigration, and when he found out what she had done, he had gone ballistic. *Ah, that explains the shouting,* Maddie mused. When she asked him why he didn't visit her in detention, he explained that they weren't married. Only spouses or relatives were allowed visitation. Then David cried like a schoolgirl. "Please forgive me, Maddie. I'll try to make it up to you. I'll be the best husband ever. My dad knows someone who will help us get a marriage license, and then we can be married. And God help anyone who tries to separate us."

For the remainder of the drive to Ian's home, Maddie hid her feeling of disgust behind a blank expression. She remained silent, but her *camera* could not; it was busy recording every sight, sound, and feeling.

When they reached Ian's apartment, Maddie was sorry to learn it was only three blocks from her nemesis. Too close for comfort!

Ian's building was no different than the one she had left behind. "Berkshire Gardens" was as cold, stark, and impersonal as Jean's Kinloch Gardens. These concrete jungles were far from glamorous. Ian told her that these residential buildings had sprung up like weeds after the German offensive in 1940. They were a far cry from the princess castle David had lied about. However, Maddie would rather live in a bat cave than in Jean's den of iniquity. Here, at least, she would not have to look at Sadie, the expired, freeze-dried Siamese. The cat did not resemble a live, peacefully sleeping pet. To the contrary, she looked spring-loaded and ready to scratch out someone's eyes. Sadie would have made a prefect "actress" in an Alfred Hitchcock movie.

Maddie stepped out of Ian's Peugeot and smiled at the harbingers of spring—robins flitting across the front lawn. She soaked in their delightful antics before entering Ian's ground-floor apartment, and sighed. She hadn't felt this good in a long while.

It was a new day, and a warm one at that. Maddie would soon fall in love with Ian's roommates, three adorable tabby cats: Lily, Sally, and Moe.

On a wet spring day in the middle of April, Maddie and David were married by the justice of the peace at Croydon Town Hall. She never asked how this was possible given she had no legal paperwork, but later she learned Ian had sought help from a forger who had "doctored" a deceased woman's identification. But the age of the deceased could not be doctored without drawing unwanted attention. Seventeen-year old Maddie was now *twenty-one!* This official, irreparable age disparity would have an everlasting and consequential effect. Maddie would live with this age discrepancy for the rest of her life.

Settled into her new digs, Maddie felt happier than a pig in poop. As spring and summer rolled by, she discovered a part of her life that had been missing. She now had a fabulous father figure. Ian was good to her, treated her like a daughter, and spoiled her rotten. And when time allowed, he taught her how to read and write. David, on the other hand, was becoming increasingly verbally abrasive toward her when his father wasn't around. Jealousy was eating at him from the inside out. "You should have married my father, 'cuz you sure don't love me like you do him."

Any feelings Maddie may have had for David, who rescued her from the streets, died the day she set foot in Jean's home.

What is love, really? This powerful emotion was yet unknown to Maddie. She had felt only outrage and hatred throughout her entire life, until Ian came along. Any tender affection she had, she gave to him.

In the fall of that year Maddie's contentment crashed down on her like a mudslide, burying her blissfulness for a long time.

One day when Maddie tried to wake her father-in-law for work, she found him stone cold dead. An autopsy revealed congestive heart failure.

At the funeral Ian's workmates came by to say their goodbyes. Anne, the woman Ian had dated, was there, but Jean was absent. Ian wouldn't have wanted her there anyway.

Maddie cried for days.

To her surprise, though, Maddie learned at the reading of the will that Ian had instructed his lawyer to use his insurance money to buy his rental from the council and put Maddie name on the title. If any money was left over from the purchase or in his bank account, Ian's lawyer was to open an account in Maddie name. His 1961 Peugeot was left to David.

That day David stomped out of the lawyer's office muttering profanities. He headed for the nearest pub. Maddie dreaded his return. Without a doubt, a stampede of alcohol-induced ugliness would escort him through the door. But what hurt Maddie most was related to Ian's beloved tabby cats—Lily, Sally, and Moe. They had mysteriously disappeared. Maddie's eyes bore into David's, and silently questioned him. "I can't find the kitties," she said. "I saw them last night cuddled in their bed. They can't have vanished into thin air!"

David's blank, unconcerned expression hid the truth. "Beats me!" he said. "Maybe they got out."

"That's not possible," Maddie argued. "They have always been indoor cats. Why would they suddenly leave the apartment, unless *you* let them out?" she added accusingly.

David did not reply, but his wry grin told her he knew something.

What if David had killed them, drove them somewhere and thrown them from the car?

Much later Maddie learned that David had taken the tabbies to the animal shelter while she was sleeping. No amount of reasoning could silence her sorrow. Those cats had played a big part in her life with Ian. She especially loved when all three would jostle for a spot on her lap. When reality sunk in that Ian's beloved pets were never coming back, Maddie cried. There is no formula for grief! Was she to be the next one to simply vanish from Earth?

When in fear, walk away!

Maddie had nowhere else to go. Life at Berkshire Gardens wasn't good, and it was going to worsen in the coming year.

Maddie's forecast was as dismal as faded leaves falling brown and dead on the dirt.

CHAPTER EIGHT

"The greater the power, the more
dangerous the abuser."

In February 1969, Maddie walked home from her latest hospital visit in frightfully cold weather. However, it wasn't frigid temperature surging through her body. It was positive pregnancy hormones. She just couldn't believe it. It had to be a miracle. She was having another baby. She felt calmness settle in her heart like never before, but then came her probing "pregnant pauses." *Will my baby live to full term? Am I mature enough to be a parent? How will David react? Will he see me and treat me with respect, as the mother of his child?*

Dr. Barazani's thoughts were also running rampant. Maddie's pregnancy was medically unexplainable—a teenager with no menstrual cycle and one remaining, impaired, fallopian tube getting pregnant *A greater force must have pulled strings to gift her with another miracle baby.*

Prajit retrieved a notebook from his desk drawer and began writing: "Madeline Blakely, a seventeen-year-old ..."

Walking home, Maddie fed some hungry feathered friends. When she arrived at David's front door, she rattled the handle. No response.

Maddie's stomach turned queasy. She tried the handle again. This time the door opened. She stepped into the dim hallway, a cavern of dark wallpaper. As her insides roiled, she belittled herself: *You're a mouse, a little black mouse! Get a grip!*

"I'm home, my dear," Maddie announced in a superficial tone. She removed her footwear but still heard only silence. This was unusual. David never left the premises unlocked when he went out. She looked at the clock on the wall and gave herself a mental slap. *Duh! It's not time yet.*

She paced persistently as she waited for David to return from the Duck and Swan pub, his favorite watering hole and one he visited daily before each evening meal.

Meals at David's house were programmed. Even though Maddie couldn't boil an egg before she arrived in England, she mastered Britain's traditional dishes by watching television—the Philip Harben Cooking Program—at David's insistence. Breakfast, lunch, and supper had to be ready on time! Or she would never hear the end of it!

Breakfast 7 A.M.: a fry-up of eggs, bacon, sausage, fried bread, baked beans, and mushrooms, accompanied by a pot of Ceylon tea.

Lunch 2 noon: two sandwiches, one tuna and mayonnaise and the other ham and pickle, served with a pot of tea.

Supper	6:30 P.M.: meat and two vegetables with another pot of tea.
Sunday	Roast meat, two vegetables, potatoes, and Yorkshire pudding and gravy. This was the only day coffee washed down the meal instead of tea.

Occasionally Maddie's controlling husband send her out to the local fish-and-chip shop around the corner. Maddie loved this respite from the drudgery of working at a hot stove, but she was not used to the stodginess of the standard British food. She often dished out for herself tiny portions, faking a loss of appetite. David's twisted sneer and disparaging words were uncalled for: "Suit yourself, but if I hadn't come along, you would be eating dog shit! You can starve yourself for all I care!"

Sticks and stones may break my bones, but words will never hurt me.

Simply untrue.

Recognizing that words can hurt and wound is one thing. Taking steps to stop them is another. First you must know the difference between light and dark. The day she met David, her wolf in sheep's clothing, his malicious intent masquerading as kindness was unrecognizable to her. She had convinced herself the "good Samaritan" was a kind, gentle, compassionate, and caring man. It wasn't until she set foot on his stomping grounds that his true character came to light, and it had not altered to this day.

David exhibited extreme sociopathic tendencies. He was a skilled manipulator—glib, superficially charming, and cunning. He was an unemotional control freak who rarely admitted he could be wrong. He would never consider talking about an issue and working through it. His obsession was *ownership*. He never backed off.

After Ian's death David dictated how everything was to be done, despite their initial language barrier. Maddie had to master the English language, and quickly. She would come to learn these phrases well: "You will do as you are told, or else! If you don't, it will be me that has you locked up again. This time you will rot all alone because I certainly won't bail you out …" It sounded as if a two-year old had stepped into an adult's shoes. "Ha, Dad's dead!" Cackling like a demented person, he added, "You are not even wanted in the country where your sorry ass was born. Go figure!"

In addition to cooking and cleaning, Maddie was to act humbly toward her master. David's learned, inhumane behavior—*the apple doesn't fall from the tree*—applied not only to the clothing Maddie wore, but also to bedroom rights—nonconsensual sex on a regular basis. David had to be slipping something, like scopolamine, a date rape drug, into her nighttime tea because in the mornings she awoke unaware of what had transpired or of where she was.

David's power-hungry control of her stretched beyond her comprehension. She was directed to stay indoors and keep everything in the house running to his satisfaction. She wasn't allowed to talk to other people, especially their neighbor Lyndsey, a single woman on the second floor of their apartment block.

Maddie's only companions were two stuffed animals—a panda and bean-filled teddy bear—cuddly playthings rescued from the Milan dumpster. She was also deprived of a pet. She missed the tabbies. Their disappearance left a hole in her heart.

The "inferior" teenager had no freedom to make her own choices, so she became a gracious hostess (and a trophy wife) to David's motley friends, who, like her husband, drank and smoked too much. Sometimes her husband hurled humiliating vulgarities at her, which his visitors found raucously amusing. Behind closed doors, verbal and physical abuse—being slapped, kicked, spat at, ridiculed, humiliated, berated, and name called—became the norm. But David couldn't trash everything. She was still in command of her thoughts, feelings, and taste buds. David tried to force her to eat food she considered awful: black pudding, pork rinds, tripe, and offal. But pork dishes made her gag. This reflex made sense to Maddie later in life when she learned she was Jewish by birth. By Jewish religious law, *halacha*, a child born of a Jewish mother is Jewish.

David was unusually late.

Maddie shuffled awkwardly, eyes frequently flicking up to the wall clock. Six o'clock came and went. Seven o'clock marched by. Eight o'clock passed. Maddie's intuition prompted uneasiness. Had Dr. Barazani phoned him? Had the hospital administrator contacted him? Both had threatened to speak to him about his lack of concern for her and the aborted baby, and now, this new pregnancy. Maddie begged them not to. "You don't know him like I do. I will speak to him when I get home. Okay?"

They couldn't have known that living with David was like having a gun pointed at her head every day. She never knew when the weapon would fire. She didn't want to continue living this way, but

David had crossed the line—used her as a punching bag. Could she bring her abuser to justice? Could she press charges? Hell, no! One could get a felony charge for a bar brawl, but a mere slap on the wrist for wife beating! Innocent until proven guilty wasn't working. It was her word against his, and, of course, he would triumph! If she managed to escape, who would protect her? The only witnesses to her abominable circumstances were the higher powers, and they had turned a blind eye!

Maddie was trapped at Berkshire Gardens, snared like an animal, a hunter's kill, just like in her previous residence. Nighttime was the scariest. Hours of alcohol-induced rants punctuated with globs of saliva spraying from David's mouth. She feared this fire-breathing dragon more than she did the legendary *chupacabra,* the "goat sucker" beast of darkness. The television documentary she watched about this mythical creature had provided food for thought. She just didn't know when *her* throat would be ripped open.

Through the eyes of survivors, tragedy is crushing, leaving deep psychological scars that herniate previous emotional trauma. For the rest of her life, Maddie would suffer in silence, refusing to offer her hand to clinically trained professionals. "Textbook Charlies," she called them. *How on earth can they relate to my distress if they have not walked in my shoes?*

Just after eleven o'clock, Maddie heard squeaking door hinges that sounded like an ancient crypt being opened. Would David greet her with pleasantries? Hell, no!

Like a scared mouse, Maddie hid behind a large wooden coat rack, her tender breasts pressed to the wall. *Stay calm. Stay hidden. Hold your breath.* Before she could clamp a jittery, sweating hand over her mouth, David was in her face. His alcohol-laden voice thundered like a mighty ocean wave bristling with profanities. "You lying, bitch! You told me you could *never* have kids. Not only did you have one aborted, you are pregnant *again!*" Possessive and jealous by nature, he accused her of cheating on him, "Whose is it? It's not f'ing mine, whore!"

Maddie glared at her drunken accuser with loathing. "I have not had sex with another man. You know that, David."

"Don't f'ing lie to me!" David's explosion echoed in surround sound.

"When could it have happened?" Maddie rebutted. "You never let me out of your sight!"

David's face turned purple, and his eyes glowed like cinders behind his glasses. "It's bad enough that I have to support your sorry ass. I am not going to support another man's f'ing kid."

Maddie's silence was sardonic. *You mean the extra money you get from welfare for having a wife?* What little money Ian had bequeathed her, David had laid claim to and spent on booze.

Maddie's head was spinning. Had doctor-patient confidentiality been breached? Maddie didn't have time to think about who had betrayed her. She blinked back her tears while a fight-or-flight response surged through her tense body.

"You are going to get rid of it, do you hear me?" he ordered. "Or I will throw you back onto the streets, where you belong."

Previous experience warned Maddie that he wouldn't back off, so she nodded in meek acceptance. But an irate, out of control David wasn't ready to let up. "I can have you committed to the nearest loony bin, a place you know well, don't you?" he threatened. "I'll get them to throw away the key. You are nothing but a pathetic whore. Anyway, what child in their f'ing right mind would want *you* as a mother!"

David's last words woke up the Goliath in Maddie! "You won't get away with it," she hissed. "I will tell them that you are a pervert, keep me under lock and key as your sex slave, and give me drugs so you can do nasty things to me!"

David's inflamed expression did not spur Maddie to back down. She was on a roll. "I've taken the forged marriage license from the dresser and hidden it where you will never find it. It's *your* signature on that document, *not* mine. I will …"

Her audacity had consequences.

Everything happened so fast.

David balled a fist and drew back his arm. Maddie felt the fierce, crushing punch strike her mouth. The impact sent her flying backwards. Blood trickled down her lips, and her head throbbed with blinding pain. But behind her injuries there was a resilient survivor. *What goes around comes around. One day you will pay for your crimes against me.*

And indeed, karma would pluck this evil weed from Earth and burn him in hell's compost heap.

Thirty-two years later, David was gunned down, discovered in a pool of blood not far from his favorite watering hole—The Duck and Swan. He had been shot multiple times. A neighbor who heard the gunfire from his nearby apartment could not identify the vehicle rushing and screeching from the bloody scene.

David's homicide remains a cold case to this day.

On this crazy, hate-filled night, the walls of their home absorbed contemptuous laughter and threats. "Bitch ass nigga," David cussed in an accentuated American tone. He had flung that derogatory term at Maddie more than once, ever since watching a violent movie portraying the KKK.

Fighting anger, frustration, and pain, Maddie lay still. Ringing sounds filled her head. Saliva sprayed as David continued his rant. "You are not going to live long enough to open your mouth again, whore." With lightning speed, his foot delivered a blow. Maddie gasped for air. The last sound she heard … his leather shoes tramping down the hallway. Maddie, a teenager, lay unresponsive on the floor, a victim of domestic abuse fueled by odious emotions. Would she live to fight another day?

Physically, Maddie lay crumpled in the twilight of unconsciousness, but her inner camera continued to operate. One day it would give her a voice and bear witness to the atrocities she suffered.

Time elapsed and folded back on itself.

The past is never dead.

Click, click, click.

CHAPTER NINE

*"Our children change us,
whether they live or not."*

The ceiling light in the hallway flickered spasmodically, as did Maddie's blurred vison. She tried to rise, but a painful stabbing in her lower back forced her back to a fetal position. Maddie heaved a muted sigh of realization. Through her camera's lens she saw her brutal beating—being punched in the jaw, kicked in the abdomen, and viciously insulted. No one should ever have to suffer this abuse. Hate-filled hearts have no conscience.

To Maddie's horror, she felt blood trickling from her vagina. As weak as a new foal, she forced herself to her feet and searched for a sanitary towel. *I dare not venture upstairs. He may hear me rummaging under the washbasin looking for the hospital's pads.*

In desperation, she reached for her cotton headscarf from the coatrack. Folding it into a square, she placed the makeshift pad into her underwear. A stabbing abdominal pain left her breathless. She was in crisis. She knew she had to leave, to seek medical intervention. For the first time in a long while, Maddie turned her throbbing head upward. *Please, whoever you are up there, I tried my best. Please don't let this precious little baby die like the other one. Don't let this treasured soul's journey into this world end by the savage actions of another.* Maddie laid bare her secret sorrow. In her young life, circumstance seemed to always make her a victim, a target of abuse for all those who lorded over her.

Maddie gently rubbed her tender belly while softly singing "Hush, little baby, don't say a word, *Mama's* gonna buy you a mockingbird ..." More stabbing pains interrupted her pregnant plea. Apart from her labored breathing, a cemetery silence pervaded the home. Where was her assailant? Would he attack her again if he heard movement? Doubled over in pain, Maddie placed both of her hands on her lower back and tiptoed to the front door. *Oh, no,* her muted voice cried. The door was locked from the inside, a habit David repeated each night. *Where is the key? Is he upstairs in bed?*

Maddie heard loud snoring spewing from the living room. The sadistic drunk, with bulbous stomach heaving, was passed out on the sofa. She was grateful for the outside light that found its way in through an opening in the drapes. David's wallet and key were beside the sofa.

Maddie removed a five-pound note from his leather wallet and picked up the key. She traveled on tiptoes down the hallway, grabbed a jacket from the coatrack, and gingerly made her way to the outer door. She held her breath as the dry hinges creaked and groaned. Would the noise awaken the monster?

With the door open wide, Maddie rested on the concrete step to catch her breath. The pain of a thousand knives pierced her flesh.

Maddie fled as fast as the pain would allow.

At 10:45 P.M., fifteen minutes before closing time, an out-of-breath Maddie, her features ghostly, staggered into the fish-and-chip shop. "Excuse me," she said to a worker. "I need to speak to Mrs. Morris."

Catherine Morris put the chip fryer basket on a clip to drain and made her way to the counter. "Well, hello, Maddie. What a surprise. You never come this late for a takeout, dearie."

"I'm not here for a takeout, Mrs. Morris," Maddie said breathlessly. "Please call me a taxi."

Catherine's gentle eyes examined Maddie's pale face. "Is everything all right, dearie? You look terrible."

"I'm okay, but I *really* need a taxi, please."

"Sure. I'll call one straight away."

A classic black Austin cab arrived. The driver, wearing checkerboard trousers, a wool jacket, and a Herringbone-tweed cloth cap, opened the passenger door. In a strong Cockney accent, he asked, "Where to, missus?"

"How much does it cost to Croydon Hospital?"

"Two quid."

Maddie heaved a sigh of relief. The stolen money was more than adequate.

As the car set off, Maddie licked the blood from her lip and cradled her sore abdomen. The pain was growing in intensity and becoming unbearable, and so was her embarrassment. She thought the makeshift sanitary towel was leaking because she felt warm blood trickling down her thighs.

Shortly after 11:30 the taxi came to a stop.

Fighting dizziness and nausea, Maddie thanked the driver, paid her fare, and gave him a generous tip.

"Much obliged, missus. I hope all goes well for you."

Maddie headed toward the hospital's automatic door ... and then her knees buckled. She lay unconscious, unaware that the doors were jammed by her prone body.

The cab driver saw her fall, rushed inside, and shouted for help.

Maddie would have been mortified if she had known that she had, indeed, left a puddle of blood on the back seat of the cab.

Maddie's eyes slowly opened. "Oh, no!" she wailed. "Not again!" The anesthesia mask being lowered over her face activated her mind's camera.

Click, click, click.

What is this room? Why have I been brought here? Black man, what are they going to do to me? Are they going to kill me? I'm so scared. I'm so scared ...

A touch of gray streaking his black hair, Dr. Barazani waited by his patient's bedside in the recovery room. He was concerned—she was taking too long to snap out of the anesthesia. While he addressed the signs of domestic abuse—a cut lip and bruised mouth, he suspected that violence had been the major factor in the child's death.

In all the years he had practiced medicine, he had not personally become involved with any of his patients, until this girl. Something about her tugged at his tender heart.

Now, the most difficult part of his profession—how would she take her latest loss, and would she react to his suspicions of abuse?

Would she clam up, like most victims do?

One thing at a time, Prajit told himself, and he reached for her hand. Holding it firmly, he said, "Wake up Maddie."

Her amber eyes slid open. Still groggy, she mumbled, "The last thing I remember is that horrible mask ..."

"I'm sorry," he said interjecting. "Maddie, I had to perform a D&C., scrape your uterine lining ..."

"Why?" This time Maddie halted his words.

No point in beating around the bush. "Your baby son was aborted."

It took a slip of a second for his words to register. "It was a *boy!*" she cried. She had not yet queried the gender of her ectopic baby, if it had been known.

Prajit hoped his consolatory words would bring comfort. "Maddie, against incredible odds, you have conceived twice ..."

"I don't want to talk about it," she interrupted. "Obviously, I'm not meant to have children. That's all there is to it. And I don't bloody need grief counseling," she ended in an escalating voice.

Prajit saw raw sorrow carving furrows into her face. Quietly, he left her side. There was nothing more he could say or do. No words could take away the heartbreak of losing a child.

Prajit was unsure how Maddie's miscarriage came about. *The baby was doing fine at her last checkup.* And he knew this wasn't the best time to discuss her facial injuries.

The loss of a second baby tore at Maddie's heart, stabbing cruelly all over again. She sobbed until tears could no longer fall from her swollen eyes.

Later, when the nurse who had previously offered her a ride

home came to take her vital signs, Maddie spoke tonelessly. "One more of my little angels, whom I have named Alexander, has passed away. It was not meant to be. But Alexander is looking after his baby sister, Sky."   Maddie's second child brought a little comfort to the mother of a baby whose sex was still unknown.

"I'm so sorry," the nurse responded. "You're still very young. Don't give up hope."

Maddie's caregiver could only imagine what she was going through. Having two healthy children at home, the nurse had not experienced the loss of a child. When Maddie was alone in her room, she touched the bronze drapery ring David had placed on her wedding finger last year. He wasn't worth the dirt under her fingernails. Would he feel guilt and remorse? Hell, no! *Leopards don't change their spots!*

There is no greater agony than bearing an untold story.

Before retiring from his shift, Prajit returned to Maddie's bedside. He had to try once more. "Maddie, I would like you to consider seeing Mrs. Phillip's. She is our clinical psychologist and family counselor ..."

"No! I don't need a shrink."

"She's highly qualified and can help you cope."

"N-O spells *no!*"

"Then please talk to me, Maddie. I'm a good listener. You can't hide the truth anymore about your past or present injuries. It's my ethical responsibility to report my reasonable suspicions, regardless of age, to the proper authorities."

"So it's *your* fault my husband beat me up ..." Her lips clenched shut. She had let the cat out of the bag. Maddie saw the discomfort in his dark eyes. She should have bitten her tongue.

"No, Maddie, I did *not* tell him!"

"Well, someone in this hospital did."

Prajit could not break medical confidentiality. Mrs. Phillips' good intentions to counsel the couple had gone horribly wrong. After learning Maddie was pregnant again, she had phoned David to encourage him to attending counseling with Maddie. Prajit couldn't let this good-intentioned blunder interfere with something more important—foul play. "Maddie, I can't stress this enough. You need protection. If you won't talk to Mrs. Phillips or me, then please speak to the police."

"No!"

Maddie, riding on a roller coaster of mixed emotions, knew bringing police into the picture was a no-win for her. An investigation would prompt an immigration inquiry. Maddie still had no documented legal status. She had already spent a day and night behind bars, thanks to Jean Blakely's malicious actions.

Maddie was certain David would not show any compassion for her or the dead baby, but she discharged herself from the hospital anyway and started walking home on timeworn sidewalks. She followed a route she could manage blindfolded. She knew every asphalt crack and every protruding beech tree root that had damaged the pavement. Surprisingly, at this late hour she was accompanied by many boisterous companions—pigeons. She reached into her pocket and pulled out a slice of toast she had saved from breakfast and a bun she had saved from lunch. Before anyone could say "Jack Robinson," they surrounded her cooing, *Hush, little baby, don't say a word ...*

This early October evening Maddie—her face pulverized and her eyes and mouth swollen, as if all her teeth had been pulled—continued walking, unaware that it was more than her feathered friends following her. From the corner of her eye, she spotted a vehicle curb-crawling. Her stomach knotted. He was the last person she wanted to see or talk to. Her intuition shrilled, *Run, run, run!*

Whoosh, she was off like a hare. But listless in her movements and physically weak—oxygen depleted from trauma—she came to an abrupt halt. Breathless, she placed her hands on her hips and inhaled deeply. She watched the car window rolling down. "Maddie, wait up," David called out. "I've been driving up and down looking for you. They told me at the hospital you left *an hour* ago."

"Leave me alone, baby killer," she shouted as loud as bolting thunder. A surge of adrenalin began to pump, and she dashed around a corner.

In blatant violation of the rules, David parked the Peugeot in a fire zone, blocking a hydrant. He took off after Maddie on foot. Catching up with her, he grabbed her arm fiercely.

"Don't touch me!" she screamed.

A nearby pedestrian rushed towards her. "Everything okay, miss? Is this gentleman bothering you?"

"Piss off! Mind your own business. She's my wife."

Maddie resisted the temptation to argue out loud in a public place. *I'm not his wife. I never wanted to be his wife, and we are not legally married.*

In the middle of the sidewalk David's anger took a turn. Teary eyed he swore it would never happen again. He confessed to having a drinking problem. It was a lame excuse. "I never remember what

I have done, Maddie. Please, please, please, I will change. I promise you. I will try harder. I'll make it up to you. Can we just bury the past, let bygones be bygones and start over again?"

Was he speaking honestly? Was he truly contrite? Hell, no!

Maddie glared at him. His pleas for reconciliation didn't fly with her. Instead, they made her furious. The shoe was on the other foot now! The frightened, shy little mouse faded into the background.

Step aside Goliath. Make room for Debra.

In a combative, warrior stance, both feet planted firmly and fists clenched, Maddie began. "You're a despicable human being," she screamed. "You and your evil mother reduced me to a feeble, sniffling idiot. But I'm not that pathetic creature anymore. I'm all grown up. And you, slimy bastard, I want you out of *my* home, a place that is legally *mine*, or I'm going to report you to the sex-crimes unit."

She was expecting his to say, "Go ahead. See where that will get you! You'll come off worse!" But for the moment he was quiet. Had her bluff worked?

Maddie was no longer playing patsy to David's lack of conscience. His bullying had turned her into a wretch and was not to be easily forgotten. Obviously, David had not considered the long-term consequences of his inhuman actions. She was positive David, the unwanted parasite, would not feel regret, remorse, or shame, would never learn from his mistakes or become accountable. He must be feigning, feeling sorry for himself.

A bevy of onlookers stood near Maddie watching the drama play out. But the next scene took "Debra" by complete surprise. The "tough," manipulative older man couldn't hold it together. He fell to his knees slobbering, "Please, Maddie. I love you. I'm so sorry for the pain I've caused you. I beg you, give me another chance. Please think about it. You won't regret it, and I promise to drive you wherever you wish to go."

Liar, liar, pants on fire ...

It was an awkward moment, but, oddly, a moving one. She stopped fighting. Innately, she was a softy filled with enough maternal instincts to console many broken, crying souls.

Maddie knew she was embracing the Devil, yet she reached out in empathy anyway. "Don't cry. Don't cry," she said, passing him her handkerchief. "Everything is going to be okay. Let's go home now."

Oh, what a sucker you are! You've fallen prey to fake remorse delivered as crocodile tears!

Maddie set aside her chiding inner voice. It was desperately warning her that her decision would result in a myriad of ramifications—future pain and suffering. Her intuition knew it was not a question of if, but when!

CHAPTER TEN

"Sometimes miracles come in pairs."

Two months passed without incident. *This* glorious Christmas day in 1969, with sunflower-colored sunlight caressing the snow-mantled ground, promised a pleasant new beginning ... or did it?

Maddie busied herself in the kitchen preparing her first festive meal since arriving in England. Although she had continued to serve David's traditional meals, *this* fare would be to *her* liking, a Christmas meal of dreams.

The aroma enticed David from the living room: glazed shoulder ham, baked sweet potatoes drizzled with maple syrup, Brussels sprouts with almonds, and buttered carrots. "That smells so good. I can't wait to dig in."

Maddie smiled pensively. They would never be best friends, but they were managing to get along. She thought if she showed him enough love (a tall order), she could change him.

Mistaken psychology! Mad men don't get better, they get worse!

For the time being, though, it seemed David *had* changed his behavior. He only visited his watering hole on Friday nights. He stopped smoking, and rarely indulged in a 'doobie.' They ate together, watched television together, took strolls in a nearby park, and slept together. David drove her to the grocery store, the chip shop, and the Adult Learning Center, where, with people from around the world, Maddie furthered her education. The living room was stacked high with medical textbooks borrowed from the library. Her ambition was to become a gynecologist, like Prajit. Though she was far from making that dream a reality, Maddie memorized pages of medical knowledge in preparation for medical school.

David raised no objections to her ardent studies. "Great! You can become the breadwinner, and I'll make the meals," he joked. But inside he was hurting. He had ambitions too. He was passionate about music and longed to become a famous musician, singer, and songwriter. He had a uniquely rich voice, and Maddie urged him to chase his dream. But he continued to make self-defeating excuses: "It's too late. I'm too old. I'll never accomplish what I want to."

Maddie assumed he simply wasn't prepared to work at it. A Chinese proverb summed up her thoughts: "He who says he can and he who says he can't are usually both right."

Maddie was rational. In her mind, there was no deadline for dreams.

Following the delightful meal, David announced, "I have a Christmas *and* a birthday present for you."

An "oh-no" expression creased Maddie's face. "David, you said there would be no gift exchange because money is tight. I didn't get you anything."

"This is a special time. I'll be right back!"

David returned a few minutes later, and Maddie's expression of surprise was worth the trip he made to his car. Purring contentedly on her lap was a male tabby kitten she instantly named Whiskers.

Maddie couldn't have been happier … but that feeling was not going to last for long.

Four weeks after Christmas, in January of 1970, the same ol' same ol' happened. Sudden, severe abdominal pain doubled Maddie over. A few seconds later, she felt vaginal blood seeping onto her underwear. "Oh, no!" she cried out before rushing into the living room where David was watching television. "David, I'm bleeding! Can you drive me to the hospital?"

"Of course, I'll drive you."

When they reached the medical facility, David accompanied her to the entry door, but he would go no farther. "I hate hospitals," he moaned. "Give me a call when it's all over."

Not a word of comfort. They were not in David Blakely's vocabulary. He just drove off as if he was dropping off a stranger, a taxicab customer.

Maddie sighed heavily. *At least I didn't have to walk this time.*

Dr. Barazani was leaving after a long shift when he spotted Maddie, shoulders bowed.

"What are you doing here?" Prajit queried.

Maddie's smile erupted into a giggle. "What a silly question, doctor!"

Prajit smiled then looked behind her hoping to see the evasive husband. No such luck!

After examining her, Prajit removed his latex gloves. In disbelief he announced, "Maddie, you are at least *three* months pregnant. And, sweet girl, I believe you are carrying twins."

The revelation swirled around her numb brain. When reality set in, Maddie cried with joy … until past doubts forced her to declare, "Doctor, I shouldn't get excited, should I? With my luck they will join my other dead babies."

"Don't say that!" Prajit remonstrated. "Think positive, Maddie. Miracles do happen." However, the same reservation hovered in the back of his medically trained mind. Prajit understood he wasn't the Creator, and he had no idea what He had in store for this skeptical eighteen-year-old. Rarely did Prajit discuss patients with his wife of forty years, but this night, when he returned home, he spoke to her about the patient who had baffled medical science, the same girl his wife had given clothing to back in 1968.

"Maybe she's an alien," his wife jested.

"No, daft woman," he laughed. "She's one of a kind!"

"You're getting soft in your old age, husband. It appears you have feelings for this girl. Maybe you are having a midlife crisis," she ended jokingly."

Prajit smiled. "I suppose I do, wife, but in a well-meaning way."

After Maddie's checkup, David did not turn up to take her home. His excuse—he didn't feel well, had a bad headache! Maddie wasn't perturbed. Pushing her doubts aside, her heart felt elated and ready to burst. *I can't believe I'm having two babies!*

The happy mother-to-be's feathered friends gathered around her waiting for crumbs from the cookies she had been given at the hospital.

As if she had strapped on imaginary dance shoes, Maddie swung her body and swiveled her hips along the sidewalk. When she got home, David's reaction shocked her right out her dancing shoes. He lifted her off her feet. "Oh, my God," he gushed. "I'm going to be a father of twins! Maddie, I love you and will love the babies. Do you know the sex?"

"Put me down before you drop me! And no, it's too early to tell. Maybe I'll know their sex after the next ultrasound."

In the following days, Maddie had nothing to complain about. Her doting husband went the extra mile to ensure she was comfortable. He surprised her, shocked her, by taking over some household chores: cooking and serving healthy foods, cleaning the house, and running her nightly baths. Her new "switcheroo" man thoughtfully gave his wife space when hormonal imbalances made her angry, weepy, tired, hungry, or nauseous. It seemed Maddie, now pampered, had become his queen!

Was he really a gracious keeper? Hell, no!

On a lovely warm day, the first day of June, Maddie went into labor. Her now less-than-attentive partner dropped her off in front of the hospital. "Call me when you've had my babies—whose sexes had never been revealed—and I'll come get you all."

Twenty-four hours later, the nurse monitoring Maddie's vitals rushed out of the maternity room and summoned Dr. Barazani.

He was at the nurse's side in minutes, and out Maddie's hearing range.

"Doctor, Mrs. Blakely has elevated blood pressure, 180 over 80. Her heart rate is 182, and her temperature, 104.

Maddie was rushed to the operating room where an emergency C-Section was performed under local anesthesia. An epidural block numbed the lower part of her body so she couldn't feel the surgeon's scalpel. With her head craned, she watched in amazement as a baby was removed.

"A baby girl," Prajit announced.

The young mother's heart filled with tenderness. There in Prajit's hands was a part of herself. "Can I hold her?"

Prajit's wide smile was apparent, even though it was concealed under his surgical mask. He could only imagine what was going through his patient's head—first the botched sterilization, then the ectopy abortion, then a residual mangled fallopian tube that defied medical science, and a baby boy's death by violence. "Of course, Maddie," Prajit said tenderly, "as soon as I've cut and clamped the umbilical cord."

Prajit handed the six-pound baby girl to the nurse, who urgently suctioned the baby's windpipe to clear fluid and mucus. The new-born took her first breath and let out a roaring wail that abruptly made the birth a reality. The sound took Maddie's breath away. Nothing she had ever heard before could compare to her baby's first cry. It was heavenly music to her ears. However, her elation over baby number one overshadowed the second child waiting in the wings.

The nurse wrapped the newborn girl in a blanket and placed a knitted hat over her coppery tufts of wet hair. Then she lowered the baby to Maddie's chest. The tiny bundle was the most wondrous sight Maddie had ever seen. It was hard for her to believe she was finally a mum. It was all she had ever dreamed of.

The nurse placed identity bracelets on both the child and the mother.

Maddie stared at her beautiful baby's flawless features: a celestial face, not a freckle or birthmark, a dainty snub nose, and pouting lips. Her upper lip was a double-curved Cupid's bow. The baby was perfect in Maddie's eyes. She didn't even notice David's traits: auburn hair and blue eyes. "I held your heartbeat in my body. I am going to give you strong roots and solid wings," Maddie proclaimed. "Doctor, I'm naming her Emma ..."

Maddie's face took on a look of alarm. She gave the doctor a curious frown. "What's going on? Why are you stitching me up? Where's my *other* baby?"

Maddie had been so engrossed in bonding with her daughter, that she hadn't noticed the nurse stealthy whisking the second baby away.

"I want answers *now!*"

Prajit, eyes downcast, responded casually. "He needed a little help breathing. Your baby is in the ICU."

Why had he, after forty years, broken the cardinal rule of professional ethics—honesty? For one, he had a tender heart. But primarily, he worried another death would send his emotionally fragile patient over the edge. He couldn't let that happen. One miracle baby was healthy, very much alive, and needed her mother. Sooner rather than later he would have to inform Maddie of the baby boy's demise.

Maddie's stillborn son had died of oxygen deprivation due to umbilical cord constriction several days before she went into labor. When she was told later that night, her agonized wailing echoed through the maternity wing, along with some blasting, berating questions:

"Why did you lie to me?"

"Why, Doctor, didn't you perform CPR?"

"Maddie, he was already dead."

"I had an ultrasound. Why didn't you see the twisted cord then?"

"The ultrasound was carried out one week before you went into labor," Prajit replied.

"Horseshit! I had it done again before the surgery." Maddie's narrowed, swollen eyes made angry contact with her doctor, reflecting her sadness and fury. "You *knew* he was already dead, didn't you?"

"Maddie ..."

"Leave me!" she shouted. "Go before I say something I'm going to regret."

Prajit, hands clasped behind his white coat, slipped out of the room. His patient's heart-rending sobs and the baby girl's cries followed him down the hallway.

Hush, little baby, don't say a word …

Dr. Barazani addressed the head nurse. "Take her baby to the nursery. See that Maddie is given this …" He wrote "300mg trazadone, administer immediately" on a prescription pad.

Prajit went to his office and made a phone call to the lab. "This is Doctor Barazani. I want blood taken from both Madeline Blakely and her newborn daughter … specific screening for myeloblastic leukemia. Thank you."

He had studied Maddie's previous bloodwork. Prior to surgery she had an elevated white cell count. Had she passed on this hereditary disorder to her child?

The powerful sedative guided the heartbroken mother into a dream home filled with dead souls. Sky, Alexander, and now Samuel, with tiny arms outstretched, were waiting for their earthly angel.

CHAPTER ELEVEN

"The loss of my babies has not defined me,
but it certainly has forever changed me."
—ANONYMOUS

Ten hours later, after the sedation wore off, Maddie looked into her daughter's exquisite amber wolf eyes, a trait Maddie was happy to have contributed. She sighed. She was a mum, and she was in love!

As Emma suckled at her breast, Maddie inclined her head and whispered, "My precious baby girl, be strong in the knowledge that this world can be a better place, not just a hideout, a cave full of tears, like your mother has known."

Silently, she added, *and your father is primarily to blame for this cave of tears. Where the hell is he?*

The nurse said she had called David four times and had left recorded messages.

Maddie had not birthed alone, but it felt like it. Why hadn't he made an effort to be by her side? After all, he had announced he was going to be the proudest dad alive!

Her dead son was not mentioned until Prajit checked in to see how mother and baby were doing. "I did what I thought was best for you at the time. Am I forgiven?"

"Of course," she answered. "Doctor, please, where is my son's body?"

"He is in the mortuary."

Tears flowed down Maddie's sagging cheeks. "Please don't leave him in that cold place."

"No, I won't, Maddie, but I need to discuss the funeral arrangements with you …"

Maddie didn't let him finish. "My husband hasn't even bothered to come and see his *live* child, let alone his dead one, and he sure as hell isn't going to pay for a funeral," she said bitterly and realistically.

Prajit lowered his head. "What about another family member?"

"I don't have any family. All I have is my baby and a tabby cat," she said in a childlike tone.

Prajit's compassionate heart ached for her. He said, "Let me think about this. I'll see what I can do for you."

"Thank you, Doctor. You are my only friend."

Prajit smiled. "Then you must call me Prajit."

"Oh, I can't do that! It wouldn't be proper."

Prajit grinned.

Her developing friendship with this kind soul would become bonded by mutual respect and love.

Miracles do happen.

Prajit paid for the funeral expenses, and baby Samuel Alex Blakely was buried in Croydon cemetery. Maddie wanted desperately to be there when her baby was laid to rest, but complications from the surgery forced her to mourn the loss from her hospital bed.

Prajit's wife took photos of the tiny oak casket and of the beautiful spray of white lilies, yellow roses, white snapdragons, and tropical foliage that adorned his tiny home.

When Prajit had asked Maddie about her religious affiliation, she had answered, "None! And my son's ceremony is not going to be led by a Catholic priest!" The acidity of her statement was understandable. Her childhood had been slaughtered by Catholic devotees.

Matthew Rider, a pastor from the Bethany Baptist church, was happy to oblige. His eulogy was comforting:

"Heavenly Creator, your love for all children is strong and enduring. We were not able to know Samuel as we had hoped. Yet you knew him growing in Madeline's' womb. In the midst of her sorrow, she gives thanks that Samuel is with you now ..."

To this day Maddie continues to mourn the loss of her children: Sky, Alexander, and Samuel, the baby she had carried to full term. She visited his grave once, briefly, and left traumatized. She had heard voices vibrating in a way that sounded like the excited babble of a crowd of rowdy football fans. Was she hallucinating? Had she been given a glimpse into a different realm? Yes. Not only did Maddie have a photographic memory, she was clairaudient. She believed her gift was a perfectly normal extension of her grief.

Maddie never stepped into a cemetery, any cemetery, again. She honored her babies' departures by planting flowering magnolia trees in the garden of every home she ever resided in.

The day before Maddie was discharged from the hospital, a nurse drew back the curtain and announced, "Maddie, you have a visitor waiting in the guest lounge."

"Who is it?" Maddie queried, hoping the father of her baby had finally plucked up the courage to visit her.

"The lady said that she is your mother-in-law."

Maddie's eyebrows shot up. "Tell her I don't wish to see her."

The nurse's brows matched Maddie's. "Okay. What exactly do you want me to tell her?"

"That I don't want to see her," Maddie repeated. "You've no idea what this awful excuse for a human being has done to me."

The nurse left to do Maddie's bidding and returned in a couple of minutes. "I'm sorry, Maddie. Jean Blakely is insisting. She says you will want to know what she has to say about your husband."

Curiosity killed the cat!

"Hello," Jean greeted, staring down at the baby in Maddie's arms. She asked, "Can I hold her?"

"No!" Maddie said curtly. "Why are you here, Jean?"

Without invitation, Jean pulled a chair close to the bed. "Well, I have a lot to tell you."

"Go on," Maddie replied tonelessly.

"David is over you. He is not coming to see you or *your* baby. He says it's not his!"

Maddie wasn't shocked, and she couldn't care less. Emma was *hers."*

"I have removed David's belongings from the flat, at his request. He has a new love in his life and will file for divorce when he returns from touring with the band."

Why bother? It's not legal anyway. I don't care if he has six women in his life!

"And there's something else you should know," Jean said in a "got-you-bitch" voice. "Before he left for Europe, he registered the baby. Her name is Joanne Jean Blakely ..."

"Whaaat?"

"You heard right!"

"You just told me David said the baby wasn't his. Why would he do this without my consent?"

"Consent!" she bellowed. "If it wasn't for my son giving you his name, you would be thrown out of this country. Are you forgetting the fact that you are still illegal?"

Maddie's blood boiled. She wanted to strangle this poisonous woman who had made her existence at Kinloch Gardens a living nightmare, and who had been responsible for her previous imprisonment. Though not devious by nature, Maddie had to think fast ...

Keep your friends close and your enemies closer.

"Would you like to hold your granddaughter?" she asked, moving the sleeping child toward Jean. "What do you think? Doesn't she look like David?"

"She is so adorable," Jean mushed, fingering "Joanne's" little face. "David must be mad. How can he say this beautiful little girl is not his! She looks just like him."

Not in a million Sundays, but if you want to say so, go ahead!

Deep down Maddie was reeling over David's chosen name. "Emma" was the name written in Maddie's heart; "Joanne" was scribbled on paper. But rocking the boat by complaining further would be fruitless.

What was done was done! David and his mother still had the upper hand when it came to her immigration status.

"Maddie, I know we haven't seen eye to eye, but I want you to know that even if my son is not in this child's life, I will be there for her and you."

Is this for real? Did this harridan have a change of heart? Hell, no!

But Maddie played along. In a sugary voice she said, "Thank you, Jean. You are so kind."

The reality of Maddie's situation didn't offer her too many choices. Yes, she did have a roof over her head and owned her own home, but how was she going to support herself and her child? She would have to get a job. Although the idea made her cringe, she thought Jean could babysit.

Rocking Joanne in her arms, Jean said, "I'm going shopping, and I'm going to buy her everything she needs."

Maddie wished she could feel genuine gratitude, but it simply wasn't there. With only limited funds to her name, she realized she would not have the baby items she desperately needed—a crib, bedding, clothing, diapers, cream, nursing pads, and more—if she did not accept Jean's offer. So Maddie fed the woman's ego by repeating, "Thank you so much. I don't deserve your kindness."

An impassive Jean handed the fretting Joanne back to her mother. "By the way, tell that Paki doctor of yours I'm going to file a complaint with the College of Physicians and Surgeons. I believe he has violated ethics by going to my son's apartment."

His apartment! Curious, she said, "I don't understand."

Maddie had no idea that Prajit had taken it upon himself to

determine why David was a no-show. But even more, he wanted to confront David about Maddie's violent injuries.

Apparently, Prajit had driven to Berkshire Gardens, the address Maddie gave on her admittance papers.

Knock, knock.

No response.

An upstairs tenant, hearing the loud rapping, had come to the balcony and shouted down, "If you're looking for David Blakely, he's not home … Oh, hi, Dr. Barazani," the woman said recognizing him.

"Hi. Do I know you?"

"You've probably forgotten me. I'm Lyndsey Locke. You pre-scribed birth control pills for me when I was a teenager."

"Oh …"

"Anyway, David is touring with his band in Germany," the forty-year-old said. "And if you're looking for his wife, she's not there either. I'm told she has returned to her native country."

Prajit retorted. "Is that a fact?"

"I have David's mum's number, if you want to call her."

"Yes, please."

Lyndsey appeared a moment later with a slip of paper in her hand. "Here," she said, handing over the telephone number. A short while later, Prajit called the number.

"Hello. This is Jean speaking."

"Hello. I'm looking for David Blakely. I'm a friend of his wife.

She is in the hospital. She hasn't heard from him, and she is worried sick about him."

"Who are you?"

Prajit hung up.

With a nurse by her side, Maddie waited in the entryway for David's mother to drive her and Joanne home. An hour passed. Maddie started to fret. Joanne was due for another feeding soon, and she didn't want to breast-feed her baby in the hospital lobby. She needed a new plan. The nurse held Joanne while Maddie headed to a payphone in the hospital's waiting room and called a taxi.

When the nurse learned of Maddie's intention, she said, "Maddie, Dr. Barazani gave strict instructions. You are to be accompanied home. I'll call him and ask if I can drive you home." Maddie's eyes flashed a mischievous glint. *Go ahead, but you won't find him at the hospital today.* Prajit had wished her well and said his goodbyes the night before. He and his wife were driving to Jesus College at the University of Cambridge. His daughter, Adeeba, was to begin her medical career there. Prajit's older children, two sons, were already MDs making their livings in private practice in the suburbs of Croydon.

Maddie spotted a black taxi waiting outside. Placing the sleeping baby under her coat, head facing upward, Maddie buttoned up the garment. With one hand under the baby's bottom, she rushed out the door.

"Berkshire Gardens, please."

As the cab prepared to drive away, Maddie removed the drapery ring from her finger and flung it out the window. Then, she removed from her coat pocket the sealed envelope that was handed to her the night before. On the outside it read, "I've put a little something in here to tide you over. I've included my private telephone number. Please, when you get home, let me know you are all right. Best regards, your doctor and friend, Prajit."

Maddie slit open the envelope with a fingernail and was speechless. Four crisp 100-pound notes were more than generous. However, the cab driver expressed concern. "Haven't you anything smaller, missus. It's only two quid."

"I'll check in the house for some change."

Maddie unlocked the door and stepped into her home. It was as silent as a concrete box. How long had the electricity been cut off? She didn't know. Was it deliberate, or was it merely an outstanding overdue bill? She retrieved a biscuit tin from underneath the bed and took out two pounds in coins and a fifty pence tip to pay the driver.

A little later, with postpartum depression kicking in, Maddie's imbalanced nervous system began to jangle. Apart from having no electricity or telephone line, she noted the bare bones look of her home. Not a stick of furniture. No crockery, pots, pans, or even a teaspoon remained. Even the drapes had been removed.

Maddie and baby Joanne sat on the living room carpet. Both were crying. Figuring out how she was going to keep herself and her baby warm in the cool September weather was daunting.

After roughing it on the carpet all night, Maddie bundled her baby in her coat, and set out to the chip shop. "Mrs. Morris, I need your help again. Where can I go to buy cheap furniture and baby items?"

In the Morris's living quarters at the back of their business, Maddie poured out her outrage and sadness. Catherine's face was as pale as the raw potatoes soaking in a bowl of water on the table. "You poor thing," she said compassionately. "Don't worry, dearie. I'll get Fred to rustle up some stuff for you. My husband knows all the secondhand dealers, and I'll call the electric company to find out what's going on, because I don't suppose you have telephone service either."

"No," Maddie returned.

Maddie and baby Joanne spent that night in the comfort of Catherine and Fred's spare room. The next morning, Maddie handed her remaining cash to Catherine, who, without her knowledge, added their own savings to buy what Maddie and Joanne needed to survive.

Maddie couldn't believe her eyes when she returned to her own home forty-eight hours later. Gratitude coursed through her veins as she witnessed the fruits of Fred and Catharine's kindness. They must have raided every secondhand store in town.

The kitchen had been provided with all the basics. New yellow drapes adorned the only window. The living room was fitted with a clean, used, two-seater tapestry sofa with matching display cushions; a round oak coffee table; a brass floor lamp; and a small television sitting on a double-shelf oak cabinet. Upstairs, her bedroom was furnished with an old-fashioned bed with hand-turned posts. Her "closet" was a five-drawer matching dresser, and it would remain empty for now. Baby shampoo, oil, and washcloths were neatly displayed on a bathroom shelf. By the side of the toilet there was hanging a large packet of sanitary tissue. But it was the decorated nursery, filled with all the must-haves, ignited a rush of happy tears.

Under the only window in the spare bedroom was a drop-side white crib with pink sheets, blankets, and bumper pads. Mounted above the crib was a musical mobile with pink, padded dangling stars designed to soothe the baby. Maddie pulled the string, and, to her delight, the mobile played *Hush little baby …*

A baby monitor sat atop a three-drawer oak dresser filled with socks, bibs, and outfits for the newborn. Against one wall was a changing table laden with cloth diapers, wipes, ointment, and everything else a baby needs. Catherine and Fred had given her the most wonderful nursery she could have dreamed of. The icing on the cake was a vintage rocking chair for breast-feeding Joanne and singing to her when she needed comforting.

Maddie hugged her loving, generous benefactors. "I can't thank you enough for what you have done for me. I'll pay you back every penny you spent."

"No, you won't," Catherine insisted. "Most of our regulars chipped in (nice pun for a chip shop) when I told them of your terrible circumstances."

Maddie was speechless. Complete strangers had come to her aid, and their charitable donations even covered the outstanding electric bill.

Her faith in humanity was rekindled.

Life was good, for now.

CHAPTER TWELVE

"Forcing a mother out of a child's
life is a hate crime."

Being an inexperienced single parent, learning how to do
things on her own was frightening for Maddie. Bathing her
newborn was the worst. Maddie was terrified of dropping
her baby. But practice made perfect, and three years later, Joanne
was busy walking, talking, and feeding herself. Maddie couldn't
believe her daughter would be attending school next year.

Though Catherine and Fred Morris had been supportive of
Maddie when Joanne was a newborn, sadly, her dear friends had
been missing from her life for the past two and half years. Fred died
of cancer a month after he surprised Maddie with the home decora-
tions. And a lonely Catherine sold the chip shop, bid her goodbyes
to Maddie and Joanne, and relocated, as a heartbroken widow, to
Portugal, where her daughter and son-in-law lived. Catherine had
sent letters regularly, always with money orders, but suddenly they
stopped.

Maddie learned from Catherine's daughter that her friend had died of a stroke shortly after she had arrived in Portugal. To add to the sadness of this loss, Prajit died in a head-on collision with a drunk driver, three days shy of his retirement.

Whenever Maddie faced a moment of weakness in her life, she thought of Fred, Catherine, and Prajit. They were her heroes.

Shortly after Prajit's death, Maddie received a call from the hospital administrator. "Mrs. Blakely, I am calling to let you know that Dr. Barazani was successful in obtaining full medical coverage for you on compassionate grounds. You'll not have to worry about any further medical costs."

Maddie was dumbstruck and grateful to the man she called her friend. She would never forget him. However, she tried hard to keep her parenting free of her sadness. She didn't want her daughter to feel her pain, so she sang her happy songs. Prajit's kindness continued in another way, from beyond the grave.

The unexpected visitor was a healing balm. "Hello, Maddie. I'm Adeeba. My father told me so much about you. I'm here to see how you are doing and if there's anything I can do to help you."

Maddie stared into Prajit's eyes. The woman was the splitting image of her father.

"Come in," Maddie invited. "I'm happy to meet you, and please don't take this wrong, but I loved your father with all my heart."

Adeeba's dark eyes twinkled. "And he loved you too, Maddie. Any love of my father is a love of mine."

Maddie sighed with the memory of what Prajit had meant to

her. He had been a knight, shining armor and all, and she loved him.

The women chatted about this and that, and then Adeeba informed Maddie of her plans. "I'm following in my father's footsteps, becoming a gynecologist. It is what he would have wanted for me. But *you* are the one who inspired me to choose this specialty."

Maddie frowned.

"My father kept diaries about you, and after his death my mother gave them to me. One entry made me laugh and pushed me in the right direction."

"What was that?" Maddie asked curiously.

In one entry my father wrote of an event that occurred shortly after the loss of Alexander, your second baby. He wrote, "My Maddie has more spunk than anyone I have ever known." The entry continues with you saying, "Doctor Barazani, I'm going to write a letter to the medical school urging them to encourage women to take up your specialty. I'm sure I'm not the only woman who is embarrassed when men look at my 'bits.' And who knows better about 'bits' than women, because they have the same parts."

Maddie burst out laughing, and so did Adeeba.

In the three years since returning to the apartment, Maddie had made ends meet thanks to Prajit and the Morris family. She had been frugal with the money, often going without so she could give Joanne everything she desired, but the money was nearly gone. Foremost in Maddie's mind was how she was going to support herself and her daughter.

Maddie set out to find a job. A "Dishwasher Wanted" sign caught her attention.

Maddie stepped into the Gentleman's Club, a members-only private club for upper class men, located not far from her apartment complex. The owner, a dodgy old man, hired her on the spot, taking advantage of her illegality. He didn't have to pay Maddie wages and benefits equal to those of a legal citizen. She couldn't earn him money as a dancer—she was an unattractive bag of bones—but she'd do fine as a dishwasher.

Maddie was given the graveyard shift—midnight to 5 A.M.

She rushed home and called Adeeba. "I got a job, and now I need a babysitter. Do you know somebody?"

"I can babysit for you when I'm not at school, and I will ask our cleaner, Roshanni, if she can take over when I'm not around."

"I'm so grateful to have you in my life," Maddie declared.

The twenty-two-year-old dishwasher avoided eye contact with men wearing expensive suits. She tried hard to be strong, not to break under the pressure of having to deal with lewd older patrons. She wondered how they treated their own sisters and mothers. But it was the exotic dancers, who used their bodies to make ends meet, that saddened her most. One veteran dancer, Sarah—an attractive, leggy blonde—made a killing at the club. Beady-eyed men rained cash down on her.

The bold thirty-five-year-old Sarah befriended shy Maddie.

One night Sarah approached Maddie and said, "Here," as she

handed over a wad of cash. "You look like you need this more than I do."

Maddie's mouth hung open. "That's kind of you, but I can't take your money!"

"Hey, there's plenty more of this," Sarah said flipping through the notes. "That bugger over there," she pointed to a fat man bedecked in expensive jewelry and clothing, "he's a millionaire. Every night he comes here trying to get into my knickers. But an exotic dance is the only thing coming his way," she ended with a huge grin.

Maddie's red, raw hands inflamed by troughs of hot soapy water accepted the cash. The extra "support" would enable her to buy magical Christmas surprises for Joanne—things that could never have been purchased before getting this job.

The back-breaking job she had accepted to make ends meet would one day be used against her in a court of law. "She is a stripper, Your Honor. She is not morally fit to have custody."

Maddie would bear this, and other preposterous accusations, for years to come, and she would be unable to defend herself against David's poisonous lies.

David's two daughters always believed him. Their name-calling—slag, slut, whore, and liar—would become routine.

In 1974, the day after Joanne's fourth birthday, Adeeba, Dr. Prajit's daughter, was frantic when she turned up at Maddie's workplace. Her dark features were pale with distress. "Your husband and his mother came to the flat, and I couldn't stop them, Maddie. They have taken Joanne. Your husband said you will know where to find him. Should I have called the police?"

"No. I wouldn't advise that," Maddie said, trying to keep her wits about her and focus on the now. "I'm glad you came to me first. Drive home, Adeeba, I will sort this out."

"No. I want to come with you. What if he hits you again? I read my father's journals. He's dangerous, Maddie. But you are correct not to involve the Bobbies. It can only bring more trouble. Did you ever sort out Joanne's birth certificate, which stated the father's full name and mother as 'unknown'?"

"No," Maddie answered softly. "How could I have marched in the registry office and demand it be put right? I'm still undocumented, Adeeba. I don't have a legal leg to stand on."

Adeeba, looking traumatized, shook her head in disbelief. Her puzzled father had written, "How can this be happening to a human being in this day and age?"

"I'll be fine, dear Adeeba," Maddie sighed. "Please go home, and I'll call you as soon as I can."

Maddie removed her apron, left the club, and ran like hurricane wind to Kinloch Gardens, the most obvious place they would have taken Joanne. Even though Maddie's insides were screaming in anger and frustration, she reminded herself, "I *am* strong. I *am* resilient. I *am* a survivor."

Panting, she arrived at number 24 and hammered on the door until she woke the neighbors, whose lights now shone brightly. "Keep it down or I'll call the police," an elderly man yelled.

Maddie wanted answers, at any cost. She knew David's life was in shambles and he was taking his bitterness out on Maddie by taking Joanne. Maddie had heard that the female singer in David's band had recently jilted him for a lead guitarist in another band.

A semi-naked David finally opened the door. "What do you want, bitch?"

Maddie heard Joanne cry, "Mummy, Mummy," but she couldn't see her. Joanne's cries pierced Maddie's soul. "I'm coming, darling."

Maddie's wolf eyes flashed dark with rage. "You bastard!" she screamed, "don't do this to me. You have kidnapped my daughter, who you said wasn't yours." Maddie tried to shove his bulk aside. "I'm coming in to get *my* daughter."

David backhanded Maddie violently. The brute force sent her body crashing into the concrete railing. She screamed in pain. Unbeknown to the evildoer, his actions were witnessed by the neighbor who had threatened to call the police.

The man lifted the telephone receiver.

"Police, fire, and ambulance, how can I assist you?" the dispatcher asked.

It wasn't David who got carted off to the police station. His account of events, narrated with a straight face, was incredulous. The police constable fell for David's horseshit … hook, line, and sinker.

"The woman is a stripper … she works at the Gentleman's Club … she's infatuated with me … just turned up at my door … tried to extort money from me … when I told the crazy bitch to get lost, she took a swing at me."

No amount of pleading her innocence—explaining that her *husband* was crazy and a pathological liar—sufficed for the law officer.

The kidnapping of her child wasn't taken seriously. Once more, David was above the law.

Maddie was charged with assault, fingerprinted, photographed, and locked in a cell far worse than the ones in the detention center. Cockroaches ran freely. The washbasin reeked of urine. Obviously, the previous inmate had chosen to urinate in the sink instead of the cell's filthy toilet.

Maddie, who once believed that all life was precious, reevaluated her feelings about her life. *I must be a bad person! Why else have I been given such endless suffering? Why have the few people who have loved me died? David is committing horrific hate crimes and getting away with them. Oh, Joanne, my precious daughter, my heart is breaking. I wish I could hold you in my arms and reassure you I will never leave you again.*

Maddie wanted to die by suicide.

The same Home Office official whom she had met during her previous lockup appeared at her cell door. "Madeline, you have been cleared of all wrongdoing. You are free to go. Would you like to press charges?"

"No," she said reluctantly. "One can't beat the devil. He is holding the only thing I want, my daughter. And he has, I'm told, legal grounds to do so. Unless my name is added to her birth certificate, I have no chance of rectifying this horrific ordeal."

To this day Maddie cannot understand why their forged marriage license had never come under investigation. But since she didn't want to draw further attention to herself, this false identification would remain her get-out-of-jail card for now.

"I understand, Madeline," the official said, "but I'm doing my best to get you legal status in this country ..."

"Really!" she scoffed. "Three years ago you said the same damn thing, and here I am, still without basic human rights!"

The official hung his head. Higher bureaucrats had argued that her marriage was illegal, and, therefore, her application for Landed-Immigrant status was null and void. The confusion of her deportation dilemma explained why she hadn't been ordered out the country already. Now, the nonexistent name on her child's birth certificate created additional headaches for the bureaucracy.

The official handed Maddie money, ordered a taxi, and said, "For now, it's best you go home—he paused thinking *at least the property is officially in her name*—and await my next visit. I promise you, I will take your ghastly situation to arbitration if I have to."

Maddie, with upper eyelids drooping and lips quivering hopelessly, entered her home. For days she couldn't get out of bed. Being separated from the only person she loved was unbearable. She didn't answer the door or the telephone. *Was her precious daughter being cared for properly? Were they feeding her healthy food? Did they read her favorite books? Did they sing to her? Did she ask after her mother?*

Not having had a father in Joanne's life, the mother and daughter had been attached at the hip!

Bang, bang, bang.

"This is the Police! Please open the door."

Maddie opened the door to a Metropolitan police officer, dressed in formal uniform: custodian helmet, jacket with polished silver buttons and black trousers, a wooden truncheon protruded from a pant pocket.

"Are you Madeline Clark?" he asked.

"Yes."

"We got a call at the station to check on you. The caller was concerned you had taken your life."

"Well, as you can see, Officer, I'm very much alive. Could you give me the name of the caller?"

"Sorry, but all calls are confidential. Have a good day."

Maddie's face was set in stone as she shut the door. The phone was ringing and ringing in the background. She decided to answer it. "Hello, Maddie speaking."

"Hello, Maddie ..."

She scowled. "What do you want, David? You have done your worst. What more can you do to me?"

"That's why I'm calling. I'm sorry for what I have done to you. Please forgive me."

Maddie was far from dumb or delusional! She had fallen for this poop before. David's narcissistic plea for forgiveness simply meant he wanted her to ignore the evil he had done. How convenient! It was his sick way of keeping control of her. He wanted Maddie's life to be a wreck ... permanently. But the painful truth was that he had possession of the love of her life, her only child. *Play his absurd, vain game, girl. It's the only way you are going to see your daughter.* She recalled one her favorite Mahatma Gandhi quotes: "You can't change how people treat you or what they say about you. All you can do is change how you react to it."

"I forgive you, David," she said tongue in cheek. "I know you didn't mean to hurt me again."

"I love you, lovie."

"I love you too, David." Maddie felt like throwing up.

She combed her hair, which hadn't enjoyed TLC for some time, refreshed her lipstick, the only makeup she wore, and eagerly awaited the return of her "missing" daughter, but not the return of the monster.

David ushered himself and Joanne back into Maddie's life. Maddie fought back tears when she saw her daughter's unkempt hair, dirty face, and crumpled pajamas, the same ones she wore the night she was kidnapped.

"Mummy, Mummy," the four-year-old cried. "I missed you. Daddy said you were sick. Are you better now?"

"Much better now that we are together again."

Click, click, click.

Maddie's video recorder stored that happy-sad day and continued to record the ongoing psychological and emotional damage David inflicted on her. Her life was mentally draining. For a period of time she experienced psychogenic blackouts—where she blanked out—from overloaded memory banks. At times her camera would shut down from the enormity of the emotional stress. In the years to come, Maddie would not recall which of her two living daughters by David was a twin, and she would vent at the wrong offspring, "You killed your brother!"

In her adult years, a brainwashed Joanne would reject Maddie, the only person who truly loved her without rhyme or reason. The eight-year-old became unrelenting. One day she said, "You're not my mother! My father is right. You're a sick bitch! I hate you!"

Maddie's journal entry—one of many—read:

> Joanne, those who hate don't win unless they are hated
> back. I can't do that because I don't hold grudges; it is not
> in my nature. I'm not even going to try to combat the *hate*
> that occupies—consumes—you and your half-sister, Mary-
> Jean. Life is too short. *Love* cannot conquer *hate*! I'm now
> convinced of that.

CHAPTER THIRTEEN

"You weren't created to be unhappy in order to keep everyone else happy."

As the years had passed, neither David nor his mother took ownership of Maddie's misery. Her mind grew resilient—no point in crying over spilled milk! She felt she had only one life to live, and she didn't want to live it as a victim of past persecution. However, it was her fate to remain in a loveless, emotionally blackmailing marriage held together for the sake of the only child she thought she'd ever have. That would prove to be wrong. But, thankfully, David wasn't around much to enforce the conditions and ultimatums he had enacted when he brought Joanne home four years ago.

"Don't nag me if I'm late coming home from the pub every night."

"Don't interrupt me when I'm watching football on the TV."

"Run my bath water when I tell you to."

"Prepare my favorite meals."

"Keep this home spotless."

"I expect to have sex every night, or whenever I feel like it."

"My mother is not to be stopped from seeing *her* granddaughter. Is that clear?"

David's last demand was the cruncher: "You and I are going to a lawyer to have my father's home put in *my* name. The poor schmuck fell for your crap when you told him you never wanted to be homeless again."

Not long after David returned to share Maddie's home, he had joined a new band that was hitting it big in England and abroad. His escapades with "groupies" and the sex they offered him were bragging points, and that was music to Maddie's ears. For now, she would not be his preferred bed mate, even though he still drugged her to get his perverted way with her when he was home. During his absences, David instructed his "spy," his mother, to keep an eye on her. Jean was a pain in Maddie's neck, telling her how to raise her school-age daughter. Nothing Maddie did for Joanne was right! Maddie spent days knitting sweaters for her daughter, and they always disappeared after Joanne visited number 24, replaced by new, expensive clothing her grandmother had bought her.

Today Maddie asked, "Where's the pink sweater and the other clothes you were wearing before you went to Nana's?"

"Nana said you make me wear ridiculous stuff," Joanne replied in a derisive tone. "I'm not going to wear thrift store clothing ever again. Nana is going to buy my clothes from now on … and I hate the silly sweaters you make!"

Maddie knew she could not change the evil mother-son pair, but at least Joanne was in her life, and that was some consolation.

Maddie was proud of her eight-year-old daughter, who never stopped asking questions. From birth on Joanne had exhibited the telltale signs of a gifted child. At five months old she tried to verbalize words. At one, she began to speak in little sentences. Joanne was quick to pick up reading skills and began to sight-read before age three. At four she was a high achiever at the preschool. She loved to read her favorite books aloud: *Once a Mouse* by Marcia Brown and *Time of Wonder* by Robert McCloskey. She was also musically talented. Playing the piano came naturally to her. A school psychologist, who examined Joanne at Maddie's request, informed the delighted mother that her five-year-old had an exceptionally high IQ but that there were drawbacks.

Joanne couldn't interact with kids her own age; she preferred the company of older girls or adults. And she, like her father, wanted control. When that wasn't possible, she had a meltdown, replete with ear-shattering and teeth-jarring screams of anger and frustration. Maddie simply ignored these childish tantrums.

Maddie's second daughter would undergo the same IQ testing and receive the same intelligence results. However, Maddie's third child would crush her perception of the necessity of educational testing. The examination led to a shocking discovery. If Maddie could have peered into the future, she would never have had the third assessment performed!

For a while life settled into "normal," and getting along with David was key. Things could have been worse. Maddie, a stay-at-home mum, was concerned about Jean's control of the purse strings—money David gave her—to pay for bills, groceries, and more. Maddie decided to look for a job she could work while Joanne was in school. She had completed her adult education, received her high school diploma—with flying colors—and was conversant in several languages, a skill she began teaching her prodigy child.

Maddie browsed through the Job Center employment listings. One placement caught her eye: "Court interpreter wanted, median salary equivalent to $28,000 U.S. per annum," a healthy wage in those days. This could be her ticket to independence, to never having to ask David or Jean for money again. Of course, there was a drawback: "Bachelor's degree in translation studies required."

Maddie sighed. She had no official paperwork she could use to enter a university to take the certification. Her yearning to become a doctor was thwarted also. About to give up on finding a job, she spotted another opportunity she hoped would not draw attention to her lack of status.

"Housekeeper wanted for retired Royal Navy officer. References needed."

Maddie wrote the number down, even though she was apprehensive about not having the references the position required. Should she wing it?

As soon as she returned home, Maddie dialed the number. "Hello, my name is Madeline Blakely. I'm calling about the advertisement at the Job Center."

On a hot summer's day Maddie, wearing a short-sleeved blouse and cream skirt, took a taxi to the address in the suburbs of West London. The impressive Jacobean country manor was in pristine condition. It took her breath away. It was the finest house she'd ever seen. Something like she had imagined David's promised castle to be.

The house was the full-time residence of eighty-year-old Admiral Thomas Neville.

After being ushered into the drawing room by a uniformed butler, Maddie waited to be interviewed by the owner. She was in awe. The room was elegantly detailed: a magnificent crystal chandelier hanging beneath a plaster rose ceiling mould, several plush royal blue armchairs, and a marble mantled fireplace, which beautifully set off the mahogany-paneled room. A pleasant odor of old leather and beeswax emanated from the built-in bookcases and the bound volumes that lined the walls.

A side door opened and in stepped a well-dressed man, slightly hunched, but free from any other obvious physical infirmity. He approached Maddie. His winter-white thinning hair shimmered under the light of the chandelier, which illuminated his deep facial furrows. But it was his gentle blue eyes that put Maddie at ease.

"You must be Madeline."

"Yes, sir," she returned demurely.

Gesturing with a thin hand, Thomas said, "Please be seated."

Maddie chose a chair opposite him.

Thomas Neville said, "You sounded much older on the phone. This is quite a surprise. How old are you, if you don't mind me asking?"

"I'm twenty-seven, sir."

"Please call me Thomas," he offered smiling.

"Oh, I couldn't do that. It would not be proper." Her answer was an echo from the past.

"Before we continue, I must tell you that I don't have any references. But I'm an excellent cleaner and will keep your house spotless."

"I'm sorry. Perhaps you misunderstood my advertisement. I'm not looking for a cleaner."

"Oh ..."

"You see, ever since my wife died I have been very lonely. What I'm seeking is a companion ..."

Misinterpreting his intentions, Maddie blurted out, "I'm married, sir!"

A chuckle reverberated through the 128-year-old room. "I'm not looking to replace my wife," he said to her surprise. "I would like someone to read me newspapers and books, since my eyesight is somewhat worse for wear."

Maddie's cheeks flushed. "Well, I'm the one," she said smiling.

Leaving the stately manor, Maddie had difficulty believing that she had just landed a great position, and without having to produce references. Thomas Neville had given her flexible weekday hours and no weekend work, which gave her time to dedicate to her daughter.

Maddie couldn't have been happier, having landed such a cushy job, and she liked her new employer.

Each weekday morning Maddie prepared Joanne's lunches,

tuna-and-mayonnaise sandwiches, which were her favorite. Her daily routine was taking Joanne to school before 8:30 A.M. and picking her up at 3 P.M.

Each morning she waited until Joanne was safely inside the school. Then she walked around the corner to wait for Thomas's uniformed driver to pick her up. Maddie never imagined that being a senior's companion, and getting well paid for it, would be so rewarding. She enjoyed her employer's company and learned so much from him. After he taught her Latin, she enjoyed reading from his vast collection of classical books. Greek philosophy and more. For the first time in a long while, Maddie was content.

Today Thomas was going to teach her to play chess. Eventually, Maddie became accomplished, regularly beating her employer at the game.

When she spoke of her passion for medicine and her dreams of making enough money to attend medical school, he remarked, "I know the Dean at Cambridge University. I could put in a good word for you."

Maddie's friendship with Thomas was solid, but she still struggled with trust issues. She hesitated to cloud their rewarding relationship with revelations of her ugly past. So she refrained from telling Thomas her life story. She was done talking about the past!

"Thank you for your offer to put a favorable word in for me," Maddie said, "but I promised my daughter I would be there when she comes home from school. Maybe when she leaves for university would be a better time for me. As you have taught me, it's never too late to pursue your dreams."

Maddie kept her day job of nearly two months a secret. When

asked why she wasn't at the apartment when Jean turned up unannounced, Maddie extemporized. "I can't be cooped up all day in the flat, so I take long walks, go window shopping, stop for tea, or go wherever else my fancy takes me."

The "spy" didn't buy it.

The morning after that deception, Jean, a scheming sleuth, went to work. She tailed Maddie and Joanne in her car. The shrew's chin jutted out and her eyes widened when she saw a vintage Rolls Royce roll up beside Maddie after Joanne entered the school grounds. A short drive later a uniformed driver doffing a chauffeur's cap opened the rear passenger door. Jean's heart pounded with curiosity as she surveyed the scene. She decided Maddie must be having an affair. When she saw Thomas hug Maddie in the mansion doorway, she muttered, "Caught you!"

Jean returned to number 24, called her son, and spilled the beans. "You're not going to believe this ..."

The next day, on Maddie's trip back from Thomas's, the Rolls became stuck in a traffic jam because of a car accident. Maddie began to panic. She would be delayed picking up Joanne from school. When she arrived, thirty minutes late, she rushed onto the school grounds. Mrs. Knightly was not wearing a cheerful expression. "I was concerned, so I called your mother-in-law. Joanne's dad answered, and he picked her up, Mrs. Blakely."

Maddie rushed to her apartment. David and Joanne were nowhere to be seen.

Her heart beating fast, Maddie jogged the three blocks to number 24 and rapped hard on the door knocker. David opened the door. Jean stood behind his bulky frame, firmly holding Joanne's hand.

"I'm so sorry, precious," Maddie said, addressing her daughter. "I was at a friend's house, and forgot the time ..."

"You're a liar!" yelled Joanne. "Go away! You are nothing but a whore! I'm staying with my dad. And I have a *new* mother now ... Lyndsey from upstairs."

Maddie sucked in a shocked breath. No wonder that woman had been snubbing her! *How long has David been having a relationship with the second-floor tenant?*

With eyes bugged out and a face like thunder, David exploded. "You heard right! You are never going to see her again. Your free ride is over. You have twenty-four hours to get out of *my* home. (Title had been legally transferred to David months earlier.) Go back to your lover!"

"It's not what you think ..."

Joanne sidled up to her father's side. Maddie noticed the horse-accented eyewear Joanne was wearing, the same pair Maddie told her she could not afford, which had triggered a hissy fit. Maddie had willingly sacrificed everything to please her spoiled child, but she could not compete with the extravagances Jean lavished on her.

"I hate you," Joanne spat. "I never want to see you again. You're a worthless piece of shit!" *I wonder where she gets that language from,* Maddie thought contemptuously. Joanne was exhibiting vile genetic markers, character traits she inherited from the Blakely gene pool. Maddie would not be able to override them.

"Get going, bitch, or I'll call the cops!" David threatened, physically lashing out at Maddie before slamming the door in her face.

Maddie's heart was overwhelmed with sorrow and anger. She cried all the way back to Berkshire Gardens. The hatred she saw in her daughter's blue eyes could never be reversed. David had won. His venom had poisoned her only child.

On entering the apartment, Maddie discovered the electricity and phone had been discontinued. Upstairs, not one item of Joanne's clothing or toiletries could be found. It wasn't a stretch to figure out who had carried out this plan. The heavy smell of Jean's perfume wafted through the room.

In her bedroom, using classical music as therapy, Maddie began packing a suitcase with Joanne's photos, scrapbooks she had lovingly pasted, a lock of baby hair, Joanne's first tooth, handmade birthday and Christmas cards in which Maddie had written "Love from Daddy."

David had never purchased any presents in celebration. Maddie's cat was the only gift she had ever received, and Whiskers was gone too. The only items she packed for herself were underwear, socks, and a thick warm sweater.

Maddie sat on her overloaded tapestry luggage trying to close it while tears rolled down her cheeks. She knew she couldn't "fight" *three* hate-filled devils, and the thought of being homeless filled her with dread.

She reached under the bed. *Oh, my God!* Maddie silently exclaimed. The biscuit tin containing her cash wages was missing. Before her desperate situation hit home, she heard the creaky front door open. She flew downstairs. Did David have a change of heart?

Hell, no!

In the hallway stood two burly men in overalls marked "Mitchells Furniture Removals." Silently, they proceeded to remove *her* furniture without a glance in her direction, as if she were a mirage.

Rays from a blood red sunset brushed over Maddie like a devil's trident as she headed forlornly for the main road. With the few coins she found hiding in her jacket pocket, Maddie headed for a red payphone booth.

"Good evening. This is Maddie. May I speak to Thomas, please?"

"I'm sorry, Mrs. Blakely. Mr. Neville will no longer be taking your calls," replied the butler in a formal tone.

"And why is that?" Maddie queried.

"I'm sorry, but as I've said, Mr. Neville is not available."

Maddie hung up. *Another soul David has poisoned.*

Unknown to Maddie, David and Jean had gone to Thomas's home and threatened to expose the prominent gentleman to a scandal, a love affair with a young woman. Obviously, her friend and employer had decided not to risk his reputation.

Maddie reached into her jeans pocket and found enough coins to make one more call: "I'm sorry, but the number you are calling is no longer in service." Maddie had kept the telephone number given to her in 1968 by the kind nurse.

Maddie's last option was Sarah, the compassionate stripper, who had shared her tip money. Was she still working at the Gentleman's Club? Maddie entered the Club through the kitchen door. An unfamiliar face greeted her. "What do you want?"

"I'm looking for Sarah. Does she still work here?" inquired Maddie.

"No. She left years ago."

"Is Mr. Cargill here, the owner?"

"No. There are new owners."

A well-built man with bleached blonde hair appeared and looked Maddie up and down. "If you are looking for work, I suggest you go elsewhere," he said rudely." With your skinny body and small tits, you wouldn't make me a penny."

"I used to work here as a *glass cleaner!*" she said, hoping her words didn't come across as rudely as his comment. "I'm in desperate need of a place to stay and will work for free if I can sleep in the back room.

"This is not a shelter. Get the hell out of here!" the man barked.

Maddie picked up her heavy suitcase and walked aimlessly through the dark night. Her thoughts were as numb as the chilly September weather. She was an unwanted soul. The temptation to end her life loomed strongly before her: *What's the point in living? No, not living, but existing in a world filled with such hatred and cruelty?*

Click, click, click.

She recalled David's bloodshot eyes boring into hers before he had lashed out: "You are nothing but human trash! You are a worthless piece of shit! You're a slut! Hang yourself for all I care! As far as I'm concerned, you are dead anyway! You will never see Joanne again, and if you even try, I will kill you and get away with it! I've spread it around that you are nuttier than a fruitcake. A liar and a thief! Do you think I didn't know that you stole from my wallet?"

After holding her thumb out, Maddie caught a ride with a trucker. "I'm heading for Manchester," he said. "That's where I'm headed too," she replied glibly, even though she hadn't a clue where to go and a few minutes ago had wanted to die.

Maddie held back tears as the friendly trucker engaged her in conversation.

"I don't wish to talk about it. Okay?"

She looked up at the stars shining like beacons of hope for the lost souls in the world.

What will be, will be ...

CHAPTER FOURTEEN

"Even in the darkness it is
possible to create light."
—ELIE WIESEL

Maddie risked her life accepting a ride from an unknown, lumber-hauling trucker. The newspapers had recently exposed the dangers of hitchhiking. The bodies of five murdered young women had been discovered at various locations along this highway. The presumed serial killer was still at large. Fortunately, her driver—a portly, grandfatherly man in his late sixties, with silver hair, a clean-shaven face, thick eyebrows, a friendly smile, and a slight stutter—was not likely to be her executioner.

"It's dangerous to be hitchhiking on these roads, young lady," said Colin.

"I know, but I have to get to Manchester. My mother is sick, and I don't have enough money for a train," she explained, cheeks reddening. Maddie had never been comfortable bending the truth, but lately white lies had become a survival tactic.

"Then hop in. I will get there in about four hours. I'm sure your mum will be happy to have her daughter home for the holidays."

Maddie nodded, avoiding eye contact.

The long-distance trucker had heard many "excuses" from hitchhikers about why they were thumbing it late at night. Like the rest, this girl's explanation didn't ring true. But experience told him not to press his sad looking passenger any further.

Colin shared his beef and horseradish sandwiches with Maddie. His wife always prepared these for him to take on long journeys.

"It saves money at truck stops," his wife always said. "And you don't need extra weight from fatty foods," she laughed, drawing attention to her husband's potbelly.

Just before daybreak the truck entered the town of Bolton, on the outskirts of Manchester.

"I'm turning here," Colin said. "Where would you like me to drop you off?"

"Oh, anywhere," replied Maddie.

"I thought you said ..."

"Right here will do."

Maddie said goodbye to a frowning Colin and was sorry for the bull she had fed him. He was a decent man.

Pounding an unfamiliar sidewalk, she saw a sign marked "Moss Bank Park." She entered the unlit playground, found a bench, and sat there, her fears of the dark nibbling at her sanity. In a fit of self-pity, she covered her face with her hands and sobbed. The unknown stretched before her, but at least she had no one to answer to.

Fall was approaching, and dark indigo clouds drifted across overcast skies. They hovered over the playground, complementing Maddie's bleak outlook. She drew her worn sweater around her shoulders and trudged onward until she found a different bench, deserted, under a cluster of trees. Sprawled on the uneven slats, she fretfully drifted off into sleep. A passing boy looked at Maddie as if she had fallen from the sky. "Mom, there's a person sleeping on our bench," he said with alarm in his voice. He made a shooing motion with his hands as he said, "That's *my* bench!"

Maddie opened her eyes to see the small boy pointing at her.

"I hope you haven't slept here all night," said the mother of the boy.

Maddie answered in a broken voice. "I had nowhere else to go."

The normal response would have been to ask "why," but instead the woman said, "If you are homeless, there is a convent not far from here. I'm sure they will help you."

"Never!" she hissed. "I'd rather sleep in the open."

"Look, I don't know you from Adam, and I don't know what brought you to sleep all alone in the park, but I would like to invite you to come home with me and my son after he rides on the merry-go-round. It's his favorite activity in the park."

Maddie's heavy heart started to ease thanks to this good Samaritan. Her thoughts went back to the Nasser Samaritans in Italy. Did they still remember her?

"I have a small spare bedroom you can stay in until you can make alternate plans."

For the first time in a long while the weight on Maddie's heart lifted.

"My name is Rosemary. This is my son, Matthew. We live down the street from here."

"Madeline Clark," Maddie responded.

Maddie entered Rosemary's modest Council townhouse. She

was given a hot cup of tea and a slice of fruit tart with custard. Then she was shown to what they referred to as her bedroom. The tiny den was tastefully wallpapered but had little furniture: a single bed with orange covers, and a small bedside table with a little lamp.

"It's not grand," Rosemary declared, "but it is yours for as long as you need it."

Maddie gave her benefactor a big hug. "I don't know how to thank you."

"Then don't," Rosemary smiled. "Make yourself at home."

Aged forty-four, Rosemary told Maddie she was a single parent, jilted by Matthew's father, her boyfriend, when she was pregnant.

In the following days, a friendship developed. When Rosemary got a job as a cashier at the local grocery store, Maddie became Matthew's babysitter. Looking after three-year-old Matthew helped fill the enormous hole in Maddie's heart. But she missed Joanne every waking moment. At night, resting her head on her pillow, tears fell. Every time she tried phoning her daughter, her calls went to Jean's answering machine. Little Matthew replaced not one, but three *lost* children.

Two weeks later the telltale sign of "morning sickness" sent Maddie rushing from her bedroom to the bathroom. She was shocked, but at the same time ecstatic. The aging Vienna schnitzel hadn't deserted her empty womb. How was she was going to tell her friend, her new older "sister," a generous woman who shared her home, food, clothes, and affection, and paid Maddie for babysitting?

In the beginning stages of their friendship, Rosemary, curious, had asked Maddie why she was homeless. Maddie replied, "I walked out of an abusive relationship," but she had never mentioned Joanne. Nor did she reveal the horrific details of her childhood or the terror of her relationship with David and his mother. All that would remain in the past for now.

After Matthew had been put to bed, Maddie decided to tell Rosemary about the pregnancy, but when the flush-cheeked Rosemary returned home from her afternoon shift, she was gushing like a teenager about a first crush. "Maddie, I'm in love. The new manager, his name is David ..."

Maddie sighed. *I can't spoil this moment for her!*

"He has asked me out, wants to take me for a meal, and, Maddie, he is drop-dead gorgeous." A mischievous smile parted her full lips. "He has a brother, Maddie. Just think of it. We can both get boyfriends ..." Noticing Maddie's blank expression, she asked, "Why aren't you happy for me?"

"Rosemary there is something you ought to know."

Maddie finally poured out the truth about David, Jean, and the loss of her daughter, Joanne. Her abominable childhood remained locked away in her memory banks.

Rosemary's compassion spilled over. "Oh my God, Maddie," she cried. "I'm so sorry. Why couldn't you trust me? You have become more than a sister to me."

Maddie, ashamed, had no answer.

Maddie gave birth to miracle baby number five, a six-pound baby girl delivered naturally on May 21, 1979. This bundle of joy—with cherub's ears, wisps of brown hair, velvety eyelashes, David's blue eyes, and Maddie's cupid lips—was a dream-baby come true. Would this baby replace the sorrow Maddie felt at losing Joanne? No.

Maddie never stopped thinking about the child who had been forced to hate her own mother. But *this* child was *hers*. The brute could not take this one from her. Maddie was pleased that she had not seen David since she had been "evicted." But her new, positive outlook would soon be undermined in a perverse way, and without penalty. David was above the law!

Maddie's next of kin, according to the Croydon hospital records, was her husband, and as there was no other documentation to state otherwise, David was notified.

Taking evil pleasure in the misfortune of others, David flaunted his power, his "ownership," and enjoyed his sadistic gloating. He traveled to Manchester, where he registered Mary-Jean Blakely as the official birth name. However, this time Maddie's name was included as the mother.

Unbeknownst to the happy mother, David had visited the baby girl in the nursery and had commented, "She's not my child, but I have compassion for my ex-wife."

Yeah, right! Maddie was livid, but, once again, she had no legal right to register the birth. It had been a long, miserable pregnancy, filled with nausea, headaches, and backaches, and a loss of appetite throughout. David's cruel gloating during Maddie's suffering would bring all three of her "enemies"—David, his mother, and Joanne—

into a court of law before the year was out.

Thanks to Rosemary's persistent interventions at the Council offices, Maddie was given a rental house, the only vacant property available. It was not far from Rosemary's home.

The house had been scheduled for demolition for some time. The conditions outside and inside were appalling. Plastic wrap was stapled over missing glass window panes, and the shingle roof looked like it would cave in under heavy snowfall. The inside was bare, no carpeting, no kitchen cupboards, nothing. But it did have an operational coin-fed natural gas meter that fired up the heater in the living room, and a coin-fed electrical meter.

"Beggars can't be choosers," Maddie muttered.

Maddie cleaned the derelict home the best she could until it no longer smelled like death. With her babysitting money and money gifted to her from her "sister," she stuffed the meters with coins and purchased the basics for Mary-Jean and herself. She placed a framed photo of Rosemary and Matthew on a windowsill. Maddie missed her "sister," who had moved 100 kilometers away to take up residence in her new boyfriend's home. Having no telephone didn't help her isolation. She felt alone, but it was nothing she couldn't cope with. She was busy working as a full-time mom.

When Mary-Jean was two months old, Maddie's financial situation became strained, so she searched for work, any kind. She was hired at a bakery, no questions asked, as a dishwasher. She scrubbed baking equipment by hand from nine in the morning until two in the afternoon, and she was paid a minimum cash wage under the table. Most of her income went to the rent and the babysitter, her friendly neighbor, Mrs. Goudie, a widow and retired postal worker.

With a minimal income, Maddie's fridge was filled with pumped breast milk bottles, but very little else. She did not consider food to be a priority for herself. Keeping her child warm and fed took precedence over everything else in this drafty home. Maddie's weight plummeted to ninety-eight pounds.

Alarmed by Maddie's emaciated body, the owner of the bakery, a Polish woman, began putting leftover baked goods into a take-home box for her employee. Maddie was grateful for her boss's thoughtfulness, but she ended up giving most of the delights to Mrs. Goudie, who had a real sweet tooth.

The summer season came and went, and in the fall equinox, on September 22, Maddie received a registered envelope requiring her signature. David had filed for divorce and full custodial rights of both daughters. She had twenty days to respond. Her mind whirling in shock, she slumped into a plastic chair. For him to demand legal separation was fine by her, but he had some nerve trying to gain custodial rights to both girls, whom he had adamantly denied were his. He had not spent one minute with Mary-Jean since the day of her scurrilous registration. Outrage and disgust raged within her. *The marriage license is a bloody forgery. How could he brazenly flaunt this in a court of law?* It was unbelievable. Maddie could not wrap her head around David's demand for full custody of Joanne. Even though she had been living with him for some time, he now wanted court-approved, legal custody of her and Mary-Jean, even though both birth certificates were missing their mother's name! It was absurd, but then nothing was logical in David's mind. He loved power and took it.

Maddie burst into tears of fear. She knew she didn't have a chance against this pathological liar and his toxic mother, who would surely accompany him to court. Being undocumented, the odds were stacked against Maddie. She had no financial statement to prove that she could support one child, let alone two. She was emotionally drowning. And she had a criminal record, had been imprisoned twice. Hiring a family lawyer was beyond her resources, but this plaintiff was not ready to give up, to lie down and die, as David assumed she would.

A troubled Maddie had no clue how she could sleep with all this on her mind, but she knew she must.

That night Maddie, snuggling baby Mary-Jean against her chest, spoke to her ancestors: *Ancestral Spirits take pity on me. I do believe I have suffered too much. Come to me in my sleep and show me how I can win against this devil.*

Maddie woke the next morning to thoughts manifested from her dreams. With reluctance she knew what had to be done. It was not something her decent heart ordinarily would have considered. But she had little choice.

She turned her head heavenward: *Thank you for hearing me. Please give me the inner strength to pull this off.*

At seven o'clock that evening Maddie put on her best thrift store dress. It hung loosely over her thin frame. She tied her waist-length hair into a ponytail, painted her lips pink, and went downstairs to Mrs. Goudie, who had fully agreed with her plan to save her children.

"I should be back before eleven, if all goes well."

"Best of luck, Maddie, Mrs. Goudie said. "My fingers and toes are crossed."

Dolled up, her insides shaking, Maddie walked to the nearest pub, The Red Lion. Sitting at the bar, she ordered the cheapest drink she could afford, a pint of shandy—light beer mixed with carbonated lemonade.

A slim gentleman, attired in a navy-blue and white Royal Navy uniform, sat down next to her at the bar. "Can I buy you a drink?" he offered.

"Sure," Maddie quickly replied.

Come into my parlor, said the spider to the fly ...

"What are you drinking?"

"Shandy," she replied.

"Ah, come on. It's my birthday so why don't we celebrate? Two whiskeys, please, bartender."

"My name is George. What's yours?"

"Madeline. Pleased to meet you," she replied, feeling a strange fluttering in her heart.

"Well, cheers," said George raising his glass. And down the contents went.

"Happy birthday ..."

A sputtering, choking sound assaulted George's ears. Many eyes turned toward Maddie.

Unused to hard liquor, Maddie's dusky complexion flushed red.

Later in Maddie's life a DNA test revealed she had a genetic condition that left her unable to metabolize alcohol. Later, when she was accused of being a drunk by one of her adult children, she laughed at the thought.

"Oh, I'm so sorry," a mortified Maddie said, wiping whiskey stains from George's pristine uniform. "Are you in the Navy?" she asked, before giving herself a mental slap. *Duh! He's wearing a RN uniform!*

"Yes. I'm a medical officer. I'm stationed at Torpoint, Cornwall, currently on leave."

Wishing to encourage small talk, Maddie spoke about her ex "companion," Admiral Thomas Neville, and how he constantly narrated his escapes at sea.

"How did you get to know him?"

"I worked for him as his 'eyes,'" she laughed before explaining their relationship.

"And what do you do here in Manchester for a living?"

"I work at a bakery."

"That's nice. I love baked goodies."

"I can't bake to save my life," said Maddie. "I'm just a cleaner." Maddie's face reddened in anticipation of her lowly position putting him off.

"That's nothing to be embarrassed about. My mother worked as a maid for a rich family until she retired. My father was a coal miner."

As the evening progressed, Maddie perked up as she warmed to her friendly, clean-shaven, light-skinned companion, whom she guessed to be about her age, twenty-seven. But a guilty conscience saturated with hard liquor is not a good recipe for "genuine" friendship. She wanted nothing more than to flee the pub. *Go, get out of here! I can't do this. It's not me!*

Her plan was to flirt, chat up a financially secure man who could become her legal "ticket" to saving her nursing four-month old, Mary-Jean, from being removed, and both girls from being legally separated from her. The vision of her baby's angelic face nearly brought Maddie to tears. She would continue her life of self-sacrifice.

The couple continued to chat about this and that. At closing time Maddie, now drunk, staggered out the door clinging to George's arm. He hailed a taxi. The cab driver asked, "Where to, mate?"

"Where do you live, Maddie?"

Maddie woke at four in the morning, fully clothed and alone in a strange bed. *Deja vu!*

Her head spun. "Where the hell am I?" Maddie looked at her watch. "Oh, no!" she cried out. "Mrs. Goudie!" She fled to the front door and opened it, but she had no clue where she was. She raced upstairs and found George asleep in an enormous bed in another room. "Wake up. Wake up," Maddie pleaded, shaking his arm.

"What's up, Maddie?" his sleepy voice answered.

"Help me, George," she pleaded. "I have to get home to the

babysitter. I told her I would be home before eleven last night."

George bolted upright. "I would have taken you to your place, but you were too intoxicated to make sense, so I brought you here to my mom's house ..." there was a long pause. "You never mentioned that you had a baby."

"I didn't think it was important. We had only just met, and we were celebrating *your* birthday."

George drove his mom's car, following Maddie's vague directions. He finally got Maddie home.

"Thank you, George. I'm so sorry I have been a letdown."

"Quite the contrary," he said. "You were the best birthday present a fellow could have asked for. I'll walk you to the door. If it's okay with you I'll come inside and take the blame for your lateness."

Maddie's stomach knotted. *Oh, no. He's a decent fellow, and I'm a bad girl.*

George wouldn't take no for an answer. Entering Maddie's home, he looked around. The bare living room floor with protruding floorboard nails was an accident waiting to happen. A bare light-bulb dangling from the ceiling and accompanied by frayed, fabric-insulated wiring certainly didn't meet electrical safety standards. He spotted Mrs. Goudie.

She was fast asleep on the only piece of furniture in the living room, a plastic chair. Maddie gently touched her shoulder. The elderly woman jerked upright with fright. "Oh, it's you, Maddie. You scared the bejesus out of me!"

"I apologize for being so late, Mrs. Goudie."

Brenda Goudie's eyes were not on Maddie but on the stranger beside her. He was slender and tall, a blonde, handsome, uniformed man with moon-shaped green eye. She said, "It is okay, my dear. I was young once! I hope you had good time," she said winking at George. She got up stiffly. "I'll see myself out."

After Mrs. Goudie left, George's natural curiosity overcame him. "How long have you been living like this?"

"For some time," was Maddie's honest reply.

"And you have been raising a child in these conditions?" gasped George.

"Yes, but she is well cared for," Maddie answered defensively. It was all too much. Maddie cascaded into despair, which brought up memories of postnatal depression, birthing a baby alone, childhood trauma, adult trauma, body mutilation, sexual and domestic abuse, grief, and racism. These things flashed through her tortured mind. She fell to her knees. Heart-wrenching sobs racked her body. Then, unable to control the trapped child inside her, Maddie bared her raw pain. "I want to kill myself, George, because I'm a worthless piece of shit!"

George looked at the person he had earlier found to be vivacious, eloquent, funny, and charming, exhibiting no traces of mental fragility or mood swings. "I want to kill myself" did not shock George. He had heard those words before, and he knew not to mouth trite phrases to a suicidal person: *Things could be worse. You have so much to live for. You don't mean that. You don't really want to die …*

Ten years Maddie's senior, Lieutenant George Harland Smith held a medical degree and worked as a consultant psychiatrist in Her Majesty's Naval Service. He counseled sailors and officers suffering from combat stress: PTSD, depression, and anxiety disorders. George couldn't let her self-destruct. He saw likely signs of childhood trauma etched deeply on her face, and he heard it in her voice.

"How can I help, Maddie?"

Maddie stared at George, confused. "Why would you want to help me? You hardly know me! If I were you, I'd get the hell out of here. You don't want to become involved with the likes of me."

George sat down on the bare floor and announced, "I'm not going anywhere, Maddie. I'm a clinical psychiatrist, and I want to help you heal from whatever is causing so much brokenness."

"You never told me you were a shrink!"

"You never asked!" George returned in a playful tone.

"I don't like shrinks!"

"Tough! You'd better like me because I'm here to stay."

"Then you're the nutty one."

Lighthearted banter continued for a while and then turned serious.

"I'm sorry for my earlier display of weakness …"

George interrupted, "Maddie you are not weak. You are hurting. Do you want to talk about it?"

Maddie closed her eyes and asked herself if she should finally open up, let out the raw pain that had shamed her for too many years to count. Her head nodded involuntarily.

"The father of my baby, Mary-Jean, who is four-months old, is taking me to court to get full custody, and he is my rapist …"

As sunlight streaked through the plastic-covered window, Maddie concluded her appalling life story to the sounds of an awakening baby. "Thank you, Dr. George, for taking the time to hear my trials of survival in a hate-filled world. But this is the last time I will repeat these atrocities to anyone. My baby needs me, and I would give my life for her. Again, thank you."

"You don't have to thank me, Maddie. I'm not here as your *doctor*. I chose to be here because I have strong feelings for you. Don't laugh. I don't want to leave your side."

Maddie looked at him with surprise. "Really?" she gasped, confused. "Even after everything I've told you? You still want to be in my life?"

"Yes, Maddie ..."

The wailing from upstairs prompted George to say, "See to your baby." He lifted himself off the floor and said, "I'll be back after lunch. Okay?"

Yeah, right! Maddie's inner voice retorted. *He'll be off like a shot!*

True to his word, George returned shortly after one o'clock bearing grocery bags filled with delights unaffordable to Maddie. Her heart filled with gratitude for this wonderful man who had cared enough not to walk away.

Although George was single, he had had many girlfriends in the past. He found himself questioning feelings he had not experienced before. Were some stealthy love hormones being released into his bloodstream? Had Cupid's arrow finally struck? His rational mind thought, *this is ridiculous!* His conscience, however, confirmed the emotional turmoil. *This has nothing to do with good looks, fate, or destiny. You have fallen in love.*

Following a fish-and-chips lunch, Mary-Jean went down for a nap. George, in a whirlwind of emotion, drew Maddie into his strong arms and kissed her passionately. Maddie thought she was going to faint. Her mind couldn't process the intensity of her feelings. It was something she had never experienced before.

Upstairs in the small bedroom Maddie shared with Mary-Jean, the baby slept soundly, oblivious of the actions of her mother and the stranger. Maddie moaned! She was experiencing love for the first time, and her first organism. She wanted to stay in George's embrace forever, but she was a realist. She had maternal responsibilities, and they had to take precedence over her newfound happiness.

At five o'clock that evening, George left to meet a sailor friend, an arrangement he'd made before meeting Maddie. She spent this absence doing what mothers do, nurturing her child. From where she lay cuddling her daughter, she had a clear view of the sun sinking behind the rooftops. She marveled at the yellow ball of fire shading into tangerine hues. As she awaited George's return, she watched the silhouettes of birds returning home to roost. He had gently kissed her goodbye on the forehead and said, "There's no turning back now, Maddie. I want to be more than your lover. I know this won't make sense right now, but my heart is filled with love for you."

Maddie had replied, "I don't know how to put into words what I'm feeling. It's as if I'm glowing inside."

Of course, George had the answer. "Maddie you feel love, something you haven't felt in a long while … or ever."

As happy as Maddie felt, she could not stop the familiar insecurity from creeping in. "You know I come with awful inner and outer baggage. I have more baggage then can fit into a jumbo jet's overhead compartments."

George's laughter reverberated. "Now that's the funny girl I met at the bar. Well, sweetheart, I can help you unpack. I have lots of patience."

It was Maddie's turn to laugh. "I was thinking you were a sailor! And now you're an airport baggage handler."

"We are going to get on just fine, darling. I'm going to take care of you and your baby. What's her name again?"

"Her name is Mary-Jean." Maddie didn't add her legally hyphenated middle name. She detested the association with David's mother, who would have screamed holy horror if she had learned that Maddie's chosen name for her daughter was Lynda, German for *snake*! In the end, Mary-Jean would live up to this original appellation!

As midnight drew close, George said, "I must leave now, Maddie. I have some calls to make, but I'll be back early tomorrow morning. We can all go out for breakfast, how's that?"

"And what will Mary-Jean order ... breast milk?" Maddie teased.

George's lips creased in a tender smile.

At 7:30 A.M. George knocked on the door, stepped into Maddie's house, and announced, "We have a change of plans. Breakfast will have to wait. Pack you stuff. You are coming to live with me ..."

Surprised by the suddenness, Maddie inhaled deeply and replied, "It's not that I don't want to leave this horrible home ... immediately ... but it's not practical. I have to give the Council notice, and your home is too far from my work."

"You can give four weeks' written notice. Tell them the rental is vacant, in case they come up with another tenant who wants to move into this slum dwelling! And you won't be working at the bakery anymore. Just call them and apologize. Say you are moving to Cornwall. That's the truth."

It was all too much for Maddie's logical brain to process, but she wasn't going to allow her mental hesitation to overcome her emotions. She had never before had feelings for a man, and the depth of it was blowing her mind. George's tenderness, as opposed to David's control, felt devoted and real. When Maddie had been living with Rosemary and her son, she told her friend, "I don't ask myself how I ended up with the devil incarnate because I know the answer: post-traumatic vulnerability and insecurity."

Maddie's heart won. She gave away her meagre furniture and bric-a-brac to her neighbor, who was thrilled. "You're such a loving and kind, lass, and a good mother," Brenda said, "you deserve a good life, and with such a lovely man, Maddie. And he's a doctor. Oh my!"

"Mary-Jean and I are really going to miss you, Mrs. Goudie."

"And I will miss you both. I hope you and your daughter will be happy. Please write to me, I would love to hear how you are getting on."

"Will do," Maddie said, "I promise."

Maddie and Mary-Jean stayed at George's mum's Manchester

home for a couple of weeks. He went ahead to Cornwall to exchange his bachelor apartment for a family home provided by the Royal Navy.

Mrs. Smith, George's mother, was on vacation, sailing on the cruise ship *The Song of Norway*. She would be returning in six weeks. Maddie was looking forward to meeting the woman George had spoken of so highly of. "You'll love her, Maddie, as I do. She is down to earth and adores babies. She usually picks on me, her only son, for not giving her a grandchild. But we can soon change that, can't we?"

Maddie's heart sank. What were the chances of having another miracle baby? Slim to none! She believed she had pushed the Vienna schnitzel to its limits. Way back when, Dr. Barazani had told her that it was only a matter of time before he would have to operate again.

Maddie never met Elizabeth Smith. She died from respiratory failure while on her cruise. George was devastated. He flew her body back to England and, with permission, buried his beloved mother at sea—in the ocean surrounding the Isle of Wight, where she had met and married his father. George's father predeceased Elizabeth. He died after fighting an unsuccessful battle with lung cancer. His early death was blamed on an accumulation of inhaled coal dust. George's father was also buried at sea. It gave George solace to know his beloved parents would remain together forever, sheltered in their watery graves.

Maddie and Mary-Jean became George's surrogate family, and he promised to make them as happy as his tenderhearted father had made him and his loving mother.

From that time forward, Maddie believed the world would become a more hospitable place for her.

But a tempest in a teapot was brewing around the corner.

CHAPTER FIFTEEN

"Laws are like cobwebs, which may catch small flies,
but let wasps and hornets break through."
—JONATHON SWIFT

O n her twenty-eighth birthday, December 2, 1979, Maddie arrived punctually at Croydon County Court dressed in a dark skirt and jacket and dress shoes. George and RN senior lawyer Lieutenant Commander James Brown, a white-haired gentleman with azure blue eyes, were at her side, both attired in their naval uniforms. Seven-month-old Mary-Jean was being cared for by George's friend Patti outside in the Lieutenant Commander's Bentley.

Maddie's footsteps echoed down the marble floor corridor. Her "mother" eyes lit up when she spotted Joanne sitting on a bench with David. Next to him were his mother, Jean, their neighbor, Lyndsey; and several drinking buddies, probably band members.

Maddie rushed toward her daughter. "Hello, my darling. How are you?" Maddie held out her arms to hug Joanne. "Mum has missed you so much."

Joanne stuck out her tongue. "You're not *my* mother, whore!"

Maddie felt a stab in her heart. She wanted to lash back with *I didn't raise you to be so disgustingly rude!* But, instead, she remained tight-lipped. She could feel tears welling up, but she knew she had to be strong, had to curtail her feelings of overwhelming sadness for the daughter she loved. Maddie had no choice but to accept that the emotionally poisoned child had been brainwashed. It was not *her* doing.

George shook his head and led Maddie away. He could only imagine the pain she was feeling. Was Maddie prepared for the hearsay statements and false allegations that would be spilling from the mouths of her adversaries? No, he didn't think so, but she had been well advised by Lieutenant Commander James Brown not to let her feelings interfere. No emotional outbursts.

When the doors opened, everyone filed in, including the swarm of hornets that followed David. His minions took their places on the right side of the courtroom. Joanne was missing. She had been in-structed to remain outside with Lyndsey until the Judge instructed otherwise.

Maddie, the defendant, stared contemptuously at the man who, by his vicious attacks, had estranged her from her firstborn child. But something else caught her eye. David wasn't court presentable. Would his attire—unwashed jeans, grubby parka, and dirty finger-nails—be a "factor" that could work in her favor? And his mother's appearance wasn't respectable either.

In fact, it was unbelievable! Jean looked as if she were off to the Ascot races. She was sporting a bizarre cobalt-blue leather dress and ludicrous headgear—an angled silver hat with things resembling shards of metal dangling from the rim. If this hadn't been a serious proceeding, Maddie would have burst out laughing.

"All rise … this court is now in session … the honorable Judge Baker presiding."

David's barrister gave his opening statement, followed by Maddie's lawyer, James Brown. Then, one by one, David's minions spilled out their lies to the female judge, whose face remained impassive.

Where did the lies end and the truth begin? Would it turn around in Maddie's favor? In practice it doesn't matter if what the other side says is true or not; the outcome depends on whether the judge can ascertain the difference. While a lie detector test would have shown signs of deception in David and his witnesses, Maddie felt she was a credible witness with no shameful secrets to hide. David could have filled a book with his numerous hate crimes.

David was cocky, arrogant, and confident on the witness stand, sneering fiercely at Maddie. His allegations were that she was a child abuser, a neglectful mother, and an immoral woman. His lies spilled fluidly from his devious mouth.

When Maddie was on the stand, she was asked, "Why do think you could be a better parent than Mr. Blakely?"

She answered directly. "Your honor, this is not about who will tuck my children in at night, make sure they clean their teeth, or who will walk them to school. No. This is about who will protect them and love them without rhyme or reason."

Judge Baker ordered a fifteen-minute recess.

"All rise ..."

Striking the gavel, the judge presented her ruling. "After careful consideration, I declare the marriage null and void due to illegal discrepancies that will be dealt with later. Accordingly, I award Madeline Clark sole custody of the minor children, Joanne-Jean Blakely and Mary-Jean Blakely, with supervised visitation by the father, David Blakely. The court approves their relocation to Cornwall."

Maddie's beaming face showed everyone in the courtroom how she felt.

David erupted in yells of rage: "F'ing Bitch ... I'm going to appeal ... she's not fit to have my kids ... she's f'ing insane!"

With a look of distaste creasing her face, the judge ordered firmly, "Bailiff, remove Mr. Blakely from my courtroom!"

"All rise ..."

Judge Baker rose and exited the courtroom.

Maddie could have fainted with joy. This was one of the best days in her life. It was over! George squeezed her hand, and James gently patted her shoulder. "Now, get your daughter, Joanne, and let's go home" George said.

Maddie, her heart bursting with justice long deserved, sprinted down the corridor toward Joanne. "Come, darling," she said extending her hand. "You are coming home with ..." The hard slap to her face smarted. "I hate you ... I hate you ... I won't go with you ... my dad is going to buy me a pony!"

Maddie was looking into young eyes filled with hatred. She

knew then that she couldn't win this evil battle. Turning away from her daughter's glare, she walked back into the courtroom and asked the court recorder, "Could you please ask Judge Baker if I could have a quick word with her?"

That day Maddie voluntarily revoked her custodial rights to Joanne and returned her daughter to David's care.

Maddie did not see her daughter for many years. When they eventually met, Joanne's deep-seated venom reemerged. "You are nothing but a stranger to me ..." Joanne was an apple that did not fall far from her father's tree. She would emotionally and financially hold her mother hostage well into her mother's senior years. "I need money for contact lenses ... I need money for rent or I'll be evicted ... Can you buy me this? Can you buy me that? ... I'll pay you back, I promise ..."

Maddie would continue to wait for her to fulfill that promise!

In the years to come Mara's pathological falsehoods would alienate and poison Joanne and Mary-Jean against their mother. Even so, Maddie always felt her children should have held in their hearts this message: "She gave me what I needed when I needed it ... without question."

Does spiritual justice exist?

CHAPTER SIXTEEN

"Nothing hurts more than being disappointed by
the person you never thought would hurt you."

ollowing the courtroom drama in December 1979, Maddie, George, and seven-month-old Mary-Jean, relocated to
Torpoint, Cornwall, a small town that provided housing for
H.M.S. personnel. Thankfully, David had lost two appeals and made
no further effort to visit his daughter, Mary-Jean.

Five Decembers passed, and not without ups and downs. The
downs had become more apparent of late. Maddie's dream to live
"happily ever after" needed a refresh button. Her contentment had
died gradually. At the beginning of their common-law marriage
(Maddie was *still* an undocumented immigrant), Maddie loved her
married life. She adored George. He was respectful, dependable,
committed, supportive, and put their family first. Maddie never
tired of saying, "I'm glad you're in my life … I'm glad you're my
partner and friend … I appreciate all you've done for me and Mary-
Jean."

Her intensive therapy sessions with George, for years now, had healed her brokenness. Not something that happens every day. The thirty-three-year-old became a bubbly, cheerful character—without the anti-anxiety pills George strongly suggested she take. "No. I will not take diazepam!" she explained. "I don't want to get looped up with drugs. I like to be in control of my mind, not lose it."

Maddie was and forever would be an anti-pill person who declined even aspirin and vitamin capsules!

Throughout their partnership Maddie considered herself a good wife, friend, mother, and third-year medical student. Her studies were being paid for by the Royal Navy, and Mary-Jean, gifted like her sister with high intelligence, was placed in a private school, also covered by the RN. Life could not have been better ... until. In 1984 Maddie's happy "married" life took a turn for the worse. Loneliness began to eat away at her. George's long counseling trips to various naval bases around the UK were becoming increasingly frequent. So were the heated arguments.

Yesterday punishing April showers had bombarded their windows, and the "weather" indoors hadn't been much better. Maddie and George had had a stormy falling out.

"I'm not putting up with a spoiled brat!" George vented. "You're getting played like a chump! Can't you see it, Maddie? She is pitting one parent against the other. If I say no, she'll go to Mummy to get her way. Her 'I'm not going to and you can't make me' has to end. Damn it! She whines about *everything*."

"George, she is only four and half! She'll grow out of it."

"No, she won't, Maddie," George argued irately. "In my professional opinion, she has all the clinical signs of attention deficit disorder and manipulative narcissism."

That day Maddie, a protective mother bear, defended her young, but later she would wish she hadn't. "She's *my* child George, and I have the right ..."

"Have it your way," George butted in, trying to keep calm. "I'm late for the airport. See you in three weeks."

This time there was no customary goodbye hug. His silence meant he was done talking.

George stormed out of the house.

From that day on things went sideways.

Maddie slumped into a living room chair. Tears of frustration stung her eyes. She realized she had rocked the marital boat by, on more than one occasion, defending and making excuses for her bratty child. But the real crux of the matter was that she was unable to give George a child of his own. The void was ruining their relationship!

"I know a fertility doctor in London," George shared a year after they got together. "I know him well. We went to school together."

Maddie didn't want to admit what she believed in her heart: her loyal Vienna schnitzel had long since passed away. Mary-Jean was the last! But for George, Mary-Jean could never replace a child of his own flesh and blood. Maddie was heartbroken. Her instincts to protect and defend her daughter had caused friction between them, again. Maddie couldn't kid herself. Mary-Jean was a handful. As a baby she learned how to manipulate to get her way, and during toddlerhood she learned how to fake affection to conceal her true intent. She tested, just like her sister. Mary-Jean was too smart for her own boots. Without a doubt, the five-year-old ruled their home. Was her marriage in jeopardy? Hell, yes!

One month later, on Mary-Jean's fifth birthday, Maddie's high-maintenance child was not happy with her gifts. She whined, "I hate the Raggedy Anne doll, and I hate the pajamas. They are horrible, and I won't wear them. I wanted a My Little Pony cake, not this stupid fairy castle one!"

George quietly slipped out of the living room, only to stumble in later that night smelling of perfume. Maddie pretended to be asleep, but her senses didn't lie. She had suspected George was cheating for some time. He was exhibiting all the classic signs. In the beginning stages she really was deceived, but today the reality hit home. *I must have "sucker" tattooed on my forehead!* Blindsided!

Designer boxer shorts and trendy clothing started to appear in George's closet.

When he left the house to go to work, he was dressed in civilian clothing.

He stopped taking Maddie to the social events at the RN base.

He took calls privately.

He no longer disclosed his whereabouts.

His affection had waned. He no longer made love to her.

He hardly spoke to either her or Mary-Jean before leaving for work.

Dump him, fast, flashed through Maddie's panicked mind.

That was not going to happen. She was solely dependent on George and had not a penny of her own. And she couldn't just walk out of medical school. She had worked so hard, studying well into the wee hours of the night. Finishing could give her the chance to be free from relying on others.

Maddie released a long sigh. She felt betrayed and jealous. Her trust was shattered. She didn't want to accept the fact that her amazing husband was capable of cheating and lying. Wasn't she good enough? Should she give him space? Who was the person who had "stolen" her husband and robbed her of happiness? She decided to do some snooping. What she learned was devastating. George had been having an affair with his coworker, a fellow doctor. His new consort was none other than Patti, who had minded Mary-Jean at the Croydon courthouse!

Maddie didn't know how long the affair had been going on. But whether it was long or short, she was becoming convinced that she'd never find true happiness again. Was she cursed … by the anti-Midas Touch?

Maddie convinced herself that the world was a cold place. *You can't count on anyone but yourself.* That bit of wisdom did not comfort her. She escaped into old emotional habits: sadness, failure, low self-esteem. She cried for days. She didn't own George, like David had owned her, so she resigned herself to a split up. Her thoughts wandered to her friend Rosemary in Manchester. Maddie could now relate. She was suffering the same feelings of jilted love.

Maddie began hyperventilating—*breathe, breathe, breathe*—but she knew where to go when anxiety got the better of her.

Outside, sitting on a garden bench, Maddie's stress was soothed by an orchestra of hummingbirds protecting the feeders, and droning bees playing in the background. But her anguish heightened when she saw George enter through the garden gate. "We have to talk," he announced.

"Okay," she said meekly while her insides signaled it was not going to a pleasant conversation.

They walked into the house and sat down opposite each other at the dining table. Not revealing she knew George had been unfaithful, Maddie opened the conversation. "I baked your favorite desert. It's in the fridge." George loved cheesecake.

"Maddie," he stated in a neutral voice, "you are a delightful soul, but I don't love you anymore ..."

Pangs of pain and sorrow stabbed at her heart, and she felt her lips tremble. She fought hard to stop the sobs begging to be released. "George, I don't understand. You have frequently told me you love me. Now, suddenly, you have fallen out of love?"

"I'm not going to beat around the bush and lie to you, Maddie. I'm now in love with someone else, and I cannot live a double life. It's not fair to you. And, truth be known, I can't stand Mary-Jean. She has serious behavioral problems that I believe have wrecked our marriage."

Maddie didn't bite at his pointed remarks about Mary-Jean; she had something else on her mind—disclosure. "I know it is Dr. Patti Caldwell," she spilled. "I'd like to know how long this affair has been going on behind my back. Maybe I'm delusional, but I thought you were happy with me.

George did not react. "I have paid the rent on this place for one year, and I will send you money every month to tide you over until you get on your feet," he said with finality.

"Well, thank you very much for your *charity!*" she returned acridly. "How damn convenient! You know I can't hire a divorce lawyer and take you to the cleaners for taking care of your every need all these years. You promised me I would get my papers because of my relationship with you, Dr. George Harland Smith! Now you want to take even that away from me! Do you realize the damage that this will cause me and Mary-Jean?" she screamed.

George extemporized. "Maddie, I tried. I hired the best people available in the legal system, but your case is more complicated than I first thought."

"So you are going to dump me, leave me to the wolves to fend for myself, when you know life will be impossible for me without your support?"

George sighed heavily. "Maddie, I don't want to fight with you. Like I've said, I will help you until you get on your feet. But heed my warning. Mary-Jean knows how to push your buttons. God help you when she grows older. I know what a dedicated mother you are, so put your foot down now and teach her *you* are the parent. It's not the other way around."

Click, click, click.

Maddie's camera dredged up the past: "Your free ride is over, bitch! Who would want *you* as their mother?" David Blakely's heartless words had never left her.

Maddie exhaled in resignation. "I have nothing more to say to you, but, with all sincerity, I wish you a better life with Patti. I hope that she bears you lots of children."

"Thank you, Maddie, and I hope you find the man of your dreams."

I thought I had!

That same day George packed his belongings and left. Maddie never saw him again.

She slept fretfully that night, but her mind was clear. Her life with George was over. It was time for her to get a new act together.

Her tear ducts ran dry. She would never cry again ... at least for years to come.

On a sun-filled morning Maddie walked to the medical school building and told them she would not be able to continue her studies. "My husband has left me, and I have a small child who needs me. Maybe one day I will return and reignite my passion for medicine."

Her tutor said he was sorry she was leaving, but he agreed that she would one day rededicate herself to the field. Wrong! She never did. But there was an upside: she doctored her children through every one of their ailments ... successfully.

The hardest part would be breaking the news to Mary-Jean, but her daughter brought it up first. "When is Daddy coming home?"

Maddie softened the truth. "I don't know when he'll be back."

As the weeks turned into months, Mary-Jean never again asked where George was. She became more possessive of her mother, now that she had her to herself.

Life in Cornwall continued, and Maddie adopted a new frame of mind. She was done with crying and bitterness. She got up every morning and did the things other mothers do—washed and ironed her daughter's clothes, made school lunches, and walked Mary-Jean to the new state school not far from their home. The monthly money orders George sent no longer covered Mary-Jean's private schooling, and, of course, she had a hissy-fit. "You can't make me go to a new school. I know I will hate it."

No amount of reasoning appeased this pompous child, who

now exhibited the same behavioral characteristics as her sister. At her former school and her new school Mary-Jean refused to interact with other kids her age, preferring older children, but it was her cruelty toward other creatures that troubled Maddie most. She received a telephone call. "This is Mrs. Morley ..."

Maddie sat down in the principal's office. What could be so bad that they told her she had to come to the school right away? Was Mary-Jean in trouble?

"Mrs. Smith, these ..." the portly woman opened her hand and presented dismembered beetles, their hard shells separated from their flesh. "These mutilated creatures were found in Mary-Jean's desk, and the English teacher informed me that the classroom rabbit is missing much of its fur, seemingly cut with scissors. The classroom scissors were found in her desk."

Maddie didn't know how to react.

On the way home, Mary-Jean was severely chastised. However, Maddie's gut told her this would not be the last telephone call she received from a school. In the years to come, Maddie would lose count of the phone calls different schools made to her home.

Being a single parent wasn't easy, and Maddie was concerned about how she could cope on her own with Mary-Jean's behavior. But then she thought: *I didn't do such a bad job when I was raising Joanne by myself.* Adding to her concerns were the monthly "alimony" payments. They barely covered household expenses—utility bills, groceries, and school-uniforms. At the beginning of the New Year, 1985, she would be nearing the end of her one-year agreement with George.

Maddie began to panic. Her own homelessness was not such a

big deal to her, but for her six-year-old child? Distraught, she knew she could not let this happen. *I'll find a job and another rental, because, as sure as Hell, I'm not going into a pub again to find a replacement man!*

Miracles do happen.

One late afternoon, a month before her free rent, and support payments were up, three men appeared at her door. They were dressed in formal black suits and ties and stiff white collared shirts. Maddie recognized the eldest, who wore a bowler hat.

"Hello, Madeline. Do you remember me?"

What brings you here, Mr. Jones?" she queried the Home Office official. "I haven't seen you in years, not since our meeting at the deportation center. Have you finally kept your word and brought me my official papers so I can feel human in your country?"

"I'm still working on it, Madeline."

"Yeah, right!" she sneered. "What can I do for you and your friends?"

"May we come in?" the taller of the younger men requested.

Curiosity killed the cat!

Foregoing her usual offer of a pot of tea, Maddie sat with the three men at her kitchen table. The taller man introduced himself. "I'm Agent SK, and this is my colleague, Agent JF. We are from the Antiterrorism Security Service."

"Do I look like a bloody terrorist?" she bristled. She made steely eye contact with Mr. Jones, whose bowler was resting on his lap. "What the hell is going on here?"

"Hear them out, please, Madeline. It's for your benefit," Official Jones urged.

Agent SK reached into a black leather briefcase and retrieved a beige folder printed "Classified documents" on its cover.

Maddie's curiosity heightened. "What's that?"

"Would you take a look at this?" Agent SK said, handing Maddie a legal-size sheet of paper. She took it and examined its contents. Her eyebrows knotted as she declared, "One doesn't have to be a rocket scientist to know this is Aramaic. But I believe there is some sort of code within the letters. I thought you Secret Service people were brainy. It begs the question, why are you showing me this ...?"

Agent SK interjected, smiling. "Madeline, you *are* that rocket scientist! You scored *162* on your Mensa test at the Adult Learning Center, and you scored well over that for linguistic skills."

Maddie smiled proudly. "Does that mean I'm an "import" in the smartest people group, and I may have a bargaining chip? One hand washes the other, right?"

Three sets of raised eyebrows caused Maddie to smile. *Gottcha*!

"Here's the deal," Maddie said with a smug grin. "I will do my best to break the code in this document, but before I do, I want my long-overdue status to reside in Britain legally granted."

Without hesitation Agent SK replied, "Agreed."

Forty-eight hours later Maddie was handed a Naturalization/Citizen legal status document that noted, "Granted by her Majesty the Queen on compassionate grounds." She stared at this piece of paper that had been seventeen years in the making. At last she had human rights!

Maddie was sworn to secrecy about the nature of her work. Using logical analysis with insightful intuition, in less than twenty-four hours she declassified (cracked), the secret message hidden within the document. The queen of code patted herself on the back. She had now joined the ranks of the "code girls" that had helped the Allies win World War II.

"I've done it, come and get it," she said over the secure telephone line.

"Wow!" That's fantastic," Agent SK remarked.

Yep. We women code breakers are superior!

In early June Maddie traveled to Thames House on Millbank where she was officially recruited by the director of the Secret Service as a high-level Naval Intelligence Cryptanalyst. She was told she would begin work, deciphering coded texts and messages, straight away and that Agent SK would contact her with the details.

Maddie couldn't have been prouder. Finally independent, she had a noble job with a decent salary, and the future belonged to her. Maddie was determined to give Mary-Jean the best life possible.

A couple of days later Agent SK showed up at her door to inform her that she was being relocated to the small village of Kilmacolm, Scotland, and subsequently "hired" out by the British Service bigwigs to a U.S. nuclear submarine base known as Site ONE, Holy Loch. This American base at Dunoon in the Scottish Highlands was set up during the Cold War. For decades it had been a bone of contention for the Scottish National Party.

Maddie didn't allow herself to frown. She understood she was under their thumb now and would have to do as she was told without question, except for the one she couldn't pull back from the tip of her tongue. "What will I be doing there?"

"You will help gather intelligence abroad pertinent to the UK's international affairs. You will monitor Middle Eastern and Russian communications, wiretapped telephone conversations, decode them, if they are in code, and hand your findings to the U.S. National Security Agency. An agent from this outfit will be working with you."

It seemed her expertise now extended beyond the British Isles.

Maddie began packing, and this time Mary-Jean wasn't opposed to the change. "I'm glad we are moving because a girl in my school told me that George was getting married to *her* mother!"

A few days before leaving Cornwall for good, Maddie heard someone knocking madly at her door. She stared at the heavily pregnant young woman. "Can I help you?" Maddie asked.

"I'm looking for Dr. George Smith."

"Oh, he hasn't lived here for some time. Is there anything I can help you with?"

"I was told you are his wife ..."

"Ex," Maddie quickly responded. The young woman, whom Maddie guessed was in her twenties, looked desperate. Maddie's compassionate heart opened to her. "Come in," she offered, opening the front door wide. "I'll make you a nice cup of tea, and you can tell me all about what's troubling you."

The woman, Candice, sat at the table and explained. "One of your ex's patients got me pregnant, and my boyfriend has run. I can't reach him by phone, and he's not at his rental. I thought the doctor could help me find him."

"What's his name and rank? Give me a day or two and I'll see what I can find out for you." Maddie's privileged position now gave her "clout" over many other citizens in the country, including George.

Candice handed over her telephone number and address and in a hushed voice admitted, "I used to be a prostitute, but when I became pregnant, I left the business. Gerry was thrilled I was no longer going to sell myself, and, instead, was going to become the full-time mother of his child. He told me he couldn't wait to become a father."

Maddie stretched her arm across the table and clasped her guest's hand warmly. "What you did before becoming pregnant is all in the past. Never look back. You won't have a future with your baby if you allow the past to rear its ugly head. Believe me, I'm speaking from experience."

Candice hugged Maddie on her way out. "Thank you for listening."

"No need to thank me. Go home and wait for my call. I'll do my best to unravel your pain and find the bugger!"

The following day Maddie woke to a noise that sounded like a baby crying or a cat mewing. At first it didn't perturb her because she had noticed a mama kitty, teats low, prowling the back garden. *The kitty must have given birth on the front porch.* Then she heard Mary-Jean yell, "Mummy, come quick!"

Maddie rushed to her daughter's side.

"Holy mackerel!" Maddie exclaimed.

There on her front porch, wrapped in a pink blanket, was a newborn baby. It didn't take much guessing to figure out who it belonged to. She carefully picked up Candice's wailing baby, held it to her chest, went indoors, and called the police. Shortly after, a patrol vehicle arrived, and a police woman took the baby and the information Candice had given to Maddie. Her heart went out to the young woman whose desperate plight had led her to leave her precious baby on a stranger's doorstep. Maddie wanted fiercely to reach out to Candice, telephone her before the police arrived on her doorstep, but she decided that getting involved would not be a good way to start her new career.

That day Maddie's memory suffered a blackout. Her mind's camera did not record that tragic event. Years later that particular "blank" memory would return to haunt her. In a heated argument with her hateful teenage daughter, Mary-Jean, Maddie would fume irately, "You are an ungrateful piece of work. I found you on my porch. You are the daughter of a prostitute." Mary-Jean would then accuse her mother of being a lot worse than a prostitute's offspring.

Many years later a brain-imaging scan would reveal a lesion on Maddie's frontal lobe, a dark spot that didn't present like normal brain tissue. The neurologist suspected blunt force trauma and queried her. But Maddie refused to divulge the truth, that she had been beaten about the head on numerous occasions. David Blakely was, indeed, an animal … period!

That brain injury, and a rare spinal cord infarction, would eventually force a sixty-five-year-old Maddie into a wheelchair.

But Maddie would once more defy medical odds. She would make her "dead" legs walk again!

CHAPTER SEVENTEEN

*"Today I close the door to the past, open the
door to the future, take a deep breath,
and start a new chapter in my life."*

During the transitional month of May 1986, prior to Maddie's relocation to Scotland, her new employer put her through a barrage of psychological profiling tests, including a polygraph exam. Much to her surprise, she passed with flying colors! Maddie had been convinced that her life of suffering and overwhelming trauma would signal instability, that she was a basket case. But when George dumped her, she had placed a chokehold on her emotions. The past was dead to her.

Maddie was given a new identity—Madeline Santini, Italian-American immigrant. Mary-Jean's surname remained the same. If David found out they had altered *her* identity, it would have opened a can of worms. When he lost the court battle in December, he became obsessed with taking Maddie down.

Maddie didn't recognize herself in the mirror, having had her appearance altered in preparation for her new role. The stylist had cropped her long hair to a short pixie cut and dyed it auburn. White porcelain caps disguised her bad teeth. Her mysterious eye color was concealed beneath green contact lenses, and she underwent a rhinoplasty that reshaped a nose deformity, a nasal cartilage disfigurement that resulted from a punch in the face by David in 1968. Madeline Blakely no longer existed. Her sudden transformation was a hard pill to swallow, and Mary-Jean was a relentless interrogator. "Why, why, why?" she asked, "You're not my mum anymore. You look strange! We don't look the same anymore!" Maddie didn't have the heart to say, "You never looked like me anyway. And ... you and your sister have inherited your father's twisted character traits, which will not benefit you as grow older."

The day they departed from Cornwall, Maddie said her silent goodbyes to the cozy rental with glorious views of long sunsets, a place where she had been happy for five years. Then *poof,* it had been flushed away by her ex-husband's self-indulgence.

In her garden, which had nurtured her soul, rays of spring sunlight bathed the flowering bulbs and danced on the bright plumage of hummingbirds and blackbirds. Bees and ladybugs busied themselves in the meadow-sweet atmosphere. "Bye, lovely garden creatures," Maddie whispered. "I hope the next tenant appreciates you as much as I have."

She said no goodbyes to the friends she and George had made during their relationship. Not one had come to offer condolences after Maddie had been abandoned.

A sullen Mary-Jean stood beside her mother, head downcast. She had no goodbyes for anybody or anything. She moaned, "I don't want to leave here. You are taking me away from all my school friends (though she didn't have any), and I'll have to go to a new school that I know I'm going to hate. I hate you, Mummy. I really do! You are crazy, talking to the birds!"

Maddie and Mary-Jean traveled to Scotland by train. They were met at the Glasgow station by Agent JF, who drove them to the Village of Kilmacolm on the Rosneath peninsula, a stunning location with views across the water to Greenock and the Farlane HM base, home of the Trident nuclear submarines. Barely in view was a U.S. submarine base set up during the Cold War. It was to become Maddie's second home. She loved the area, but she was about to be disappointed—blindsided!

Kilmacolm had a lot of farms and a lot of cows! Her new residence wrinkled her eyebrows. Maddie was speechless as her eyes scanned the timeless stone building and lichen-encrusted roof. Nesting swallows chittered on rotting eaves. Wizened oak trees lined the long pathway. Spring grass and purple Scottish thistles crayoned the window panes. The shutters drooped. The ancient gamekeeper's lodge was situated on a large estate owned by the Duke of Argyll. It was spooky looking. The exterior dilapidation mirrored the building's interior.

Maddie walked into a silent shrine with dusky hallways. A larder of dank odors assailed her nostrils. The few items of furniture scattered throughout the two-bedroom home were old and shabby. The slate-mantled wood-burning fireplace sitting in the small living room was an arachnophobic's worst nightmare. Cupboard spiders—creepy, dark purple, and eight-legged—were weaving their fresh spring webs in the nooks and crannies. Although Maddie did not fear spiders, she suppressed a claustrophobic anxiety attack in the confined, musty setting. She turned to Agent JF. "You don't expect me to live here," she groaned in a phony American accent. Mary-Jean grumbled, growled, and stomped her feet as she added, "I'm not staying in this disgusting house. I want to go back to our old house. I hate you for bringing me here! I'm not going to listen to you anymore! Why are you talking in that funny voice?"

Agent JF, a father of four, glared at the belligerent child. *What a rude brat!* Observing Maddie's flushed cheeks, he decided it would not be prudent to remark on her daughter's rude behavior.

Maddie reprimanded, "Hush, Mary-Jean. Go and explore. I bet you'll find some interesting stuff. Pick out a bedroom, and Mum will turn it into a fairy castle for you in no time."

"I'm not a kid, Mum," she answered in an acidic tone. "I'm seven!"

Maddie stifled a laugh. "Then you are old enough to have an adventure on your own. Go on while I talk to JF."

In a temper-tantrum mood, Mary-Jean's sandaled feet stomped off down the corridor.

Agent JF addressed Maddie, pointing out facts. "You were well briefed in Cornwall, Mrs. Santini," he said using her new identity. "You know full well, it is to avoid drawing attention to yourself or the "outfit." You are a single mother leaving a troubled, marital relationship. This residence is all that you can afford, correct?"

Maddie's prolonged sigh spoke more than words. *What have I gotten myself into?* She had been feeling enormous pressure regarding how to make ends meet. George's "charitable" payments had ended. Now, with Lady Luck smiling on her, this cushy job would be her bread and butter.

Agent JF's next sentence caused Maddie's eyebrows to arch in surprise. "You will have two roommates, submarine base workers, who will help pay the rent and utilities and keep your undercover work more plausible."

"I thought the rent and the rest of it are being covered by the 'outfit.'"

Agent JF sighed. "They are, but that's not for anyone else to know."

Maddie scratched her head. The house had only *two* sleeping quarters. Tension heightened. "I was informed that I would have *one* minder, not two! Where are they? And you may have noticed there are only *two* bedrooms!"

"Change of plans. Get used to it," he responded brusquely. "You will meet them tonight, after you have settled in. I will return tomorrow morning and escort you to your workplace."

"What about my daughter? I can't leave her here alone."

Agent JF puffed out his cheeks. "That's all taken care of, Mrs. Santini. She is to start school tomorrow. She'll be collected by ..."

Maddie interrupted. "I have always accompanied my children to school. Mary-Jean will freak out if a stranger takes her on her first day at a new school! Why can't I go to the base after I have taken her to school, wherever it is?"

"*Mrs. Santini,*" JF replied in an exasperated tone. "You have signed Her Majesty's Secrecy agreement and are dutifully bound to honor your contract. You now work for us. Normally the "outfit" doesn't accept foreign recruits with children, but you are the exception. As I've said, we can't allow your cover to be blown, so you are just going to have to get used to some changes."

Maddie exhaled a long breath. She had to do what she had to

do. She now had a fake personal life and would have to use intelligence and street smarts to keep up the façade. She nodded her head in acquiescence. However, her thoughts were on her strong-willed daughter. *Oh boy, I hope Mary-Jean's escort has ear muffs!* Her thoughts turned toward herself. *Each new chapter of my life required an old part of me to be discarded to make room for a new part to arise—new habits, new life!*

Maddie found cleaning supplies in the small kitchen, provided by the "outfit," and an antiquated fridge packed with fresh food.

She made a jam sandwich for Mary-Jean, who had returned home after exploring the extensive six-acre property. Mary-Jean's cheerful attitude pleased Maddie. "Mum, you should see the lovely rose garden, and there's a greenhouse … it needs some work, but we can grow our own vegetables."

Maddie smiled. Mary-Jean detested most vegetables! But she was fond of baby carrots baked in butter.

Following their improvised lunch, Maddie started applying her "neat-freak," OCD ways to their new home. By four o'clock that afternoon the house and the bedroom they would share smelled much better. She inhaled the fresh air that entered from the open sash windows. Columns of vintage dust bunnies had flown out of the windows and into the nut-brown forest adjacent to the house.

That evening, around 7 o'clock, Maddie's new lodgers arrived. She was leery but also pleasantly surprised, and she knew how to carry herself.

The first lodger, wearing a pristine U.S. naval officer's uniform and packing a sidearm, walked up to her. Maddie sized him up: a Paul Newman look-alike. The difference was he was over six feet tall, of burly physique, and sporting a navy buzz cut. "Hi there," he greeted in a beguiling voice with a trace of southern accent. "I'm Nate Silver, and you must be Madeline."

Maddie stared into blue eyes as clear as a mountain stream. With a megawatt smile and an extended hand, she replied, "Call me Maddie. I'm pleased to meet you." Nate gripped her hand so firmly Maddie thought her fingers might break. He turned to his thin-faced companion, who had Nordic-gold hair, wintery blue eyes, and was wearing civilian clothing. "This is Wojchiech. We call him Wally."

"Hello, Wally," Maddie greeted, extending her hand. His handshake was limp.

Maddie immediately warmed to Nate and thought she could easily build a friendship with him, but for some unknown reason she felt the opposite about Wally. Why? That unanswered question would reveal itself in the future.

Nate handed her a small box. "For me?" she exclaimed.

"Well, put it this way, it's not for Wally," he laughed.

Maddie open the elegant velvet box and gasped when she saw the sparkling diamond earrings. "But I don't have pierced ears!"

"Ah, that can be fixed at the base," Nate offered.

Maddie gave her new "boyfriend" a warm hug. She took his arm and pulled him aside. Mistrusting by nature, she whispered, "Is there something wrong with Wally? He has a brain-damaged stare."

"You hit the nail on the head, Profiler MS. Nate explained: Wally was a crew member aboard a nuclear submarine, and a darn good cook. He could rustle up the best grub ever. Unfortunately, he sustained a brain injury from a fall down a hatch, and he has been on sick leave ever since. He has cognitive problems, trouble speaking coherently, but other than that, he has some normal brain function, as well. As his Chief of Watch I offered to take care of him until I'm instructed otherwise. You see, he's a Polish refugee. Came here as a kid and has no family in Warsaw."

"Poor fellow," she responded. "We must make him comfortable, *boyfriend!*"

"Yes, we must, *honey!* But we will have to work on your Brooklyn accent. It sure ain't going to fool a Brooklynite!"

Peals of laughter made this night memorable, for now!

Yes, Maddie was aware that if she didn't master the American twang, she could unmask her position. A pressing thought surfaced. *Why have I been "sold" to the Americans?* But she was a *British* intelligence officer, and that's what mattered.

After some small talk, Nate bid her goodnight with a soft kiss on the cheek. "I'll see you tomorrow on the base, and we can have griddle cakes for breakfast."

"What the heck is that?"

"Pancakes, my honey," he smiled. "You are going to have to get used to American sayings, and quick!"

Wally retired to the spare bedroom after informing Maddie he was to be Mary-Jean's minder while she was at work. He would be Mary-Jean's walking-to-school buddy.

They'll get on well, Maddie thought. *Both have "miswired" brains!*

Maddie woke in the silence of dawn. She dressed quietly so as not to waken the Sleeping Beauty. It was Monday morning, Maddie's first day on the job. From her newly acquired wardrobe, courtesy of the "outfit," she selected a tasteful lightweight, pinstriped two-piece pantsuit and flat black shoes.

She tiptoed past Wally's room, opposite theirs, and headed for the kitchen, where she prepared breakfast and lunch for Mary-Jean. Mary-Jean's school uniform was already laid out at the bottom of her single bed. Wrapping her daughter's sandwiches in wax paper, Maddie felt a pang of sadness. On Mary-Jean's first day, she'd be taken to school by a stranger. *Ah, that's the way the cookie crumbles!* Maddie was Mary-Jean's sole provider now, and Mary-Jean had little choice but to go with the flow if they both hoped to survive the harsh reality of being "dumped."

At six o'clock Nate appeared. "You ready?"

"Ready as I will ever be."

The drive to the Kilmacolm ferry landing took only a few minutes. Nate and an apprehensive Maddie boarded. The sound of waves slapping furiously at the ferry's hull ...

Click, click, click.

I can't do this. I will die, flashed through Maddie's mind.

Don't be frightened, lovie. You'll be okay, she reassured herself.

Maddie concentrated on deep breathing as the wind-tossed waters threatened to bring up her breakfast. Halfway across the Loch, the Scottish captain slowed his ferry then brought it to idle in U.S. territorial waters. He allowed a tugboat displaying the U.S. ensign on a gaff-rigged pole to come alongside. The Master at Arms greeted the Chief of Watch and Maddie. Then Nate led Maddie to the Jacob's ladder. She took one look at the dangling vertical ropes and experienced an acute stress reaction. Her heartbeat accelerated like a race car, and a swarm of butterflies in her gut put on their dancing shoes and performed a Highland jig. But she couldn't think of being overcome by fear on her first day on the job. Gingerly, she climbed down the swinging ladder to the boat below, one rung at a time. Could she face the upcoming sea voyage without vomiting? Thanks to her gripping toes and flat shoes, she was not tossed into the cold water.

"You're a pro," Nate remarked when they were safely on-board.

"Not really. My stomach is in my mouth!" a pale Maddie replied.

The men laughed good-naturedly.

With submarines stealing past her in the blue waters of the bay and the inlets of the Firth of Clyde, Maddie disembarked onto U.S. territory. Sailors saluted their Chief and politely greeted Maddie. "Good morning, ma'am." She was tickled pink!

Nate and Maddie parted company when a dark-skinned, black-suited gentleman introduced himself. "Hi. I'm Agent Omar. Please come with me."

He escorted Maddie to her workplace, a small, brightly lit room at the rear of the tax-free Commissary store. She was shown to a desk, one of only two in the room. Omar explained her assignment. She was the Trojan horse, he said. Her job was to take down terrorists by listening to wiretaps of Middle Eastern and some U.S. telephone conversations, mostly spoken in code.

"You come highly recommended by 'The Big Kahuna,' so welcome to Operation Catch the Bastards," he laughed.

Maddie would never learn his true identity, but years later he would vouch for her credibility in a court of law after learning that her last-born, adult daughter intended to file a lawsuit for slander against her own mother.

Maddie and her Syrian-born counterpart forged a great working relationship. But even though she wanted to climb the ladder to a high-ranking position like the one Omar held, she never took credit for *her* deciphering of coded messages of terrorist plots. One was the June 14, 1985, hijacking of TWA flight 847 by Shiite Hezbollah terrorists. She went international for that one and was flown to Beirut. The stakes were high and dangerous.

In the hotel room Maddie assumed her disguise: the Lebanese thawb—a loose, long-sleeved, ankle-length dress covered with an abaya—a black cloak masking her face and auburn hair, and a niqāb, discrete black veil. She was driven to the Canadian Embassy where she spent many hours listening to radio messages between the Hezbollah fanatics. Her warning, determined from the translated transcripts, eventually led the Canadian embassy to evacuate all personnel.

After returning to Scotland, Maddie was on call 24/7. She followed the same daily ritual: get out of bed in the morning, make school lunch, ride the ferry and tugboat, then return home at seven o'clock in the evening. It was such a demanding and stressful routine that Maddie took up smoking. She inhaled her first menthol cigarette, offered by Omar, she coughed deeply, expecting her burning lungs to punch out of her chest and land on her desk. When smoking became easy, it developed into a habit; yet it still did not stop her exhausted, frayed nerves from threatening to shut down her worn-out mind and body. She often said, "I would rather put nicotine in my bloodstream then antidepressants."

On top of Maddie's work stress, Mary-Jean's behavioral issues escalated.

Within months of living in Kilmacolm, Mary-Jean's challenges increased. She was rude and cold, and she refused to be cuddled. Maddie received a constant flow of letters from the elementary school. "Mary-Jean did this ... Mary-Jean did that!"

Even timeouts had negligible effect on her. But Mary-Jean did talk to Wally. She would run to him saying, "Mummy is being horrible to me ..."

Mary-Jean would only eat food prepared by Wally, the former submarine cook.

Maddie spoke to Nate about her rascal daughter.

"I would put her in a boarding school," he advised. "It might straighten her out."

Maddie blamed herself for her daughter's behavior. *If only I didn't work such long hours.* But Maddie's weekends were dedicated to Mary-Jean and the places she loved: parks, museums, and more. Maddie indulged her daughter with her favorite treats, and at bedtime, she read the many new books she had purchased for her. Even so, the child distanced herself from her mother. "I love you, Mary-Jean" was always met with, "Well, I suppose I love you, but I'm not sure!"

Mary-Jean's response broke Maddie's heart. But the situation was what it was. Maddie had failed miserably when she tried to "fix" Joanne with an abundance of love, so she realized this was an emotional battle she could not win. This child inherited the same Blakely character traits her sister did.

Committed to her job, Maddie's loneliness had taken a backseat. Now that she was starved of a healthy relationship with her child, she turned to Nate for comfort, love, and intimacy. His reaction was not what she expected.

"Maddie, nothing would give me more pleasure than to become involved with you. But honey, I simply can't."

The word on the Kilmacolm streets that the couple was "tight" ended.

Nate had accepted this "babysitting" assignment because of the generous top-up he would receive in wages by the British "outfit." Nate planned to marry a woman back in the States.

"I feel like such an idiot," she admitted to Nate. "What was I thinking?"

"You are far from being an idiot, Maddie. One day someone is going to appreciate all that love you have inside you."

The autumn leaves weaved a quilt of color. They sat patiently, waiting for the seasonal winds to send them to their next resting place. On this morning Maddie's ferry pickup was late. When *The Queen of the Clyde* arrived, Maddie climbed aboard and was greeted by a young man of average height. He was sporting a five o'clock shadow with a slick brown goatee. He had large, molten-brown eyes and dark, wind-tousled hair.

"Where's Peter?" Maddie asked.

"My dad is ill. I've taken over until he's better."

"I'm sorry to hear that. By the way, my name is Maddie."

"I know who you are. My dad never stops talking about you. He calls you the weird Yank from the U.S. base."

"Oh, that's *nice*," Maddie said with a grin. "I'm not weird, you know!"

"No, you're definitely not!" In a devil-may-care tone he added, "I think you're a damn good-looking lass for a weirdo!"

Maddie blushed. "What is this world coming to when a school-boy comes on to an older woman? Are you old enough to be cap-taining this ferry?"

"Don't be fooled by my boyish looks. I'm a couple of years younger than you."

That widened Maddie eyes. "And how do you know that?"

"I asked the Master at Arms. He said you split up with your boyfriend and that I should go for it," the man said mischievously. "My name is Gordon McCullum, and I would love to take you on a date!"

Maddie glared at this whippersnapper and returned icily, "Now you are pushing it! I've not split up with my boyfriend." She made a mental note to have a serious chat with the patrol officer, who needed to be reprimanded. Though she was not a rat, he was going to get a tongue lashing from her when she came to work on Monday. For now, she was grateful to be the only passenger on this ferry ride home. But Gordon's antics were not over.

"No, you don't have a boyfriend. He's gone back to the States," Gordon declared with a steady gaze. He waited for Maddie's reaction, and he got it! Her icy glare finally shut him up.

But Gordon McCullum wasn't going to go away easily.

On the Sunday morning following that ferry ride, the phone rang. "Hi, lass," he greeted. "It's Gordon. I owe you an apology for my rudeness. I'm quite harmless, you know."

"Think nothing of it," Maddie snapped.

"Look, I want to make it up to you. I've noticed that your lawn hasn't seen a mower in a long time. How about I come and mow the grass for you?"

"Thank you, but no. I'll get Wally to do it."

"I've already spoken to Wally. He tells me that he is your daughter's babysitter, not a gardener."

Maddie brooded on the neglected garden, and she accepted. "Okay. But come later. Mary-Jean is still asleep."

October came and went. Maddie and Gordon were opposites— he was a gregarious and she was reserved—but they were now getting along amicably. They had a lot in common. They loved gardening, when time allowed. They each had a wicked sense of humor, and they both enjoyed cooking and fishing. Mary-Jean thought the sun shone out of her new playmate's rear. Wally was toast when Gordon was around. When Gordon wasn't working on the ferry or keeping up with the cottage's lawns, Mary-Jean was constantly by his side. Her cold-heartedness thawed, but not toward her mother.

Gordon often overheard Maddie trying to placate her angry child. "Sweetie, you can't walk to the village on your own. If you give me a minute, I will walk you. We can stop at the store and buy ice cream."

"You make me sick!" Mary-Jean hissed. "I hate you."

A shocked Gordon defended Maddie. "Don't talk back to your mother like that; it's disrespectful. If I ever spoke to *my* mother like that, she would knock me flat on my arse."

Mary-Jean stomped off.

Following that incident, Gordon and Maddie's friendship drew closer. She no longer felt lonely, and she seemed to have a glow about her. When Gordon invited her to be his partner at his friend's birthday party, she readily accepted. Big mistake!

Mary-Jean wasn't too happy about Gordon's attention to Maddie. She became withdrawn and hardly talked to the pair. Mary-Jean spoke only to Wally, who commiserated with her. He, too, was losing a companion, having had Maddie to himself since Nate departed.

The night of the birthday bash arrived. Maddie knew the risk of being the object of attention; she understood the partygoers in this close-knit community would pry. But her personal and work lives were not up for grabs! She had been well coached in minding your own business.

Allister's November 3rd birthday party was in full swing when Maddie and Gordon arrived. They were welcomed as a couple. A waterfall of malt whiskey flowed, and the food was to die for.

Maddie danced her feet off, but as night progressed into the wee hours, her old arch enemy, genetic alcohol intolerance, came a calling. Her dark skin flushed red and her breathing became wheezy.

She still swayed, but no longer to the music. Now she was swaying towards lights out! She didn't remember much after that.

Maddie woke naked with a thumping headache. Her dulled eyesight scanned a small room she did not recognize. Then the penny dropped! *Oh, no, not again!*

The door opened, and Gordon entered, holding a porcelain tea cup in his hand. Maddie pulled the bed covers up to her neck.

"I've brought you a warm cup of herbal peppermint tea," he said through smiling, puckered lips. "It has always helps me with hangovers."

With awkwardness and a good dose of disappointment in herself, Maddie recalled the whispering of sweet nothings in the night, and, at one point, Gordon declaring his love for her. She had responded that she wasn't ready for a relationship and that their "no strings" friendship was all he could hope for.

"Did something happen?" she asked.

It was a stupid question because the telltale signs had adhered to her inner thighs.

"Oh, yes. You're my lass now, and you look so beautiful when you sleep."

Shame filled Maddie's soul. Was she just another notch in his belt?

Debra awakened!

Maddie's voice was warrior thunder. "Gordon, I'm *furious*! You took advantage of me when I was drunk. That's criminal. Do you know that?"

Gordon pouted like a schoolboy. "If that's how you feel, I suggest you leave. This relationship is over."

"*Over!*" she snarled, her top lip curling upward. "How dare you suggest that I gave you permission? Now get out. I would like to dress in private!"

Maddie's face was as ruddy as a strawberry when she passed what she presumed to be Gordon's mother sitting in a chair near the front door. "Morning, lass," she said with a smirk.

Maddie raced up the hill to her home as if a demon were following her. And it *was!*

CHAPTER EIGHTEEN

"If you keep a secret, it will
forever hold a piece of you."

D ay broke on the unsettled third week of November 1986.
In the distance, forked lightening streaked across the roiling sky as peals of thunder resounded.

Early Monday morning Maddie felt fatigued and sluggish as she went about her normal routine. She had been up all night with an upset stomach, and she suspected food poisoning, probably from the salmon she purchased from a local fisherman. She had baked it in the oven, but perhaps not completely. She wasn't concerned about Mary-Jean having the same symptoms, since she hated to eat fish or any other seafood. Mealtimes had become battles. Mary-Jean's fussiness disrupted many meals.

Maddie slipped into the bedroom where Mary-Jean was sleeping. She planted a soft kiss on her daughter's forehead and left the cottage for work. Maddie worked hard, and she had no digital tools to help her. Her tasks were written by hand and then meticulously typed on an electric typewriter.

She was pleased to see a recovered Captain Peter at the helm instead of his son, Gordon.

Descending the swaying Jacob's ladder, Maddie felt discomfort in the back of her throat, and forceful contractions in her stomach muscles. Her retching and the expulsion of her stomach's contents nearly toppled her into the choppy waters. The Master at Arms' strong arms grabbed her, gripped her firmly, and lowered her into a seat.

"You okay, ma'am?" he asked, concerned.

Oxymoronic! Do I look okay?

Maddie was mortified, and her clothing smelled of putrid ejections. She answered, "Sorry about that, but I ate some bad fish last night."

"Yep. Happens to me on occasion," he said in a commiserative tone. "Strap up and I'll get you over as quickly as I can. Captain Petraeus can give you something to stop the vomiting."

Maddie had often crossed paths with the navy doctor, but had never had cause to be his patient, until now. She had learned from Omar that he was a seasoned clinician and surgeon, a member of the Medical Corps during World War II. At this U.S. base he treated the base personnel for a variety of general conditions, including assorted fungal, parasitic, viral, and bacterial infections common among sailors. He also dealt with more serious conditions, such as congestive heart failure, and had performed various surgeries for such things as fractured skulls, mangled fingers, external ulcers, and more.

Taking on a pea-green tone, Maddie waited for the elderly doctor in a sixteen-bed sick-bay equipped with extensive medical equipment—X-ray machines, body scanners, and other diagnostic instruments.

"Good day, Mrs. Santini," the doctor greeted with smiling eyes. "I'm told by the Master at Arms that you threw up on the way to work."

I need to have a serious talk with this booger, Maddie mused.

She told Dr. Petraeus she suspected uncooked fish was the culprit.

"I would like to run some tests," he said, fingering his handlebar moustache. "Meanwhile, I'll give you something for nausea and diarrhea."

Petraeus leafed through Maddie's bulging medical file, which he had no time to digest fully given the short notice. Pulling out a Croydon Hospital lab report, he said, "I see you have a history of blood cancer, so I will need to do some extensive testing. Is that okay with you?"

"Sure. It's been some time since I've had any tests done, but I'm sure my nasty *gremlins* will have the last say in this matter."

He smiled, accentuating the dimple on his chin.

Maddie said, "I don't believe they are here to snatch me away because I've had no symptoms for many years. Apart from this food-poisoning, I am as healthy as an ox."

Maddie's blood and urine samples were submitted and sent to the off-base laboratory.

Sent home on sick leave, Maddie's condition worsened. She developed a high fever, was dehydrated, lost her appetite, and made frequent trips to the loo. While her stomach muscles cramped, she began to suspect E-coli or Salmonella.

Maddie's test results came back two days later. She was pregnant, and her gremlins had enlisted an army of myeloblastic white cells!

Maddie was catching up on some paperwork when the phone rang. "Hello."

"This is Dr. Petraeus. I am calling about your test results."

Maddie was silent. She then asked breathlessly, "Yes?"

Dr. Petraeus's voice was gentle. "You are three to four weeks pregnant."

"How can that be?" she queried in disbelief. "Have you read my medical file?"

"Yes, I have, Maddie, every medical note Dr. Barazani wrote. It's incredible, but once more you have defied medical odds."

In shocked, angry denial, Maddie said dryly, "Then you must know that pregnancy is impossible. I have *no* fallopian tubes, or, to put it another way, one dead one still exists. The tests must have been misinterpreted. Even if I am pregnant, I've had no symptoms of abdominal cramping, spotting, tingling breasts, or morning sickness. I would certainly know because I went through hell with my former pregnancies."

Dr. Petraeus didn't want to delay, even in the face of his patient's denial. He said, "I've ordered the base helicopter to pick you up; it will land shortly on the grassy area behind the cottage."

"What on earth for!" she said snippily. "I'm telling you …" there was a brief pause, and then, "I'm *not* bloody pregnant!"

Unperturbed, the doctor continued. "I would like to perform an ultrasound, and then we will see."

The conversation ended.

Fifteen minutes later Maddie arrived at the base. Keeping her head low to avoid having her head chopped off by rotor blades, she walked directly to the sickbay.

Dr. Petraeus's head tipped to one side in greeting. "Come and lie down," he said.

Thubalep … Thubalep … Thubalep …

There was no mistaking miracle baby number three's hoof beats.

Maddie's mouth dropped open. "Heavens!" she exclaimed. "It's real?"

Click, click, click.

"You took advantage of a drunken woman, Gordon McCullum. Do you know it's a criminal offense?"

Maddie's reflections dominated her mind, but they were by-passed as quickly as they appeared. Dr. Petraeus's next words were, "Yes, Maddie, but …"

Now came the hardest part for the doctor, informing his patient of the other life-altering findings. It was of great concern to him how she would handle the unwelcome news.

He had entered the field of medicine long ago hoping to help his patients stay healthy and feel better; however, now he had to deliver tough news. Most medical schools don't offer their students much instruction on this task.

Dr. Petraeus sighed. "As your primary physician, I'm referring you to an oncologist at Glasgow Hospital. Maddie, you have chronic myeloid leukemia. Your white cell count is dangerously high."

Maddie showed no immediate reaction because she had heard

this more than once before. She didn't look glum or start to cry, as most folks would have done. Saving herself at the cost of her baby's life was not an option for her. The cancer diagnosis was devastating, but she wouldn't allow herself to dwell on it.

In a tone as harsh as the stormy weather outside, Maddie vented anger, not shock. "No, I won't see an oncologist! I'm opting out of cancer treatments until my baby is born. I will not undergo chemotherapy that will poison my baby. She chose me. She needs me, and I need her—because the two kids I've already brought into this world don't want me."

"But Maddie …" Dr. Petraeus felt anything he could say would have no medical effect.

"If you have fully read my file, you learned that I'm a long-term cancer survivor, so I'll take my chances. If it's meant to be that we both die, then we will be with my deceased children in baby Heaven, if there is such a place!"

The image of her dead babies was frozen in her memory. Between pinched lips she said, "So be it."

On her way home, Maddie imagined the whole village would be abuzz with her news. Suddenly, she jolted in realization. She had forgotten to ask Dr. Petraeus of the potential risk—could the gremlins harm her baby? Other musings rushed through her mind: How would Mary-Jean take the news? Should she tell Gordon? Her most pressing thought was about her job. Would she be fired? If so, what then?

It was all too much for Maddie. She closed her eyes, cradled her weary head, and for the first time since her Cornwall days, sobbed herself empty.

Could she now start each day with a grateful heart? Would this unborn child be the miracle that would make Maddie's life complete?

Hell, no!

CHAPTER NINETEEN

"Such a big miracle in such a little girl."

The no-pregnancy rule specified in her Oath of Loyalty was forgiven, and Maddie was provided with full-pay maternity leave. She remained at the old gamekeeper's cottage rent free, and she was thrilled. She loved her high-level intelligence work, and asked Agent JF if she could work during her leave from home.

Holding his hands wide apart, he responded, "I doubt it, Madeline. In the many years I have served in the Secret Service Agency, I've never known them to break the no-pregnancy clause. Don't push your luck!"

"Yeah. I guess you're right. I'm fortunate to still have a job."

"You didn't hear this from me, but I understand that you will be sent to Aldershot Army base after your leave of absence, and you will continue counterintelligence operations there."

You guys own me so do I have a say? No!

She answered, "Yes, sir!"

The *real* reason for her transfer was obvious. She had been hired as a "shadow figure," but now she was drawing attention to herself. The "outfit" did not want to deal with wagging tongues as her Brussels sprout grew into a watermelon! Maddie's detractors were already having a field day:

One woman squealed, "I bet it is Gordon McCullum's baby."

Another one added, "Even his mother believes it, but she doesn't want her son to be involved with a shady lady!"

"His dad told me that he has no doubt in his mind," another tattled.

"She's lying. It's not some doctor's kid from New York," another griped.

"That's just as well. Gordon has a good wife now who told me Gordon told her the Yank on the hill is an American spy."

"You think she's a spy?"

"Why else would a helicopter land on her property?"

"She's a sly one, for sure."

Maddie was glad she would no longer be bothered by the continual requests from Gordon and his mom to buy tax-free cigarettes and booze from the Commissary, for which they never paid her back.

Six months into Maddie's high-risk pregnancy complications developed: high blood pressure, gestational diabetes, leukemia, and more. She also had a history of miscarriages. Thirty-five-year-old Maddie was feeling sad and hopeless. She had neither a partner to offer physical support nor willing ears for emotional sustenance.

She was not eating or getting enough rest or exercise. In addition, there was little in the way of fresh air and sunlight during the drab winter months. She tried acting upbeat and cheerful, but she was facing so many medical challenges. Also, she was now managing Mary-Jean's childcare fulltime, and Mary-Jean had made it clear she was not taking well to the coming baby ... and she missed Wally. He had been phoning regularly to speak with Mary-Jean, but after a while she transferred her affection to another confidant. Maddie was not pleased when she discovered it was Gordon's younger sister, Abigail, who was Mary-Jean's lunchtime supervisor.

Maddie had previously met Abigail—an inebriated Abigail—at that fateful party, and she had taken an instant liking to her. Abigail's bubbly personality was like fresh air, and she had Maddie in stitches with her Scottish and Irish jokes. But her fond memories completely changed when Mary-Jean said, "You lied to me. Gordon is your baby's daddy. Abigail told me, and I believe her. Why didn't you marry him when he asked you? I could have had a *real* father!"

Keeping a neutral face, Maddie responded, "Well, for starters, he never asked me, so that part is untrue, and it's not his baby!" she lied feebly.

"You're a lying cow, and that's why no one likes to be around you." Mary-Jean placed her slender hands on her hips, straightened her back, and glared. "I wish you *weren't* my mother! I wish Abigail was!"

Where had Maddie heard that before?

Click, click, click.

"I've a new mother now!" Joanne had hurled at her.

Mary-Jean's words were a stiletto to Mattie's heart. She was being stabbed all over again. This dreadful child could have been Joanne's twin.

At least you have a mother, child! One day when you are my age, you will realize that your mother is the most important person in the world to you, because real mothers never close the door on their children when they need them!

Tears glazed Maddie's eyes. Time had not healed the motherless child within her. Growing up with an absent mother was a traumatic, bitter pill to swallow. She had not yet discovered the truth about why her mother had abandoned her. This would come to light much later in Maddie's life. She had no photos, no baby books, no baby diaries, and no family. She was often overwhelmed with jealousy and envy when she was presented with a mother-daughter duo, and she always searched for dark-skinned female faces in a crowd, wondering if one of them was her mother! Not knowing whether her mother was alive or dead not only defined her, it shaped her. She convinced herself long ago that her absent mama *had* influenced her life, had wanted her to be a soldier, to fight and be strong.

For the rest of her years Maddie felt empty on Mother's Day. She would have given her life to hug her birth mother and show her how much she was loved. But sadder still, for the rest of her life Maddie's Mother's Days would be uncelebrated by the adult daughters she had with David.

Mary-Jean was testing her patience. "Watch your mouth, Mary-Jean," she admonished. "Go to your room until I tell you to come out!"

Stamping footsteps echoed down the hallway.

Maddie sighed knowing that "tough love" could never cure her daughter of David's traits, the footprints he imprinted in this child's DNA.

Her thoughts reverted to former times. Initially, she had been pleased that Gordon and Mary-Jean were bonding, but in time he had not proven to be a proper role model. Mary-Jean became as foul mouthed as he was. When Maddie made it clear she was uncomfortable with his language, Gordon had laughed it off saying, "She'll learn it at school soon enough."

Maddie's thoughts turned to Wally. A week before her pregnancy results were announced, he was decommissioned from the Navy and relocated to London, where he was being cared for by a Polish family who received his work-related compensation every month.

But Maddie *would* cross paths with Wally again, when the Navy-JAG represented him in a judicial proceeding initiated by Maddie. She knew Wally was a strange individual, but he had never used bad language, and he had doted on Mary-Jean, taking a lot of child rearing duties off her shoulders. When Mary-Jean accused him of molesting her, Maddie went to war to have Wally put behind bars. *That* trial would haunt her for years to come!

Time marched on. When Maddie was six months pregnant, she learned from the village handyman who used to perform odd jobs around her house that Gordon had married a Jehovah's Witness worshipper from Rosneath. She found it hard to believe that Gordon had found his "Come to Jesus" moment and was attending services at the Kingdom Hall regularly. He had stopped smoking and drinking, which made Maddie laugh. From sinner to saint overnight! *I wonder if it was his new wife or Jesus who stopped his sewer mouth!*

Two days after she had moved into the cottage, religious crackpots started appearing on her doorstep with religious pamphlets in hand. Maddie often seized the opportunity to have some fun. "If you can answer my question, I will happily join your religion."

They fixed their happy eyes on hers.

"Am I right or wrong?" Maddie began. "The *Bible* says God made Adam and Eve. They begat two sons, then they took wives. Tell me, where they hell did these wives come from?" Maddie grinned in mirth. "Maybe God decided to remove a couple more of Adam ribs? Incest is a sin, is it not?"

The JWs never darkened Maddie's doorstep again.

Feathery snowflakes fell on Maddie as she waited at the village center for the Dart bus to Glasgow Hospital, where she had an appointment for a checkup.

To her dismay, as she was boarding, she spotted Gordon and his supposed new wife—a plump, blond woman—sitting in the back. It was an awkward moment, but Maddie pretended not to see them. She kept her eyes forward, ignoring the passengers who were craning their necks. Maddie heard one woman say, "Oh, this should be interesting."

Unexpectedly, Gordon touched her shoulder, causing her body to jerk. "How are you, Maddie?"

"Well, thank you," she replied coolly.

"How's *our* baby coming along?" he asked, touching her swollen belly.

Maddie slapped his hand away and snapped, "How many times do I have to tell you, Gordon, it is *not* your child?"

Throughout the bus, eyebrows raised and ears opened.

"You can fool everyone but me, Maddie," he said reaching once more to touch her belly.

This time she grabbed his finger. She would have snapped it in half if he hadn't hastily withdrawn it. "Leave me alone, Gordon, if you know what's good for you. I'm sure your wife is not happy to see you talking to me and hearing your ridiculous claims. If I were her, I'd slap you down to size!"

With an inane chortle, like a village idiot on laughing gas, Gordon returned to his seat.

Flushed with anger, Maddie exited the bus at the next stop. She completed the next leg of her journey by taxi and decided to return home the same way. It was worth paying the expensive fare to avoid sitting in the same bus as that buffoon!

In the hospital waiting room a cloud of *black* engulfed Maddie. Her inner struggles about keeping the baby versus putting the child up for adoption were traumatic and ongoing. However, her internal scars due to the loss of her previous babies spoke more loudly. Suddenly, Maddie grimaced. "Ouch!" Her baby had been using her as a punching bag, but this kick was different. It felt like a vicious, deliberate karate blow. Maddie was angry at herself. She knew the baby's reflex had not been triggered by excess noise or bright light, both of which can stimulate such movement. Instead, it was the unborn child telling her off: *Don't even think about it!*

How correct was the baby's assessment?

According to the pediatric literature, babies who are hyperactive in pregnancy will run your feet off your feet when they are toddlers. Correct!

On a humid summer night, the first day of June, Maddie experienced agonizing cramping followed by a *whoosh* of warm liquid running down her inner thighs. "It's too soon!" she cried. Moving unsteadily, she made her way to the telephone in the kitchen.

"Fire, police, or ambulance?" the dispatcher asked. "What is the emergency?"

In a fit of panic, Maddie implored, "I need an ambulance at number one Argyll Road. Please, hurry! I'm pregnant. I am hemorrhaging badly and am having contractions."

"An ambulance is on its way, but don't hang up," the female operator said.

"I'm sorry, I have to. I've only one telephone line, and I've got to make another call. My young daughter is asleep, and I can't leave her here alone."

Ring … ring … ring … the repeated tone was crunching Maddie's nerves. "Pick up," she mumbled. Finally, a sleepy voice answered, "Hello."

"Abigail, this is Maddie. I'm so sorry to disturb you this late. I've had to call an ambulance. I'm bleeding profusely. Could you, please, come to my house and mind Mary-Jean for me?"

"No problem. I'll be there in a few minutes."

In a blare of sirens and flashing orange lights, the ambulance sped toward the closest hospital, one unfamiliar to Maddie.

"I think my baby has decided it's time to move out of my leukemia-riddled body," Maddie said to the EMS attendant, who was monitoring her vital signs.

"You and your baby will be fine. We are nearly there," he comforted. "It's a great hospital. I was born there. According to my mom, they have the best maternity nurses in the world."

Maddie couldn't manage a smile. Her heart was pounding in panic; she was fearful this baby was about to join Sky, Alexander, and Samuel.

Some medical staff awaited at the entrance as the ambulance pulled up to Dumbarton General Hospital. Maddie was rushed to the ER.

She was in agonizing pain as her blurred vision attempted to focus on the dark face of a woman dressed in a professional coat. Her mind spun. *It can't be! Yes, it is!*

"Adeeba, my dear friend," Maddie managed to say.

"*Maddie!*" Adeeba exclaimed, embracing her father's special patient. "It's been a long time, lots of catching up to do, but first things first."

Standing next to Adeeba was a tall, slim doctor whose origin Maddie guessed was Middle-Eastern, possibly Egyptian. She said in Arabic, "Please save my baby."

A smiling Rashid was, indeed, from Egypt. "Not a lot of folks around here speak Arabic. Where did you learn my language?"

"It's a long story, but enough chitchat," Maddie stressed. "Do something before I tear all my hair out from the pain."

Maddie was subjected to a barrage of tests. Dr. Rashid's eyes were compassionate as he informed her, "Maddie, your baby is in a breech position. This sometimes occurs in premature births."

"Then perform external cephalic," Maddie snapped. "Manually turn my baby into the head-down position."

Not only is she fluent in my language, she either has a medical background or has endured a breech before. There was no way of telling, as her medical file hadn't yet arrived from the Glasgow hospital, where she had received her checkups.

"It's too late to preform external cephalic. Your uterus has already expelled the baby. He or she will come out bottom first."

In an agitated state, Maddie snapped, "Then do a bloody C-section, and quick."

"It's too late for a C-section, and even if I could, you have scar tissue. It can't be done, Maddie. This baby will have to be birthed vaginally."

Maddie panicked when she heard the hoof beats pounding like thunder. "Oh, my God!" she cried. "My poor baby is in fetal distress."

Adeeba gently spoke to her friend. "It's going to be okay. I will see you through this with Dr. Rashid. He's the best there is, Maddie."

No, I beg to differ. Your dad was the best!

During her medical school days, she had learned that few practitioners were willing to exercise the skill of delivering a breech vaginally. However, Dr. Rashid El-Heely was not your average physician. Born in Cairo, he achieved the highest honor in his field of neonatology. He was an adept specialist in premature births.

Maddie couldn't have been placed in better hands. She begged him, "Please, give me analgesics. I can't take this bloody pain."

"Sorry, Maddie," he commiserated, "I can't do that. We don't want to make your baby sluggish because we need the baby out immediately!"

Lying flat on her back, writhing in pain with a third-degree tear, Maddie screamed. She didn't feel Rashid perform the thirteen-inch episiotomy or place his gloved hands into her vagina.

With Maddie's permission, student maternity nurses entered the delivery room. A breech delivery was a rare condition to observe.

Drenched in perspiration, Maddie writhed in agony. She believed her baby was paying her back for her thoughts on the Dart bus. Now, she would do whatever was necessary to deliver this baby because everything seemed to be going to hell in a hand basket!

"Push ... Push ... Push ..." Rashid ordered loudly. Then he turned to Adeeba and whispered something in her ear. She came to Maddie's side. "Maddie, listen to me. This is now a life-threatening situation. You are losing too much blood and are in critical danger. You are going to die soon. To save your life, Rashid must terminate the baby."

"No ... Fucking ... Way!" she shrieked. This language was a first for her.

"Doctor Rashid, you will bring my baby into this world no matter what the cost to my life. If I die, so be it."

To the shocked Adeeba, Maddie said, "Save my baby, my friend, and see that she has the best adoptive family in the world. I had another daughter, after birthing Joanne. Her name is Mary-Jean, and she is also to be adopted, along with this baby, if it survives ..."

Those were Maddie's last words. She felt her life ebbing away. Unconsciousness closed her heavy eyelids. Maddie was prepared to sacrifice her life for a child she didn't even know.

At 4 A.M. on June 2, 1987, Maddie's last involuntary contraction pushed the baby's bottom then torso. The head emerged. It was a girl.

The four-and-a-half-pound baby received oxygen. She had a bruised bottom, but, thanks to Rashid's expertise, her tiny head had not been squashed. She was rushed from the delivery room to the Pediatric ICU. The fragile newborn was placed in an incubator, put on respiratory support, and monitored by trained nurses.

In another area of the hospital Maddie was at the brink of death. She had suffered cardiac arrest and been resuscitated. After slipping into a coma, she was placed on life-support. A ventilator tube was inserted into her mouth and down her windpipe, forcing air into her lungs.

While Maddie was in this vegetative state, she underwent surgery to remove the remaining ruptured fallopian tube. Maddie's' faithful Vienna schnitzel finally bit the dust.

Adeeba sat by her friend's bedside daily, hoping and praying for a miracle. Even if Maddie physically recovered, Adeeba knew there was no guarantee of a positive emotional outcome. Adeeba felt certain, though, that if Maddie survived this ordeal, she would be thrilled to learn that her baby girl was healthy and doing well.

Two weeks passed, and Maddie's condition worsened. Her bodily functions were progressively failing, creating a dilemma for her caregivers—if and when to stop life support. Maddie had no family members who could make the legal and ethical decision whether to withdraw treatment or not. The machine would just have to beep away until a court ruled for the hospital.

The day following the baby's birth, Abigail arrived at the hospital with Mary-Jean. "Are you family?" she was asked.

"No. I'm a good friend, and this is her daughter, Mary-Jean."

"I'm sorry. Only family can visit." A hospital staff member pulled Abigail aside. "We can't let the child in right now. I'm not supposed to tell you this, but her mother is in the ICU in critical condition."

Abigail crossed herself. "Jesus, Mary-Jean, and Joseph!" she cried. "Did she give birth?"

"Yes, to a beautiful baby girl now being looked after in the neo-natal ICU. After being birthed, the baby was also struggling for her life, but she is doing so much better now."

Abigail took Mary-Jean's hand and said, "We have to come back and see you mum another day …"

Pouting, Mary-Jean cut Abigail's sentence short. "Why can't I see my mum?"

"Your mummy and your baby sister have infections," Abigail lied. "We *will* come to see your mum and baby sister when they are better. Okay?"

DEAD PEOPLE CAN COME TO LIFE!

CLICK, CLICK, CLICK.

THE MOURNFUL CRIES OF A HEBREW GIRL

SHATTERED THE BARREN DESERT: "HEAR,

O ISRAEL, THE LORD OUR GOD ... SAVE MY

HASSAM, MY TRUE LOVE ..."

"I'M GOING TO MARRY YOU ONE DAY ..."

Maddie started breathing on her own three weeks after they placed her in an induced coma. She suffered no damage from oxygen deprivation to her brain, kidneys, or other vital organs. And, incredibly, her platelets and white cell blood cell tests came back normal. She was leukemia free! However, Maddie was not quite out of the woods, due to a ventilator associated pneumonia infection.

The first words out of her mouth were, "Where the hell am I?"

Adeeba was thrilled to greet her friend, having feared she would not make it. She told Maddie the good news, that thanks to her courage and selflessness, her baby girl was alive and kicking, gaining weight every day.

"Please, take me to see her?"

"Not just yet, my dear. We have to make sure the infection is gone."

It dawned on Maddie that she had forgotten someone who was dear to her heart. "Adeeba, could you please call this number and ask for Abigail McCullum. If she is there, please, ask her to bring Mary-Jean to the hospital."

The intimidating look of the ICU and seeing her mother hooked up to all sorts of equipment sent Mary-Jean fleeing from the room. Shrieking, she was heard saying, "I hate my sister! I don't want to see her. She tried to kill my mummy."

The nearly four-week-old baby Santini, not yet given a first name, was brought to Maddie's hospital bed and presented to her mother. Maddie took one look at the sleeping infant's tiny face and fell instantly in love. She had her mother's midnight-black hair, an olive skin tone, and the cutest button nose and dainty ears. The baby made Maddie proud. "I can't believe it. She looks just like me," Maddie said to the nurse. "I gave birth to two girls before and neither one has even a freckle belonging to me," she laughed. "This one is mine."

When the baby's eyes opened, and Maddie screamed wildly, "Take this *thing* away! Take *it* away, before I throw *it* out the window."

As calm as a millpond, the nurse retrieved the wailing baby from the foot of the bed, where Maddie had cast it, and walked out of the room. In the nursery, she paged Dr. Barazani.

Maddie was hysterical by the time Adeeba arrived.

"Calm down, calm down," Adeeba instructed. "Whatever's the matter? The nurse told me that..."

Maddie took a deep breath. "I know you will not believe me and you'll think I'm crazy, but I've given birth to a dark entity, a dybbuk! I'm not talking about devils with tails and pitchforks that fall from the heavens cursed by God ..." Maddie searched Adeeba's face for a reaction. There was no verbal response, but her mouth hung wide open.

Maddie continued ranting. "There is an old saying: 'The eyes are the windows of the soul.' Well, I just looked into the eyes of the baby I've given birth to, and they peered at me with hate! She's a preternatural being, a demon, an evil spirit, whatever you want to call it ..." Maddie paused. Adeeba's mouth remained open.

Maddie raved on, as if her life depended on it, and it did!

"I'm not delusional or hallucinating. I don't have a sick brain that needs psychiatric intervention! I'm a smart person. And this is not a metaphysical assumption either. She is a vengeful spirit. And demonic possession should not be placed within quotations marks here because I've seen it with my own eyes."

A shocked medical professional finally spoke up. "Maddie, it's not likely that you are dealing with possession by an evil spirit, as you believe. You have just come out of a three-week coma, and I believe your brain is playing tricks on you."

"Be as skeptical as you want," Maddie huffed. "But I'm telling you this is not my baby anymore."

"Maybe you should speak to our counselor ..."

"Your dad asked me to do the same thing many years ago. I don't need a bloody shrink or counselor!" she exploded.

Adeeba Barazani quietly left the room, trembling slightly. This wasn't the woman she babysat for all those years ago, the one who loved her as much as her father did.

Against her wishes, Maddie was administered a powerful sedative.

Did she truly have a glitch in her brain? No.

Sinking into unconsciousness, Maddie heard her baby angels—Sky, Alexander, and Samuel—weeping.

Hush little baby, don't say a word ...

CHAPTER TWENTY

"F.E.A.R. has two meanings: Forget Everything And Run,
or Face Everything And Rise. The choice is yours."

M other and baby were examined by a locum physician.
When Maddie asked him why Dr. Rashid was not in
attendance, he replied, "Dr. Rashid and Dr. Adeeba are
on vacation. I believe they are traveling to Egypt."

Maddie frowned, thinking, *Why has my dear friend not come to
say goodbye, and why didn't she tell me they were an item?*

Instinct told Maddie that Adeeba, a devout Muslim, was reluctant to talk about Christian beliefs such as the devil or fallen angels,
and she didn't want to face Maddie after her outburst.

Maddie would not see either of them again, but she would come
to learn they had relocated to Cairo, married, and eventually had
five children, all boys.

At noon on July 4, 1987, Agent JF drove off with Maddie and the baby she had named Mara, meaning "bitter" in Hebrew.

Maddie had wrestled with her conscience but, in the end, couldn't find it in her heart to give this miracle infant up for adoption, her earlier plan. She was convinced that *love* was what it would take to raise this child, a true and intense maternal love. Perhaps the dark entity she believed inhabited this child would get the message and leave. *Love* conquers all!

Maddie had been assigned this mountain of darkness, and she planned to prove that the mountain could be moved!

There was little conversation with Agent JF on the way home, and Maddie was grateful. She was wracked with tension and was hoping to crawl into a cocoon of silence when she arrived home.

But she was in for a major surprise.

The car pulled into the driveway, and JF helped Maddie and Mara out. He opened the front door to the house. When Maddie stepped in, she heard a collective "*Surprise!*" as a greeting. She looked stunned. The living room had been decorated with pink balloons and a *Congratulations* banner. Her colleague, Omar, smiled and said, "Welcome home." It seemed that half the base was cramped into this small space, all of them echoing his words. Maddie's next surprise was a real shock.

"Hi, there, Maddie," she heard from a familiar deep voice. "Congratulations, and welcome home."

"Wow! Thank you, Nate. What on earth are you doing here? I thought you were enjoying married life somewhere in the States?"

"To cut the story short, it didn't work out, so I'm back to babysit you and the new addition."

Not wanting to verbalize her real response—something like *no you are not*—because other ears could hear, she said, "We will talk about this later …"

There was a rap on the door, and Nate opened it. Mary-Jean, accompanied by a smug-looking Abigail, entered.

"Hello, my Mary-Jean," Maddie said lovingly as she approached her daughter to give her a hug. Mary-Jean shrunk back, grabbed Abigail's hand, and spat out, "I don't want to live with you. I want to live with Abigail."

Click, click, click.

She knows how to push your buttons, Maddie! George, the psychiatrist, had stated.

Maddie's attention was now focused on Abigail. "I can't thank you enough for all you have done for me and Mary-Jean. I hope you won't find this offensive, but I would like you to leave. We will talk later. Okay?"

"I understand," Abigail said. "No offense taken. But can I see the baby?"

Maddie pulled the flap back from the portable car seat. "Oh, my God, she's adorable. She looks like my brother!" Abigail blurted. Maddie's look could have sunk ships.

Dropping the flap, Maddie took a firm hold of Abigail's arm and marched her to the door. Tersely she said, "Goodbye." Maddie turned to her silent, wide-eyed guests. "Thank you so much for making my homecoming so delightful, but I really need to be alone now. Would you all mind leaving? And thank you again."

After her guests departed, Maddie sent a sulking Mary-Jean to her room and set about preparing Mara's feeding. So far the new mother had only been able to breast-feed a couple of times. She swore Mara was deliberately biting her, not suckling as Joanne and Mary-Jean had done.

In a perverse way Maddie was thankful when she developed subareolar abscesses—bacteria infected lumps on the skin of her breasts. She had consented to the pus drainage procedure, a painful experience, but she was an anti-pill person and refused to take the high dosage antibiotics the professionals suggested. Instead, she had doctored herself with a cloth-covered ice pack, antibacterial soap, and antibacterial breast pads in her bra.

Maddie filled the baby bottle with store-brand baby formula, the closest one to breast milk she had been able to find. She lifted the wailing Mara but reached her wits end when Mara refused to drink. She preferred, instead, to howl like a coyote. Holding the screaming infant in her arms, Maddie called Dr. Petraeus.

"This is quite common, Maddie," he assured. "Try feeding her with goat's milk. It has proven to be a good replacement."

Maddie didn't really know the farmer down the road, but it was worth a shot.

Ten minutes later, the man's wife was on Maddie's doorstep holding a jug of warm goat's milk. "I raised five of my children on this," said the ruddy-faced woman, who had chicken feathers adhering to her coveralls and cow manure sloshed onto her gumboots. She handed the overflowing jug to Maddie. "Let me know how you get on? There's plenty more with this came from," she smiled.

"I will, and thank you," Maddie replied.

Maddie hurried into her kitchen and strained the warm milk though a muslin cloth.

The warm elixir worked like a charm. Mara was a happy camper and now slept soundly between feedings—but not before hearing her mother crooning *Hush little baby ...*

Every day Maddie sang, read fairy tales, and told her child she was loved and wanted. Mara's once soulless eyes now gave Maddie joy. She saw her own unique wolf-eyes, rich cognac amber in color, peering from her daughter's face. It was a trait Gordon could not claim!

Maddie settled into the business of raising an eight-year-old and a three-month-old. She was on her own until Nate moved back in. Maddie knew better than to question the "outfit's" motive for bringing Nate back into her life. She was sure they had a reason. Nevertheless, it still embarrassed her to think that they could be more than friends. A long, late-night telephone conversation told the tale. Nate admitted he cared about her more than she had thought and that his feelings for her were a factor in his failed marriage. He couldn't get the code-breaker out of his mind.

Maddie was looking forward to a renewed relationship and a helping hand, someone who could help care for the baby when she needed a break. Help with the baby meant she could spend more time with Mary-Jean, whose jealousy-fueled temper tantrums had worsened. The day Nate moved in, Mary-Jean's emotions built up to a point ready to erupt.

It was a glorious summer day. Maddie rested Mara in her stroller and let her sleep in the fresh air outside the kitchen window, where she could keep an eye on her. When Maddie looked up from washing dishes, she saw, to her horror, Mary-Jean release the hand brake on the stroller and give it a strong push. Maddie had ignored two cardinal rules of motherhood—first, protect your baby and never leave her alone; second, teach your older child how to interact gently and lovingly with her new sibling. Maddie had encouraged Mary-Jean to interact with her baby sister during bath times, feeding sessions, and diaper changes, but Mary-Jean's jealousy toward what she saw as competition for her mother's attention was hampering Maddie's efforts.

Rushing out of the kitchen, Maddie grabbed hold of the runaway stroller seconds before it was ready to tip. Maddie could hear Mary-Jean chuckling as she hid behind the privet hedge. Emotionally distressed, Maddie was furious. "You could have killed your sister! Time out! Go to your room *now!*"

Maddie had never laid a punishing hand on her child, but this time she lost it. In the bedroom Maddie slapped Mary-Jean's backside several times with the sole of her hard slipper. But all that accomplished was to increase the power struggle between spoiled Mary-Jean and her mother.

Shocked and tearless, Mary-Jean yelled, "I hate you! I wish that you were dead, and my half-sister Mara too!"

That same evening Mary-Jean was caught bombarding a sleeping Mara with soft toys scattered around the floor. Mara wailed loudly. Picking up the baby and soothing her, Maddie shook her head in despair. She just didn't know how to ride the waves of Mary-Jean's anger. She had succumbed to Mary-Jean's demands for years. She had always let Mary-Jean do pretty much anything she wanted to, without question. How was Mary-Jean ever going to adapt to her baby sister and the changes around the home?

Hi-ho Silver to the rescue.

Though Nate Silver did not have children of his own, he had been raised with nine siblings, all younger. After the evening meal, Nate took Mary-Jean into the living room, sat her down, and said, "Oh, boy, your baby sister cries so much, doesn't she? Cry, cry, cry. Geez, I bet you were *never* that bad!"

Wearing a huge grin, Mary-Jean hugged Nate and whispered, "I'm glad you're back. I'll have someone to talk to now."

"Honey, I'll be here for you whenever to need to vent your troubles. Okay?"

As Maddie was getting used to staying home with her children, her work life—which she had been holding as a distant memory—returned with a vengeance. She was being relocated to the largest military base in the country. Aldershot, in southeast England, was a military town, home to the British army. Once again, she was to assume a new identity: Madeline Anderson, a duel citizen of Britain and Canada. Whew! Maddie could keep her American twang, which was similar to the Canadian twang, and was thankful she could get rid of those darned blue contact lenses that caused her eyes to smart.

When Nate arrived home from the base that evening, Maddie

was agitated. "You know, Nate, I wish I had never signed my life away," she grumbled. "My strings are being pulled by puppet masters, and there's nothing I can do about it. And the worst part is that you're not here to join me!"

Nate sighed heavily. "Yes, I know, and I'm very sorry, but I too have my American puppet masters, far worse than the British ones, I assure you. I'm being shipped to the United States Pacific Command at Kaneohe Bay in Hawaii."

Maddie ached with pangs of separation from a man she had grown fond of. "I will miss you, Nate. I tried giving up my position because I'm needed at home with the kids, but they refused to accept my resignation."

"Maddie, *they* work like that! You and I signed on the dotted line, and now they own us. Don't you get it? Now, I have something to say, and I'm darn sure you are going to freak out."

"Okay. What could be worse than this bloody upheaval?"

"Maddie, I was *ordered* to sign Mara's birth registration. I'm officially the father on record ..."

Maddie's eyebrows stretched to their limit. "What the hell!" Maddie shrilled. "Not again! It seems I have no rights to any of the children I have brought into the world ... alone."

"Yes, you do, Maddie," Nate argued. "Your name is listed as the mother and mine as the father; that's all. And Mara's name is the name you chose. At least David Blakely didn't put that one over on you!"

"One day I'm going to write about all of this!" Maddie announced in a scornful tone.

Nate reminded her, "You can't Maddie. You are sworn to secrecy."

"Then I will have it published after my death."

On October 1 Maddie began her new work at the British military base. She lived outside the perimeter of the army base in a private, furnished rental. It was a fair-sized, two-story gable front with bay windows and a picket fence, the organization's civilian residence.

Once settled in, an unhappy Mary-Jean was sent to a boarding school not far from the base, and four-month-old Mara went into daycare provided by Maddie's employers.

Every day, while sitting at her desk, Maddie felt like a wreck. She felt guilty leaving her baby in someone else's care, but she worried even more about being separated from Mary-Jean, who needed her the most. But if she didn't work, they would all starve. Maddie missed the confident, charismatic Nate. Their late-night, long-distance phone calls helped ease her loneliness, but they could not protect her from the isolation she felt at work. Her new colleague's demeanor was the opposite of Omar's friendly, helpful, and respectful one. "My new boss is an annoying pain in the butt!" she told Nate.

Major-General Morton Smith, close to retirement, was a chauvinist who looked down on his female counterpart with disdain. There wasn't a day he didn't find fault with her work, yet she was always the one who produced the decoded Intel on time. Morton lazed at his desk, sipping from a silver flask and dragging on a cigar, which annoyed Maddie because she had not smoked since becoming pregnant with Mara.

On a mid-November afternoon, with keening north winds nearly blowing her off her feet, Maddie was escorted by Agent SK to a windowless black van.

Maddie stared at the vehicle, which reminded her of a decommissioned prisoner transport vehicle, and jested to SK, "I see we are traveling in style, today. So where are my handcuffs and leg shackles?"

Maddie wanted to bombard the agent with more serious questions—where are we going and what is our task?—but prudence intervened. She remained silent, something she had become proficient at.

Maddie and Agent SK sat opposite each other behind the driver's seat in a segregated area. Maddie had no idea the driver was following a circuitous route and secretly transporting her to an undisclosed destination. An hour into the journey, after struggling with little air circulation, Maddie's heart started thumping. Jagged, flashing auras of light shimmied across her range of vision, and her high blood pressure rose to her ears. *Thump, thump, thump.* In a state of panic Maddie cried, "SK, please tell the driver to stop. I need air!"

"Chill out, Maddie!" he answered. "We are getting there!"

Goliath awakened. "If you don't tell him to stop right now," she screamed while clenching a fist, "I'm going to punch you in the jaw, you pompous ass!"

Agent SK glared at her and then tapped on the window that divided the driver from the passengers.

After inhaling deep breaths of chilly outside air, Maddie straightened her back and quipped, "Okay, Mr. 007. I'm ready. Let's go."

Maddie would suffer from panic-attacks (always refusing prescription medication) for the rest of her life.

When Maddie got back into the van, she mused, *Come to think of it, you do resemble Roger Moore, but he's a darn sight better looking.*

An hour and a half later the van came to a halt.

Maddie alighted and frowned at the sight of an abandoned building, with aging concrete crumbling.

"Come," said Agent SK. "Follow me."

Maddie stepped through the open steel door. A thick layer of dust sat on the ground floor, untouched for many years, but she could not see a speck on the out-of-place, six-seater table, which bore a strategically placed buff folder.

Two men, one a tall African-American, the other a short Hispanic man with a beer belly, stood up when she came forward. The Hispanic man spoke first. "Good afternoon, Madeline. My name is Julio Gomez, and my colleague here is DeShawn Williams. "Hello, Maddie," he greeted in a Virginian accent. "We represent the Central Intelligence Agency. Please take a seat."

Her head was reeling. *The CIA! What did they want?* Agent SK's face bore a blank expression. Maddie couldn't put her finger on why she had been brought here, and the suspense was killing her. "What's this all about?"

DeShawn started. "Madeline, we shouldn't have to remind you that you have been sworn to secrecy."

Secrecy had been pointed out so many times that Maddie was fed up. But she complacently nodded her head in agreement. "Sir, I'm well aware of my oath." She scowled inwardly. *I'm a code-breaker, not specifically trained in counterintelligence.*

"You will be working with our investigative team and the UK Secret Service to investigate Major General Smith, who has been purchasing expensive paintings, top-of-the-line vehicles, and other luxury items well out of the range of his monthly salary. Intercepted Russian intelligence indicates the Major is selling them sensitive, highly classified information relating to our allied forces, so we need someone to get close, and I mean close!" A wry smile crossed his dark face. "Who better for this task than the woman who works for him? We would like you to gather intel for us."

Maddie's instinct was to protest, but she knew better!

Julio continued. "We want you to search his office and home for notebooks, documents, or anything else we can nail him with. And time is of the essence. He is due to retire shortly, and we won't get another run at him without a court order."

Maddie could no longer hold her tongue. "Sir, I don't know him *that* well! I've only been working with him a couple of months." She wanted to say, *I'm a cryptologist, not a female James Bond! And even if I agree to this, how am I supposed to gain access to his house?*

"Well, Madeline," Julio said, "I've been informed that you are one helluva smart operator, an Einstein equal, or we would not be having this conversation. You will figure something out, I'm sure."

Maddie's impulses seethed. *I should have gone back to medical school and become a doctor rather than a walking, talking puppet, and now a bloody spy!*

On the silent journey back to her living quarters, Maddie focused on one key factor. The extra pay, a great deal of money in U.S. currency, was enticing, to say the least. Working for the CIA would be a feather in her cap and a bargaining chip, if needed.

Maddie loved entertaining, so she invited her boss to dinner. "Major, I hope you don't think it would be inappropriate, but would you care to have dinner at my home this Friday at six o'clock?"

Come into my parlor, said the spider to the fly ..."

His reaction was totally unexpected.

Morton Smith's loam-grey eyes lit up with the dirty thoughts of a pimply eighteen-year-old boy. He pinched her bottom and made a puckered-lip lunge. She quickly evaded his crude attempts to familiarize himself and felt like cracking his head open with the nearest heavy object, but she had been given a mission. She forced a playful response to the lustful old man with liver spots and a wrinkled neck. "You dirty old man."

"Yes, I suppose I am," Mr. Perv confessed in a stentorian voice. "I'm nearly sixty-five, but still very interested in sex. Is that a problem?"

Maddie bridled her tongue. *Dirty old bastard!* "No, that's not a problem at all," she said with bile rising.

"I live alone," Morton admitted, "so how about you come to my place after I've walked Maggie, my dog, and I'll cook a meal for you. You'll love Maggie. She's a soft, cuddly St. Bernard."

Maddie had never met cuddly Maggie, but her owner might as well have been a drooling, lecher in a dirty brown Macintosh lingering outside school gates, for all she cared.

Click, click, click.

"And I mean get close ..." Julio had implied.

Maddie accepted Mr. Perv's invitation. She made a mental note to purchase a can of pepper spray before entering his den.

After eight long weeks of evading the Major's lecherous advances and forcing down the indigestible meals he cooked, Maddie uncovered the conspiracy, his traitorous pact with the enemy: handwritten notebooks found in his UK home and his holiday residence in Spain, and a taped telephone conversation in Russian between Morton Smith and a diplomat based at the Russian Embassy in London. Maddie passed the damning evidence over to her CIA contacts.

This once distinguished soldier, decorated for bravery during World War II, was found guilty beyond a reasonable doubt. For his treason against Queen and Country, he received the maximum sentence—incarceration for the remainder of his natural life.

Major Morton Smith died of heart failure in prison at age eighty-six.

Maddie was on a winning streak. She received carte blanche permission to enter the United States at any time, and a fat paycheck that would help her finance her next relocation.

Maddie penned in her journal:

The best cure for all my past suffering is massive success. I've found what I'm especially good at, and someone to pay me for doing it! And I have finally figured out who I am—a precious human being, not a worthless piece of dung, as I have been told.

Maddie's resilience, confidence, and intellect would be tested by her children's constant, insufferable, sick games. Would she possess the mental toughness to endure the daily physical abuse that would continue well into her senior years?

Not having her motherhood recognized or appreciated was an almost unbearable form of violence!

CHAPTER TWENTY-ONE

"The hardest part of parenting must be witnessing your child go through psychosis and not being able to fix it."

Four-year-old Mara had the loving sweetness of an angel, coupled with the darkness of demonic possession and evil. Maddie would have had her exorcised, if she believed in the ritual. Mara's psychological assessment, conducted by her elementary school, failed to open Maddie's eyes to the truth. Maddie had always believed psychological testing was advantageous and would point her children toward success at school and in life. Joanne's and Mary-Jean's evaluations of their weaknesses, strengths, and potential for intellectual achievement had been a source of pride to Maddie. But that was not true of Mara's. Her school psychologist arrived at a diagnosis and *treatment* course that floored her mother.

Click, click, click.

Prior to Mara's psychological assessment, Maddie's little chatterbox had rambled on nonsensically: "One day I will have a farm, and I will fill it with mice and rats."

Maddie suppressed a shudder at her daughter's outburst. *This* child had been different from the day she was born. She had been weaned at three months, potty-trained at ten months, and spoke complete sentences at fourteen months. She toddled, never crawled. And at four months, Mara's baby teeth started to appear, with minimal problems. But it was Mara's laughing that creeped Maddie out. At age three-and-a-half, Mara started hysterically cackling in her sleep. Whenever Maddie entered the bedroom, she found a wide-eyed Mara staring at the ceiling. Suddenly, her dark, soulless eyes would focus on to her mother, and on a number of occasions the child would say in a menacing voice, "I don't feel like killing you right now!"

On hearing this Maddie would fight to regain her composure before responding. "Now why would you want to kill Mummy? I love you, and when you grow up, we will be the best of friends."

"Because you're not my mummy, and I don't love you! I'm never going to be your friend, *ever!*" snarled Mara.

Was this a glimpse into the dark soul of a monster, or was it mental illness?

Maddie's eyes shed no tears, but her heart cried copious ones. She had experienced dreadful and dysfunctional behavior with Joanne and Mary-Jean, but Mara was something else. Maddie didn't understand what she was dealing with.

Wearing horse blinders, Maddie soldiered on and clung to the hope that Mara would get better. With this guiding belief in mind, she thought, *where there is deep, unconditional love, there is a cure!*

It wasn't long before Mara developed an aversion to mirrors. She screamed bloody murder about them until Maddie removed every mirror from their home.

On Mara's second birthday, Maddie bought her a portable, battery-operated electric piano. Mara was thrilled with her gift, and to Maddie's surprise immediately started plinking away at a tune, *Twinkle, Twinkle, Little Star.*

But Maddie was in for another mysterious surprise!

One day, when Maddie was in the kitchen preparing the evening meal, she heard a classical tune that she knew well. Mara was tickling the ivories to Rodrigo Concierto de Aranjuez. Maddie rushed from the kitchen, and Mara, with a smug smile, immediately withdrew her plump little fingers from the keyboard.

"Don't stop playing, sweetie," said Maddie, dumbfounded. "It is Mummy's favorite tune."

"Don't you think I know *that!*" she said, her voice as cold as snow.

What Mara did next rendered Maddie speechless. She strolled over to the fireplace, lifted a heavy poker out of its stand, and proceeded to smash the piano. "Look what you made me do!" she hissed, dropping the poker on the floor.

From that moment on, Mara began lashing out at her mother by biting, hitting, pinching, spitting, pulling hair, and throwing things. A torrent of verbal abuse accompanied the physical abuse: "Stupid," "Bitch," "Slut." *Where did she learn such words?*

How Maddie refrained from knocking the crap out of this abhorrent child is anyone's guess. Maddie restrained herself because she was overly sensitive to her "special" child's needs. She responded to Mara's behavior by refusing to show rage or revulsion. She didn't want to take a canon to a knife fight!

Maddie chose to use the same style of diplomacy on Mara that she had on her other girls. "Mara, sweetie," Maddie said, "if Mummy called you bad names, wouldn't you be angry?"

"Me and Cassie don't care," was the child's flippant response.

Quizzical, Maddie asked, "Who is Cassie, sweetie?"

"She's my best friend, and you can't see her. She hates you too!"

This was the first time Maddie had learned of Mara's imaginary playmate. Following this revelation Mara started showing an awareness of information that she could not have known, such as: "Are you going to throw me in the garbage like your mummy did to you? I don't want to be a doctor, like you wanted. I won't ever beg on a street because I'm going to be rich and famous one day."

It never crossed Maddie's mind that this *bad seed* might be beyond psychological redemption!

Maddie took a bus to town, located the library, and borrowed several thick psychoanalysis textbooks written by Sigmund Freud and Carl Gustav Jung. After hours of late night reading, she decided they were nutcases themselves. Freud and Jung did not shape Maddie's twentieth-century mind. She summarized their theories in one word: "Balderdash!"

One week before Mara started Aldershot School, Maddie had walked her there for psychological testing. Maddie waited in another room while a sulky Mara was marched off to the elderly professional's office. The evaluation lasted two hours.

While Mara ran up and down the school corridors, Maddie met the psychoanalyst. Mrs. Henley removed her horn-rimmed glasses and in a dour voice announced, "Mara is bright, but her IQ score indicates she is slightly below average intelligence. Her cognitive test results indicate a DID, Dissociative Identity Disorder."

Maddie refrained from frowning. She already had a hint of the diagnosis from the psychotherapy books that she had read. But she was not letting on. "Please, go on, Mrs. Henley."

"Mara's memory, identity, emotions, perceptional behavior, and sense of self will likely interfere with her mental functioning. She has within her two, or more, identities, each with its own discrete personality. This is likely to manifest itself as a severe psychological disturbance. Furthermore ..."

Maddie didn't have an impolite bone in her body, but she had heard enough. She cut Mrs. Henley off midstream. "My daughter has not been exposed to overwhelming trauma, such as physical or sexual abuse, I can assure you," she adamantly stated.

"That's good to know, Mrs. Anderson, but there are other triggers that could be responsible for this disorder, such as hereditary factors."

"Well, that makes some sense. It may be bad genetics. Mara's paternal grandmother, Gordon's mother, had been in and out of psych wards for years, and Gordon isn't mentally-grounded either. I discovered after our relationship ended that he had tried to commit suicide a couple of times."

Mrs. Henley's expression was passive. "In my professional opinion, Mrs. Anderson, Mara requires psychotherapy, cognitive and dialectical behavior therapy, for her severe mood volatility. I can help her with this. And I suggest a prescription for antidepressant pills."

The word "pill" did it! Maddie slapped the desk and snapped. "I'll never allow any pill to go down my child's throat, and, you know what, I will become her therapist."

"What do you mean, Mrs. Anderson?"

"I'm going to smother her with love and understanding and help her through whatever genetic disorder that nutty McCullum family bestowed on her, because it sure isn't coming from *my* genetics!"

That night, with a quote from Magic Johnston crossing her mind—*"All kids need a little help, a little hope, and someone who believes in them"*—Maddie sat on Mara's bed and said, "Sweetie, don't get mad at me, but there is a little wire that is not firing properly in your brain, and Mummy is going to try to fix it. Okay? You are not going to go to school here. Your mental health is more important than your grades. I'm going to find you the best therapeutic residential school money can buy so you can achieve any dream you want. Okay?"

Mara's wolf eyes made glaring eye contact with her mother, as if her mum was an inert statue or an earthenware dog, ripe for destruction, like her piano. What Maddie said meant nothing to her.

Maddie the know-it-all, who had denied there were any serious problems with her daughter, would come to regret not taking Mrs. Henley's advice.

Because she would soon learn that *her* own life would be endangered by an untreated, adult Mara.

The following day Maddie placed a telephone call on her secure line.

"This is Agent MA from the Aldershot base. Please connect me to Agent SK. It's urgent."

"Hello, Madeline. What can I do for you?"

"SK, I need to take an extended leave. I've lost focus and am not functioning efficiently. Mara needs me full time right now."

"Madeline, you are not seeing what everyone else can see. I have a copy of Mrs. Henley's report. Mara is a ticking time bomb, and in my opinion, she needs to be institutionalized."

Maddie wasn't comfortable expressing her thoughts out loud to such a powerful man, but his last statement touched a raw nerve and was a humiliating slap in the face. "Over my dead body!" she spat. "If you are not going to help me, then I will go over your head. I need *out!*"

"I will see what is possible, Madeline," was his subdued response.

"Thank you. I appreciate it," she replied shortly.

With a feeling of trepidation, Maddie entered the office of the staff psychologist. A dapper gentleman with thinning silver hair and a pleasant manner stood up from behind his desk to greet her. "Come in, Maddie. Please take a seat."

Maddie settled herself in the leather upholstered chair opposite the doctor.

"I am Dr. Creighton, the 'outfit's' token psychologist, so to speak," he announced with a humorous smile. Gesturing toward the slim green folder on his desk, he continued. "I have reviewed your file; not much wrong there, I think! I am intrigued. Why did you request to see me?"

Folding his hands in his lap, he looked questioningly at Maddie.

"It's my memory, Doctor. I have always had the ability to recall past events in vivid detail: visual, auditory, and olfactory. These recollections resemble mental snapshots when they surface. Lately I have been having blank spells, and I think they are stress related, not from my work but from my personal life."

"Yes. Your Psych Profile suggests you possess such abilities. It's really nothing to worry about, though," he announced in a reassuring tone.

"It's a matter of curiosity," said Maddie. "These memory events have been occurring with increasing frequency."

"Hmm," he muttered. "Strange thing is memory... extraordinary and complex. Even today there is much to learn about how the brain processes and records sensory inputs. Give me an example of a memory that is particularly vivid to you."

For an hour Maddie related several such recollections, to an increasingly excited listener.

Adopting his best lecturing style, Dr. Creighton continued. "Absolutely amazing!" he stated, "your powers of recall would appear to be almost photographic in nature. We know that the hippocampus area of the brain is associated with the processing of inputs from our various senses. It integrates this sensory information into coherent memories of our past and present experiences. Memory can be categorized into types. For example, autobiographical memory, as the name suggests, relates to memories of our own life experiences. This would include facts about ourselves, which fit into a category we call semantic memory, a subset of autobiographical memory. Quite normal so far. From the perspective of your memory, a more interesting form of mental activity might be that of episodic memory. Are you familiar with the term?"

"Not with that particular term," a puzzled Maddie replied.

"Episodic memory relates to the unique and complete recollection of past events that have occurred in your own life, combined with commonly shared experiences between you and other individuals you have encountered. It is a relatively recent concept proposed in 1972 by Dr. Endel Tulving, an experimental psychologist and cognitive neuroscientist researching human memory. He is a Professor Emeritus at the University of Toronto in Ontario, Canada. Of course, the boundaries between our definitions of memory types may be somewhat vague, but it would appear you seem to possess a rather extreme form of episodic memory. The mind as a video camera ... an interesting possibility! I would have to conduct some further tests to be absolutely certain ..."

"Extreme?" queried Maddie, in a worried tone.

"Nothing to concern you unduly with, my dear," he commented. "It is not a pathological condition. In fact, I imagine such ability would be useful to a spy!" he finished humorously.

"Thank you, I think." responded a somewhat bemused Maddie.

Maddie left the doctor's office none the wiser as to why she was experiencing "blank" spells. But one thing she was sure of—she wanted *out* of the "spy" game.

Where there's a will, there's a way ...

CHAPTER TWENTY-TWO

"It isn't always a change of scenery that makes life better.
Sometimes it simply requires opening your eyes."

While Maddie awaited the "outfit's" decision on whether to set her free for an extended leave, she took Mary-Jean out of boarding school, choosing, instead, to homeschool her children. Maddie received permission to opt out of the British legal school requirement because of her official status. Thankfully, Mary-Jean was not the out-of-control brat she had been prior to entering boarding school. She was now well mannered, polite, and, though she was still not cuddly, respectful toward her mother. *The school's discipline had been worth every hard-earned penny,* the proud mother thought.

Unknown to the Maddie at the time, her middle, vengeful child was merely hiding her claws, pretending to be a pleasant, harmless teenager. Maddie was deceiving herself. None of her children would ever come to truly appreciate their mother's sacrifices, or unending love, until it was too late to make amends.

Leopards don't change their spots!

Mary-Jean's little sister, Mara, was a different kettle of fish.

There were times when little Mara *was* adorable. "I'm going to brush your hair, Mummy, so you can look pretty like me." Maddie enjoyed the attention, as Mara's hairbrush stroked her long black hair.

One day Maddie caught Mara balancing precariously on a stool in the kitchen. As she instinctively grabbed for the wobbling stool, Maddie asked, "What on earth are you doing?"

"I was going to make you a nice cup of tea, Mummy, but I can't reach the kettle."

"Ah, how sweet of you," Maddie gushed, hugging her third miracle child. "Do you know that I love you to the moon and back?"

With a lightning fast mood shift Mara hissed, "No, you don't. You love Mary-Jean more than me!"

"You are wrong, sweetie. I love you both equally."

Long into the future the disquieting incidents would outnumber the "adorable" moments.

Bedtime rituals became hell. Mara accused her mother of attempting to scald her in hot bath water and of sprinkling itching powder on her pajamas. She refused to dress in the nightwear Maddie selected. Instead, Mara chose to sleep naked, even during the chilly months.

Matters came to a head one Sunday night in October 1992 at 11:30 P.M. Maddie opened her sleepy eyes to find her loaded, government-issued firearm an inch from the bridge of her nose. She didn't stop to think of how her five-year-old could have obtained the Beretta from a locked gun cabinet. Maddie's primal instincts told her to keep calm in front of the gun-wielding child, to remain passive. Any sudden motion on her part could be fatal.

"Hi, sweetie," she said passively. "Couldn't you sleep? Did you have a bad dream? Do you want to climb into bed with Mummy?"

"Yes." Mara responded briefly.

Maddie breathed a sigh of relief as she heard the thud of her firearm falling to the floor. With a pounding heart Maddie wrapped her arms around her child and waited until she fell asleep. Maddie rose quietly, retrieved the weapon, and headed for the gun cabinet.

The metal door was ajar, its key inserted in the lock. Maddie's eyes took on a troubled, baffled look. How could this small child have reached the top shelf of the tall bookcase, where the key had been hidden?

The flummoxed mother climbed onto a dining chair and ran her hand over the top of the bookcase. The zippered pouch was missing.

Maddie discovered it later on Mara's bedroom floor.

Maddie made a mental note to call in a locksmith to replace the old locking system with a keyless remote version.

If Maddie had known she was dealing with an embodiment of evil, she may have considered death to be a better choice.

Mara's fascination with death was deeply disturbing.

One day Maddie was cleaning her daughter's bedroom, which, unlike her sister's room, was always a mess. Maddie constantly reminded Mara about the state of her bedroom, to which Mara always retorted, "I hate cleaning my room! Anyway, it's my space not yours!"

No amount of suggestion worked.

On this day Maddie placed Mara's toys neatly onto shelves and into toy bins, and collected an abundance of strewn candy wrappers. She reached under Mara's bed to retrieve dirty clothing but recoiled in horror as she pulled out a decapitated, featherless baby bird wrapped in a bath towel.

Click, click, click.

The headmistress in Scotland had called Maddie to her office. *"Your daughter, Mary-Jean, has disemboweled these poor little creatures. And our school rabbit is missing most of its fur."*

Mary-Jean's mercilessness had been bad enough, but Mara's act of savagery was unfathomable.

Maddie, a bird lover, was beside herself with sorrow for this little creature. She decided the best course of action, the one she had taken with Mary-Jean, would be to talk with her five-year-old and encourage her to feel empathy for animals.

But the lecture failed ... miserably.

"The stupid bird was already dead," was Mara's callous response.

What would be the long-term effect of this dreadful behavior pattern? The overwhelming desire to gain power and control in her adult life! Especially over her mother, whom she came to regard as nothing more than a stepping stone to fulfilling her needs, nothing more than wallet!

Should parents take "demonic possession" seriously? Ask Maddie!

The phone rang. Hoping it was Agent SK, Maddie eagerly lifted the receiver. "Madeleine Anderson speaking," she said calmly."

"Good afternoon, Mrs. Anderson. This is Lieutenant Marks, Judge Advocate General. I'm calling you about the sexual misconduct complaint you filed on behalf of your daughter, Mary-Jean Anderson, with JAG against navy sailor Wojchiech Barankewicz, or Wally as he is commonly known."

"Well?"

The military officer continued. "Wally has been discharged, cleared of molestation misconduct, found not guilty …"

Maddie inhaled deeply.

"The child-abuse allegation was fully investigated. He underwent a lie detector test, and our expert polygraph examiner determined Wally to be truthful. He was given several forensic psychology tests and passed all of them without deception. I'm sorry to say this, but your daughter accused an innocent man. May I suggest …?"

This startling revelation tested Maddie's resolve. "Thank you, Lieutenant Marks, for letting me know, and I think I'll handle it from here"

Standing erect with lips clamped tightly, a rush of dismay passed through Maddie. Preoccupied with her disturbing thoughts, she didn't hear footsteps approaching from the kitchen. She jumped out of her skin when Mary-Jean touched her and casually remarked, "What's wrong, Mum? You look like you have seen a ghost."

A fast-talking Maddie responded, "Nothing's wrong, sweetie. Go get your sister. Lunch is ready."

It's natural for a mother to believe her child, but why had Mary-Jean intentionally lied, falsely accused her friend, Wally, of a serious crime he didn't commit? The supporting evidence had spoken loudly. In disbelief, Maddie, who had been a *real* victim of sexual abuse, felt like unleashing her feelings, bearing her fangs, cussing her daughter out at the dining table. She wanted to let her daughter know her blatant lies could have put an innocent man behind bars. But not even a spark of dialogue passed through Maddie's lips. She chose not to confront Mary-Jean. To bring this up could trigger Mary-Jean to revert to her old ways. The girl would make it seem like her mother had gotten it wrong!

A self-absorbed, grown Mary-Jean, who never cared about anyone but herself, would continue to live in denial well into the future. She continued to think everything revolved around her, and she believed Wally had molested her. Maddie intercepted an email from Mary-Jean to her grown half-sister, Mara. "Every man Mum had in her life has molested me."

Did that include Gordon, her own father, or Mary-Jean's father, David?

The adult Mara would become a habitual false storyteller. With no grasp on reality, she would live in a fantasy world, delusional and dangerous to others. She was cast more than a shadow of fear on her mother.

Maddie would silently suffer from these demoralizing behaviors, this unimaginable parent abuse, well into her seventies, until that torturous chapter in her life came to an end in 2018. This "imperfect" mother had her blinders removed after a Haida Gwaii shaman revealed the shocking truth about her three "miracle" children.

There is no greater sorrow than a mother's crushed heart.

In a battle of wits and survival, Maddie wished to pick up the pieces of her troubled motherhood in a new country. But before this could happen, she needed permission to leave England. She still had not received a clarifying phone call about her request for a short leave of absence.

Juggling homeschooling, household chores, and documents she had to decipher, Maddie decided to put plan B into action, just in case!

Maddie had excellent writing and communications skills. Aided by her photographic memory, she began to study at home at her own pace for a journalism degree.

Finally, the call she had been waiting for arrived.

"Hello, Madeline. I've got good news and bad news, "Agent SK said. "Which would you like first?" he teased.

"Either. I don't care," Maddie replied flippantly.

"As of the end of December, your services will no longer be required. But, as you are aware, your Oath is permanently in force."

"I'm fired?" Maddie queried in a surprised tone. *I am not getting an extended leave. I am getting fired!*

"In a nutshell, yes," he stated. "You will need to hand in your handwritten resignation for the record. Please report to the base at nine o'clock tomorrow morning for debriefing. They can help you with the letter then."

Chapter Twenty-Two

"Why am I being let go?"

"It seems that you have become more of a liability than an asset. Anyway, it's probably for the best. Now you can get on with your own life, raise your kids."

"That's the bad news. So, what's the good news?" she fired back.

"You will receive an excellent pension when you reach sixty-five," SK announced in a humorous voice.

Maddie smirked. "Ha! That's if I live long enough to see it!"

"Good luck, Madeline, and for what it's worth, you were the best damn decoder since the World War II operators. By the way, don't forget to leave the house keys with the duty officer before you vacate."

Click, click, click.

David Blakely had spat, *"Your free ride is over..."*

Maddie's' gravest concerns were where to go and how to support and cope with not one, but *two* malevolent children by herself. She had no job prospects. Though she had amassed a tidy sum of money in her savings account, how long would it last if she couldn't top it off with an income?

Two weeks before leaving the rental, Maddie defied the odds. She took her journalism course exam at the University of Guilford and passed.

Where there's a will, there's a way ...

CHAPTER TWENTY-THREE

"A woman is like a tea bag; you cannot tell how strong
she is until you put her in hot water."
—NANCY REAGAN

A
t 3:30 P.M. on Christmas Eve 1992, British Airways flight
896 came to a rubber-burning stop outside the Vancouver
International Airport Arrivals terminal.

It had been a long, nine-hour flight, and Maddie had had her
hands full. Both girls wrenched and whined throughout the long
trip. When they finally arrived on Canadian soil, Maddie was mentally exhausted.

After getting something to eat and drink from the airport's
food court, the three British passengers stepped outside the airport
terminal and onto a carpet of glistening, icy sparkles. Maddie had
researched Canada's harsh, long winters—snow, ice, freezing rain,
sleet, and sub-zero temperatures—but she was not prepared for the
feel of *minus* 10-degrees centigrade. She knew for sure it was going
to be a white Christmas.

"I'm freezing," Mara moaned while shivering. Mary-Jean echoed
a similar sentiment.

"We are going to take a taxi to our hotel, where you girls will be toasty warm. Okay?"

The downtown Vancouver hotel, with its nearby affordable restaurants, would be their home until Maddie could buy a home of her own. She had scoured through tons of real estate listings, and, to her disappointment, her savings wouldn't even cover a one-bedroom condo. She admonished herself. *Dumbo checked the bloody weather but not the buyer's market!*

Back to the drawing board, she thought. Her camera started to roll.

Click, click, click.

The day before their departure from England, Agent JF, the nicest of the *Men in Black* heavyweights, arrived at the Aldershot rental armed with farewell gifts. "I'm going to miss you, Agent MA." He gave her a warm hug and a folded note. "Here's my home address and private telephone number, and that of my cousin. He lives in Burnaby, a city east of Vancouver. You'll get on well. He's brainy like you, a history professor at the University of British Columbia. I've spoken to him, told him all about you ..."

Maddie's eyes widened.

"No, silly," JF said, observing her startled expression. "Not about your job with us. I told him you were a journalist looking for a fresh start in Canada. He mentioned that if you and the kids needed a place to stay, he has a large, fully furnished basement suite."

Maddie had never seen a basement suite. An image of a dank dungeon with stone walls and floors and iron shackles came to mind.

She shook her head. She had told no one of her journalism

endeavors! Nothing in her life was sacred. The "outfit's" spies were everywhere.

JF had more to say. "I don't know what your long-term plans are, but remember you cannot use the Canadian identity and passport afforded you while you were employed by the Secret Service. It must be destroyed. You must only use your British passport in the name of Madeline Clark. I believe that surname also appears on the kids travel documents, correct?"

Maddie nodded in the affirmative. "We are tourists, and before the six-month visa expires, I will apply for Landed Status."

Agent JF frowned. "Remember, Maddie, you can't put your previous employers on any Application you may need to file."

Without thinking, she blurted out "And why not?"

"Gee whiz!" JF huffed. "I thought you were smart. You no longer work for us. If you had read this clause in your Oath, you would know it states, 'At no time can you validate your Secret Service employment to gain immigrant status in another country, unless it is officially approved.'"

Maddie sighed.

"I'm sorry, but you are on your own now with no backup from us," JF stated. "And heed this sound advice. The "outfit" doesn't take kindly to whistleblowers. So watch every word."

Being fired from a job she loved and was good at felt like an amputation, but Maddie wasn't stupid. She knew that in this new era of electronic wizardry, her manual decoding had become a thing of the past. Why hadn't they trained her to operate their new computer systems? Their reasons didn't matter.

Maddie was determined to make her new beginning in Canada

a success. She had arranged for a job interview with a prominent newspaper for a position as an investigative journalist. She was apprehensive. She had no journalistic experience and had not written an article since cramming for and passing the exam.

JF's voice droned on. "You will be arriving during a Canadian winter, damn cold, so make sure you and the children have good winter gear. Don't forget to look up my cousin. He's dying to meet you. Well, good luck, Maddie, and keep in touch, unofficially, of course."

Maddie's family spent Christmas Day at the hotel, but the kids were giving her grief. "I don't want to live here forever. I want my own room and a garden to play in."

The taxi pulled up outside a stone-walled, historic, beautifully maintained home on a large corner lot. What an enchantment. Maddie was greeted at the door by a jolly middle-aged fellow in his early sixties. "Can I help you?" Thomas Perkins asked.

"I'm Madeline ..."

"Please, come in. Any friend of my cousin, Joseph Francis, is a friend of mine," he said warmly.

Maddie learned JF's Christian name for the first time. She baited Thomas. "Yes, he's a great person. Sometimes I've difficulty in pronouncing his surname."

Thomas frowned. "You have a problem with O'Malley. It's a fine Irish name."

Maddie smiled. *Gottcha, Agent JF. You're a leprechaun!*

They chatted over a mug of coffee. Maddie's taste buds were not quite ready for the strong coffee the Canadians consumed by the gallon.

"You and the children can live here rent free until you get on your feet, Madeline. I live alone, never married. Sharing some intellectual conversation with company is a bonus to a lonely bachelor."

Click, click, click.

Admiral Thomas Neville's jolly face smiled out at her. "I'm looking for a companion ..."

The two elderly men who had wanted her as a companion shared a first name and lived in homes that looked too large for a single occupant. Maddie immediately warmed to this new Tom, as she had done with the Admiral. She had never held it against him when he had turned his back on her.

"Thank you so much, Tom, but I would like to pay for our board and keep."

The day after Boxing Day, the Clark family moved into Tom's elegant basement suite on Burnlake Drive. Each of them had their own room. In the passing days, to Maddie's surprise, both girls warmed up to Tom.

When he was not working, he read to them, and he taught them how to play countless Canadian board games. He delighted their taste buds with Canadian cuisine: hotdogs, burgers, and French fries with ketchup.

A couple of weeks into their relocation, Tom spoke to Maddie privately. "It's not my business to interfere, but I would like to bring a grave concern to your attention."

"What is it?" Maddie asked, noticing his face saddening.

"I caught Mara hitting poor Miss Tittles (Tom's elderly cat) with a stick outside in the garden. When I told her that Miss Tittles was old and it was wrong to hit any animal, she laughed in my face."

Maddie, shamefaced, felt sickened. "Oh, I'm so sorry, Tom. I will have a strong word with her about this."

"Shame on you, Mara. What were you thinking?" Maddie admonished, trying not to raise her voice in anger. "How would you feel if I beat you with a stick?"

The telling-off was like water rolling off a duck's back. Mara just laughed. Maddie felt like taking the same stick Mara had hit the poor cat with and knocking some sense into her, but she believed violence was not the cure for a child who was beyond redemption.

"I'm giving you a writing punishment. Go to your room and write twenty sentences: I will never hurt an animal again!"

Mara gave her mother a snarly, defiant smirk, headed downstairs to the basement, and pulled the stuffing out of her favorite toy, Paddington Bear.

On January 3 of 1993, Maddie took the bus to the Visa and Immigration Center in downtown Vancouver. There she filed and paid for the necessary applications for Mary-Jean's and Mara's student visas. It was Maddie's intention to enroll Mary-Jean in Carvier High School and Mara in Seaforth Elementary. Both schools were close to their home. In her rush to get the kids enrolled, she had forgotten she needed a work visa!

Bad luck does come in threes!

About six o'clock that evening, following her trip to the immigration center, Maddie heard a loud rapping on the basement suite door.

She was looking at the face of an RCMP Constable.

"Are you Madeline Clark?"

"Yes. What can I do for you?"

"I have your daughter, Mara, in my patrol car," Constable Lytton said. "She and your neighbor's daughter have been picked up for throwing stones off a highway overpass. Fortunately, no one has been hurt. This doesn't excuse the fact that she could have caused bodily harm or even death."

Maddie was mortified. Embarrassed. Devastated. Humiliated.

The policeman continued. "As she is a minor, no charges will be brought. Miss Clark, you need to know where your child is at all times. Okay?"

After the constable left, Mara laughed heinously. "That was fun, Mum!"

And still Maddie didn't take a whip to her. Miss-Fix-Everyone, who thought the answers lay in unconditional love, was flogging a dead horse!

Unbeknown to Maddie, this metaphorical "aging mare" *would* face death when bad luck number three revealed itself!

Catastrophe number two occurred the night before. Her teenage daughter, Mary-Jean, had snuck out of her bedroom window. Maddie was frantic with worry when she discovered it, so Tom drove her up and down the Burnaby streets looking for her delinquent daughter. Finally, they spotted Mary-Jean in the company of a couple of boys her age. They were walking out of a convenience store, and Mary-Jean was holding a can of cola in her hand.

Maddie had set curfews for her daughters when they arrived in Canada, but she knew screaming at Mary-Jean now for breaking the rules wasn't a solution to her fraught nerves. She realized Mary-Jean must have been bored. She had been cooped up at home and unable to attend school, since the student visas had not yet arrived. Maddie treaded softly. "This behavior is not acceptable. You are grounded for a week!"

Maddie wanted to instill an awareness of the "dangers" that lurked around corners in a big city, but she chose not to. She was a single mother with jangling nerves. She needed a good example to follow, a role model, and someone to be there for her when she reached the end of her tether.

Mary-Jean released a sigh of teenage rebellion. She knew she would be punished, but she had an I-don't-care attitude. While Mara had proven herself to be an accomplished, ruthless, unemotional liar, Mary-Jean had appeared to have changed her ways. Or so her mother hoped.

Maddie bought Mary-Jean a bike and a can of pepper spray.

On the day of Maddie's interview with the *Vancouver Tribune*, January 10, 1994, she was struck by an intoxicated driver who sped into a pedestrian crossing. In critical condition, she was rushed by ambulance to Burnaby Hospital. Under general anesthesia a twelve-hour operation was performed, a discectomy that removed the ruptured C-6 disc in her spine. The surgeon replaced the herniated disc with a cow bone replacement, a Cloward Fusion, cementing the C-6 and C-7 vertebrae together. During this critical surgery, Maddie was resuscitated not once but twice. Forty-eight hours later, she was back in surgery where a splenectomy (spleen removal) was performed. The removal of this small but important filtration organ would leave Maddie with an increased risk for infections and immune related disorders.

Once again, Maddie was resuscitated during the surgery. When she finally learned of the procedures she'd undergone, she responded with humor: "Well, I'm missing a few body parts, but I still have my gremlins. They will come out fighting if I get an infection! And, thanks to the bovine bone in my neck, I can now *moo* like a cow!"

The incisional scar from her splenectomy was added to her list of abdominal scars: C-section, appendectomy, and laparoscopic removal of the Vienna schnitzel.

"Oh, boy," she expressed to the nurse. "Guess who is never going to wear a bikini again!"

Maddie's positive outlook was soon to be quashed.

An RCMP officer came to her hospital bedside to take her statement. Maddie learned her hit-and-run driver had been arrested *but* had no insurance. To make matters worse, neither did Maddie. She had planned to take out traveler's medical coverage before leaving England, but "Doctor" Maddie didn't think it important enough at the time. *That's something I can do later, once we settle in Canada.* Wrong move!

Maddie was hardly compos mentis after her first surgery when a well-dressed woman, the hospital director, appeared at her bedside and demanded, "I need your credit card details, Miss Clark."

The hospital bill was a staggering $56,000. It nearly wiped out Maddie's savings.

Click, click, click.

Maddie's application for permanent residency was denied for health reasons. It seemed to her that an AIDS patient could be granted permission to the land, but someone with cow bone in her neck and a missing spleen was not eligible. Maddie filed an appeal. However, the student visas were granted ... for five months only.

On day two of Mara's elementary school, Maddie got a phone call. "We have had an altercation involving Mara and a classmate. Could you please come to the school?"

Wearing her surgical neck brace, Maddie entered the principal's office.

"Mara stabbed a classmate with her pencil. Fortunately, the girl's mother is not pressing charges. Mara will be sent home, but she can return to school tomorrow. I suggest you have a good talk with her about unacceptable behavior."

Outside the school, Maddie glared at Mara. "Why on earth did you do that?"

"She said I wasn't *cool!* She said I was a hillbilly and dressed like a farm girl!"

Though this was a serious incident, Maddie couldn't help but feel for Mara. In Britain she had been used to wearing the same school uniform as the other girls, but in Canada kids wore *cool* designer-labeled clothes to school.

Maddie shopped. She spent a small fortune for popular, fashionable clothing so her children could be *cool*.

But the phone calls kept coming. It was like déjà vu: Mara did this ... Mara did that! Not Mary-Jean, though. She was an exemplary student.

The irony was that Maddie's two girls were granted extended student stay after their five months expired. Maddie's appeal against Immigration Canada for discrimination was pending; therefore, her children were legally entitled to remain in Canada. But Maddie was technically *illegal!* She was about to discover the consequence of this status.

In August 1994, two immigration officials turned up at her home, one at the front door and one at the rear door. They had an arrest warrant. Her explanation regarding the delayed appeal process fell on deaf ears. Maddie had little choice. "Is it okay if I make a call to have this matter dealt with over the phone?"

The time difference had slipped her mind. She heard a sleepy voice reply, "Yes?"

"Agent SK, I need your help or I'm going to prison ..."

As instructed, Maddie handed the phone to the arresting officer. A few minutes later, the officers apologized and departed.

Maddie redialed the number. "I don't know how to thank you."

"It's my pleasure, but you *are* going to work this debt off. Oh, I was sorry to hear about your accident. I hope you are feeling better."

His soft, compassionate tone took Maddie by surprise. He had never spoken to her like that before, ever. "I'm going back to sleep now. Catch you later, Madeline," he finished.

The following day, a van appeared outside her suite. A delivery person got out and brought her the latest in technology: a computer, fax machine, cell phone, and other office equipment. It did not take long for Maddie to become proficient in the use of the new equipment. Back to the business of doing what she did best—cryptanalogy.

Maddie and her children were granted Permanent Residency Status in October 1994. They continued to be special houseguests at Burnlake Drive. Maddie juggled her work hours around her domestic chores: laundry, cleaning house, cooking meals. She also found time to nurse Tom, who had recently suffered from a minor heart attack.

A year passed, but not without increasing emotional turmoil for Maddie. Mara was expelled from school, and Mary-Jean was breaking every imposed curfew. One evening Mary-Jean's aboriginal school friend, Aiyana, turned up at the door in tears. "Mary-Jean just called me. She said she was going out with some friends, but she had promised to go with me to a Mariachi band tonight."

That was news to Maddie. She didn't realize that Mary-Jean liked Mexican music.

"I'm sorry, Aiyana. Where is the venue?"

"At Rio Rio's. It's a nightclub, and the group is only here in Vancouver for one evening."

"*Really!*" Maddie gasped. "Aiyana, that's against the law. You have to be eighteen to gain entrance!"

"I know, but don't you think I could pass for eighteen?" Maddie looked at the almost six-foot tall girl. Yes, she could wangle the age limit, but not Mary-Jean with her baby face.

"That's not the issue. You would be breaking the law. Is your mother aware of this?"

"Yes, but she doesn't care. A whiskey bottle means more to her than I do," Aiyana confided. "Will you take me *Aunty* Maddie?" she begged with a twinkle in her eye. "You will love it. They are fantastic singers."

"Sweetie, I'm not a nightclub person, and I'm not into Mexican music. Besides, your mother would kill me if she found out I took her underage daughter to a nightclub!" Maddie had met Norma at a high school function, and she was a *big* woman, built like a muskox. Maddie wasn't about to risk a black eye.

But Aiyana was not going to take *no* for an answer. "Please, please, please, Aunty Maddie." She started to cry.

Maddie, a sucker for other people's tears, caved in. "Okay, but just for an hour. I'm in for a nasty surprise if your mother finds out! I'll get dressed. I don't think my wooly PJs will go down well in a nightclub!" she laughed.

"Great," Aiyana said happily, wiping the smudged mascara from beneath her lower eyelids. "Don't worry about my mom. She likes you. She wouldn't say anything."

"I'll go find something to wear."

Maddie went to her closet. She didn't own a nightclub outfit. She chose, instead, generic informal wear: a blue-denim mid-length skirt, and a denim shirt.

On this pleasant October evening in 1995, with an autumn chill in the air, their taxi pulled up to the downtown nightclub. Maddie's nerves started to get the better of her. Aiyana was *fifteen*! The bouncer requested identification. Maddie brazenly challenged, "You want *my* ID! This young lady is eighteen, and I should know. I'm her mother."

The situation was laughable. Here was a nearly six-foot Native girl accompanied by a petite white woman pretending to be her mother.

Anxiety knotted tightly in Maddie's throat as the two of them made their way to a booth near the bandstand. They sat down, and Maddie cautioned in a protective, motherly tone, "If a guy comes up and wants to buy you a drink or asks you to dance, you better say *no*, or I'll box your ears!"

Maddie didn't really want to consume alcohol, but when in Rome ..."

A soft drink and a small glass of red wine were delivered to the table. Maddie sipped while she waited for the music to begin. Yes, she'd broken the law, but getting out of the house was a refreshing respite.

The band started playing. Maddie was impressed, as were her

shoes, which were tapping away under the booth.

From the corner of her eye, Maddie spotted an olive-skinned young man staring in her direction. He did not seem to be Italian or Jewish. Maddie concluded he was Hispanic. When the seductive figure of the man sauntered across the floor in their direction, Maddie's mother bear activated. She warned her teenage companion, "There's a young guy heading towards us. Aiyana, don't look at him, and don't accept a drink or a dance. If you do, you'll be in big trouble!"

His snazzy white shirt glowed beneath the UV lighting as his molten-brown doe eyes met hers. An inexplicable sensation came over her: Had they met before? Maddie's photographic memory told her that was unlikely.

"May I buy you ladies a drink?" the man asked with a cosmic smile.

There was no doubting his origin—Cuban-American.

With her penchant for languages, Maddie politely replied, *"Gracias, pero no."* Then she fibbed, *"Estoy conduciendo."* She didn't own a car, but she pretended she was driving, hoping that would prompt him to leave.

"Your Spanish is *perfecta, Sēnora.* Have we met before?"

"I don't think so," Maddie responded evasively.

The aroma of his aftershave was intoxicating, together with his dashing personality. Maddie couldn't help but notice muscular shoulders that spoke of strength. She asked, "Do you work in construction?"

"Wow! Yes. I'm a roofer." he replied while pulling a vacant chair up to the table. This made Maddie somewhat uncomfortable, and she wanted to kick herself for enticing further conversation.

"My name is Hernando Esteban. I was born in Cuba. My father is Cuban and my mother is Canadian, so here I am. Are you and your lovely friend Canadian?"

Maddie *really* wanted to kick herself!

"Well, it's been nice chatting with you, but we have to leave now," she said quickly, grabbing Aiyana's arm. "Come on, daughter. It's time to go home."

"Your daughter is very beautiful, but you are a princess!" Hernando announced, patting Maddie's hand.

Maddie experienced a hot, nervous current thrilling through her body, like needles piecing her skin. She didn't know what to make of it, but her voice spoke volumes. "What's the matter with you? Do you get a kick out of flattering older women?"

Aiyana giggled.

"No, but you have captivated me," Hernando responded intensely.

"Get out of here!" Maddie flipped. "We are *leaving*, and don't even think of trying to follow us."

Once outside Maddie checked her watch. "Bloody hell," she squealed. "It's nearly midnight! Your mother is going to murder me!"

"*Taxi*," she shouted when she spotted a yellow cab. It rushed right passed her.

"You won't get a cab at this time of night," the bouncer informed. "The pubs are all closing."

Maddie's heart raced, and her breath caught in her lungs. Her anxiety was about to balloon out of control. She had to think fast.

There was no point ringing Thomas. His driving license had been revoked after his heart attack.

"Stay here, Aiyana. I have to go back inside." She said to the bouncer, "Please watch her. I have to make a call."

Guess who she bumped into on *his* way out of the club!

Observing Maddie's sweat-beaded forehead and the worry etched on her face, twenty-eight-year-old Hernando asked, "Is everything okay?"

Twenty-five minutes later, Hernando's red truck pulled up to Aiyana's and Norma's home, a building in disrepair in a not-so-nice neighborhood. "Your roof looks like it needs my touch," Fernando said.

Maddie hadn't been thinking clearly when she asked him to drive them home.

The jig was up when big Norma appeared at the front door yelling, "Aiyana, it's late! Get to bed. You have school tomorrow." Then she addressed Maddie. "I hope you had a good time, and thanks for bringing my daughter home."

Flushed red with embarrassment, Maddie invited Hernando into her basement suite. "I'll make you coffee because you must be over the alcohol limit."

It was nearly four in the morning when her new best friend got up off the sofa to leave. "I'll be back later with some real Cuban coffee," he laughed. Obviously, Maddie's instant coffee granules were not to his liking. She received another electric shock when he hugged her goodbye. "Are you sure we haven't met before?" he asked.

"No, we haven't, but it feels like I've known you forever. Is that a good thing or a bad thing?" she smiled.

Their bond was cemented.

Though she was worn out, Maddie couldn't sleep. She had opened herself up to a complete stranger, poured out her heavy heart, leaving no past stone unturned, except for what she did for a living.

True to his word, Hernando returned five hours later bearing a bag of Cuban coffee beans, a coffee grinder, red roses, and several Cuban music CDs.

Mary-Jean and Mara stared at the stranger in their home. Maddie introduced him. "This is my friend Hernando. He was born in Cuba, and he's going to teach me how to salsa dance."

Both girls looked at their mother as if she had gone insane. She had never listened to any other type of music than classical. Then they promptly left the room, acting as if their mother didn't belong to them.

Maddie was a born dancer, and the magical rhythm of salsa came naturally to her. Hernando made her feel so young and energized. What happened next was like an out-of-body experience. Hernando drew her toward him with a strong embrace, kissed her on the lips, and whispered in her ear, "My desert beauty, you know that I'm going to marry you one day."

Click, click, click

Maddie's recurrent memory faded back into the sands of the Middle East desert, where it had all begun, back to the Kingdom of Judah.

"I'M GOING TO MARRY YOU ONE DAY, LELA."

"IF IT TAKES ME UNTIL THE END OF THE EARTH, I WILL FIND YOU, HASSAM EL DIN."

Lela's prayers had been answered.

On December 2, 1996, Maddie's forty-fifth birthday and Hernando's twenty-ninth, the reincarnated souls, who were born on the same day and month, were married. She was now Mrs. Madeline Esteban.

Following their private wedding ceremony, Maddie penned in her journal:

After spending decades being unwanted, desperate to belong, I have been reunited with my soulmate, a ray of sunshine. My version of the old proverb would be this: *Beside each woman, and not behind, stands a great man. It is this man who helped me become the woman I am today, and I thank him with all my heart.*

CHAPTER TWENTY-FOUR

"No need for revenge. Just sit back and wait for those who
have hurt you to eventually screw up themselves.
If you are lucky, you will watch it unfold."

M addie lived alongside her beloved husband, the surrogate "Hassam," for twenty-five years. While the
psychoses in her hate-filled children, fueled by their
failures, ensured that Maddie was never able to truly enjoy a happy
married life, the strength of her bond with Hernando enabled them
to survive all the trials and tribulations.

Throughout their years together, Hernando had stood loyally
by his wife's side, been there for her during the darkest chapters in
her life—the endless struggle to rise above the insufferable hurt
inflicted by her children.

Hernando supported Maddie when Mary-Jean got pregnant a
month after her mother's marriage. Hernando paid for her flight to
Guatemala to marry Javier, father of her child, an exchange student
in her high school. Hernando didn't know Mary-Jean was calling her
mother daily asking for money. Her excuses were she had lost her
purse or her mother-in law was too poor to offer help or something

else. Lies, lies, lies! But Maddie had a soft heart for her daughter and not a bad bone in her body. She often walked twelve blocks in dreadful weather to the Money Mart, where she would send cash she had squirreled out of her grocery allocation.

In February of 1997 Mary-Jean called, crying and begging for her mother's help. "Mum, I want to come home. Javier is a dickhead. He refuses to marry me and doesn't give a damn about his son, *your* grandson. Please, please, Mum. I can't stay here another day. I hate this place. It's uncivilized. If you don't help me, I'm going to kill myself and your grandson!"

Maddie's heart tugged empathetically. "Don't do such a foolish thing, Mary-Jean. I will see what I can do to help."

Was Mary-Jean manipulating her mother's heart strings? Hell, yes!

Maddie placed a call to the British High Commissioner in Guatemala City. Using her "clout," baby Carlito was eventually granted British Citizenship by descent from his British-born mother. This concession would permit Mary-Jean and her baby to leave the country without obtaining permission from the natural father. Maddie paid all the expenses associated with the registration. Then, at Maddie's pleading, an unenthusiastic Hernando took time off from work, flew to Guatemala City, and collected Mary-Jean and seven-month Carlito. Maddie inquired, "Did you have any trouble at Customs?" Hernando laughed. "Nope. The kid is as dark as me, and they probably thought he was mine!"

Maddie had only two days to prepare for their homecoming. She went out and purchased every baby item they could need, and also some nice gifts for Mary-Jean. Hernando wasn't happy that these extra costs were put on their credit card, but he supported Maddie's desire to make life comfortable for her daughter and grandchild. Over the ensuing years Maddie would learn the hard way that her adult children, lacking financial responsibilities, wouldn't suddenly change from their just-one-more-loan mentality.

Maddie never did receive gratitude for kindness to and support of her children.

Sixteen-year-old Mary-Jean walked through the door, deposited her seven-month-old son onto Maddie's lap, and announced, "I'm going out for a jog. See you later."

Mara wasn't thrilled about her half-sister's return home. Attention was being diverted from her selfish desires by *two* people. Mara hated Hernando. She told a friend at school, "My mother is crazy. She has married a *boy*, and I'll never accept him as *my* father!"

Maddie fell in love with her dark-skinned, sweet baby grandson. She became Carlito's only caregiver as Mary-Jean began to spend more time with Aiyana and her other friends. Naturally, Grandma Maddie pitched in. She was proud and hands-on. She bathed Carlito, fed him, played peekaboo, read and sang to him, and snuggled with him until he fell asleep. Hernando and baby Carlito were the center of her universe, but Hernando felt differently. He wasn't the doting type when it came to children. Though he was extremely fond of his grandson, he disagreed with the way Mary-Jean was neglecting her child. She was too busy partying to take full parental responsibility. One night when Mary-Jean arrived home in the wee hours of the morning, Hernando was waiting for her. She was falling-down drunk. He gave her an ultimatum: "Take responsibility for your own child or get out!"

In a slurred voice she screamed at him. "You can't tell me to f'ing leave! It's my mother's house, and you're not my f'ing father!"

Hernando was so angry that he could have choked her, but from the corner of his eye he saw Maddie standing in the doorway with tears trickling down her face.

"Please, I beg you. She's my daughter, and I can't see her or my grandchild on the streets."

This plea for mercy would be repeated by Maddie on many future occasions.

A month later, Mary-Jean dropped a bombshell! She informed her mother that she was pregnant with Javier's second child, Maddie was in despair. How was she going to drop this bombshell on Hernando? There was enough tension in the home between him and Mary-Jean, and that did not even include the overbearing, condescending interactions and heated arguments he had with Mara.

Maddie had to be level headed when she was in the same room with her husband and daughters, each turning to her to solve their problems. Drawing boundaries failed miserably. There was *no* happy middle ground to be found. She wasn't even trying to win anymore. She'd already lost!

It takes two people to argue, as the saying goes, but *three* was the reality.

Maddie's anxiety attacks flew off the Richter scale.

Maddie's husband continued to stand by the love of his life. So when Mary-Jean latched on to a local mechanic, Maddie and Hernando breathed a sigh of relief. Mary-Jean said they planned to move into an apartment together, and Rocky would raise Carlito and the coming child as his own.

But it didn't take long for Mary-Jean to manipulate her mother. "I need maternity wear, I need rent money. I need this and I need that!"

When Maddie asked Mary-Jean why her boyfriend wasn't paying for these things, Mary-Jean answered, "He's an apprentice mechanic. He earns peanuts. So I need additional support from you."

Maddie had never kept any secrets from Hernando, but now, thanks to Mary-Jean, she was hiding things from him.

Mary-Jean informed Maddie it was *her* duty to pay for her upcoming wedding because she had no father to do so. Maddie protested. "I have had no journalistic work for a while, and I have no savings left." She wanted to say *because you have bled me dry!* "I'm totally dependent on your stepfather, until my circumstances change. Sweetie, I can't ask him to fork out money we don't have. The construction business is slow, and we are barely making ends meet. And I still have your sister's needs to consider. She'll need new school clothes when classes start next month."

Maddie did not receive a wedding invitation. In fact, she was told by an aggressive Rocky to stay away from his wife, Mary-Jean, and the children. They were *his* family now, and she wasn't wanted in their lives. Maddie didn't need to guess why he had turned on her like a pit bull. Mary-Jean and her older sister, Joanne, were pros at manipulation!

Imagine Maddie's shock when she received a hospital bill for baby Javier, Jr., for $6,235. When she saw it, Maddie suffered a severe panic attack that left her struggling to breathe. She broke down when Hernando returned from work. He was as angry as a wounded animal. "Why should you pay for the birth? It's not your child. The bitch is married to a Canadian. Let him pay for it!"

Maddie was placed into a debt collection agency for the outstanding hospital bill. It seemed Mary-Jean's husband had not filed for spousal Immigration status, so Maddie was left holding the baby, so to speak!

Hernando saved Maddie's good credit rating by taking out a loan from the bank, visiting the collection agency office, and telling them the truth. Maddie's good name was cleared ... but not for long.

The doorbell chimed. Maddie opened the door and saw a smartly dressed Asian woman standing on her doorstep. "Hi. Are you Madeline Esteban?"

"Yes. How can I help you?"

"My name is Ding Mi. I'm from the Ministry for Children and Families. We have received a complaint, and I believe your daughter, Mara, may need protection. The claim is that she is being physically abused, kicked in the back."

Blinded by shock, Maddie protested. "That's crazy! I've never kicked any child, let alone my own! You better come in," she offered. "I would like to get to the bottom of this false allegation. Who has made the complaint?"

Entering the home, Ding Mi continued. "I'm sorry. Under our confidentially rules, I can't tell you the name of the caller."

Maddie was informed by Ding Mi that Mara had been taken out of her classroom and interrogated! The accusations were unforgiveable, and a brokenhearted and devastated Maddie said, "Give me a moment. I need to place a call so I can be vindicated of all wrongdoing."

Maddie called the "outfit" and spoke to Agent JF. She passed the phone to Ding Mi.

Her face was quite pale when she responded. "Thank you for this information, Sir."

"I'm sorry to have troubled you, Mrs. Esteban. Please accept my apology."

"No problem. You were just doing your job."

Agent JF did some official digging on Maddie's behalf. She was shocked but not surprised when he confirmed Mary-Jean had placed the call. Why?

Her mother had said *no* to being scammed out of money, and had told her "NO. No more financial assistance."

Maddie could have spent time in prison for child abuse, and Mara would have been taken from her and placed in foster care. Unbeknown until many years later, Maddie learned that it was Mara who had encouraged her sister to make the false accusation. Mara had wanted to have a sleep over with some school friends whom her mother disapproved of. Mara had obviously not thought of the consequences of her actions, removed from her home.

A week later Maddie received the following correspondence:

Dear Mrs. Esteban,

It was a pleasure to recently meet you at your home.

I have now completed my investigation into a report that Mara Clark was believed to be in need of protection. This will confirm that I have found no reason for any further involvement by the Ministry for Protection and Families and will now be closing the file on this matter.

Should you have any further questions or concerns, please call me at 660-518-0605. Thank you for your cooperation.

Sincerely,

Ding Mi, Social Worker

Ministry for Children and Families

Heartless, vengeful Mary-Jean and Mara weren't finished making their mother suffer, yet Maddie, blindsided, still couldn't turn her back on or hate her miracle children. Of course, they did not admit the heinous deed.

The day after the apology letter arrived, the phone rang.

"Mum, can I come and see you? I need some help, Mum!"

Maddie lived every day with gratitude, not hate, in her heart. She gave Mary-Jean a genuine hug when she arrived with her two boys in a twin stroller. It was the first time Maddie had seen Javier, Jr. Her heart glowed with love. She made her daughter a cup of tea, played with her grandsons, and chatted to Mary-Jean about her problems.

Evidently Mary-Jean and Rocky were fighting. He had threatened to kick her and the boys out of their apartment and call Immigration on her.

"Mum, I hate him!" Mary-Jean snarled. "You have to help me or Rocky will deport me and my boys back to Britain. And where would we stay, Mum? I have no home or money over there. You see, you have to help us."

Maddie informed her, "Javier, Jr., was born here, Mary-Jean. Immigration can't deport a Canadian child!"

"You forget, Mum, Carlito isn't. He has a Guatemalan birth certificate, and I've no permanent residency status here. You have always been able to pull rabbits out of hats, Mum. I know you will think of something. In the meantime, can we move back here?"

Maddie's heart sank. *This could be the end of my marriage.* Hernando had made it quite clear, "I never want to see that bitch in my home again."

Maddie had to put her thinking cap on, and fast. "What about your sister, Joanne? Are you two still in contact?"

"Yes. As a matter of fact, I wrote to her recently and got a reply. In the letter she asked me not to give you her address."

Maddie sighed. "I'm okay with that, but it is sad that her first-born child has no love in her heart for me. I took care of her on my own until she turned twelve. I have no choice but to let her get on with her life, without me."

Maddie purchased airline tickets on her credit card and paid for three new British passports so Mary-Jean and the kids could return to England. Mary-Jean said they would stay with Joanne until they made other plans. She added that she was entitled to get welfare assistance over there.

Eight days later Maddie received a telephone call from Joanne, the first time she had heard her daughter's voice since the acrimonious custody trial. "I want her out of my home. She doesn't take care of her kids and expects me to babysit all the time. Her bloody kids are wrecking my place. My husband is going nuts!"

Maddie had no clue Joanne was married or had any children. She chose not to probe any further. But a lump rose up in her throat just hearing her daughter's voice. Maddie's inner camera took her back to the times she had spent a small fortune in cab fares driving up and down Joanne's high school street hoping to catch a glimpse of her miracle baby number one. In the end, it had been in vain.

"Put Mary-Jean on the phone please, Joanne," Maddie said.

Of course, Mary-Jean presented a different side to Joanne's demand to remove her. "I hate Joanne. She's bossy and so mean to your grandsons, and they are unhappy. We want to move back in with you."

Oh, no. This is not happening!

Maddie wasn't falling for this "cry wolf" approach ... again. She said, "I'll call you back tomorrow after I have slept on it. I'll give you my answer then."

"Why do you need to sleep on it?" Mary-Jean raged. "I'm your daughter!"

"I'll call you tomorrow, I promise," Maddie ended.

Maddie immediately called Rocky and balled him out. "*You* are responsible for your wife, not me! I can't bail out Mary-Jean financially any more, or I will lose my husband."

Rocky's voice was subdued. "I've no money to pay for their return. But if you can help me out with this, I'll pay every cent back. I've missed Mary-Jean and the kids."

Rocky met Mary-Jean and the children at Vancouver airport, their flights paid for by Maddie. However, the telephone call Maddie received after they returned was ingratitude at its worst. "You're a shit, mother!" Mary-Jean spat. "You put that *dick* back into our lives, and I'm never going to forgive you! You'll never see me or your grandchildren again!"

She was wrong!

Maddie was no longer being subjected to Mary-Jean's emotional blackmail, no longer held for ransom for monetary handouts, or forced to watch as her grandsons were used as pawns. "You can see your grandsons, but they need this and that ..."

Maddie got on with her life.

She still withheld *one* secret from Hernando she had sworn not to reveal—her true profession. The concealment was eating her alive. She would make a phone call and hope she could finally remove the burden of keeping this secret from her beloved husband.

With some trepidation Maddie placed her call. At long last her "debt" had been paid. She was free. But what Agent SK added would haunt Maddie for the rest of her life ... because she did not have the answer!

"Thank you for your loyal service," SK had said. "But there is something I need to get off my chest, and you are not going to like it. However, it must be said. You are one of the smartest people I've had the privilege of working with, and yet you are also the dumbest ..."

Maddie scowled.

"You'll never have a life of your own while you pander to every whim of your narcissistic children, who don't deserve you. You don't

seem to see it, Maddie, but you are being *used* by master manipula-
tors. But God help you when they really *are* adults."

It was now paramount that Maddie make a fresh start, a new
beginning, away from city life and the overwhelming suffering she
had endured in Burnaby at the hands of her offspring.

The night of SK's phone call, she poured her heart out to the one
person she knew would understand. Hernando adored his wife and
would do anything to make her happy. "I can get work anywhere,
my darling, so let's go for it," he agreed. "And I'm proud to be married to a secret agent," he finished with a smile.

That night, Mara kicked up a stink. "Damn it! I don't want to live
in the boonies! I don't want to go to another school. I'll miss all my
friends." She only had one friend, and she was as dysfunctional as
Mara.

"Tough!" Hernando said. "You can go to boarding school and
come home on the holidays."

That threat worked.

Mara went to her bedroom and started packing her belongings.

In 1998 Maddie received a severance payout, and along with the
refund from her cashed-out life insurance policy, she was able to
purchase a spacious three-story house in the Slocan Valley, located
in the Kootenay region of British Columbia. This small community,

nestled between the Selkirk and Purcell mountains, was a hidden gem: nature, beauty, warmth, friendly people … and freedom!

Maddie set about turning the first floor of her new home into a bed-and-breakfast operation.

Hernando found work as a subcontractor.

Mara was enrolled in the local school.

Life was wonderful, until …

One year later Maddie received a strange call. "Is this Madeline, Mary-Jean's mother?" the caller asked in Spanish.

"Yes. Who is this?"

"It's Javier from Guatemala. Where are my children?"

"What do you mean where are they?" Maddie asked rather puzzled. "They live with Mary-Jean and her new husband in Burnaby, British Columbia.

"No, they do not. I just called there."

"Javier, I'm not a magician, but I will try to get to the bottom of this. Give me your phone number."

With Agent JF's assistance, Maddie found out Mary-Jean had abandoned her sons with Rocky and his Portuguese family and had run away with a British musician to England. Their exact whereabouts were unknown at this time, JF told her, but he would look into the matter for her.

Chapter Twenty-Four

Maddie went to war.

It took eight months and $62,000 in legal costs to win the court case. Maddie was given full custody of her minor grandsons. She removed them from Burnaby and brought them home to live with her. Their mother uttered not one word of gratitude for saving her children. But Maddie wasn't finished. She was informed by Immigration that she would now have to adopt the child born in Guatemala for him to enjoy Canadian rights under her protection and at her cost.

Maddie was enraged. Taking out an equity loan, she hired an international affairs lawyer to file an out-of-country human rights violation against Canada with the European Court of Human Rights in France. This lawsuit risked her Canadian residency, but Maddie had to do whatever she could to grant Guatemalan-born Carlito the right to be her *grandchild*, not her adopted *son!*

Her tenacity in fighting Immigration Canada eventually paid off. However, when the MA402 law was passed one year later, it automatically gave grandparents rights. They did not have to adopt their abandoned grandchildren.

And still no appreciation from Mary-Jean.

Maddie had no intention of raising Mary-Jean's boys as her own. She made it clear to Mary-Jean that once she got her act together, Maddie would travel with the boys to England and reunite the family.

Using her clout, Maddie contacted Family Services in the UK

and asked them to check on Mary-Jean, whom Maddie believed *was* finally behaving like a responsible parent. She married the musician (guess who paid for that expense?), and they obtained a council home in London.

When the Family service officer informed Maddie that Mary-Jean was expecting a child, she decided it was time to make the abandoned boys whole by letting them be there when their brother or sister was born.

Mary-Jean's response to Maddie's thoughtfulness was that her mother didn't want her kids so she brought them to her in England!

The flight to England was a nightmare with two rambunctious kids to look after. But Mara was there to assist Maddie, and she had a scolding tongue that could break glass.

When they arrived in England, Mary-Jean did not hug her mum or show any gratitude, but Maddie was beyond believing her child ever would. Mary-Jean saw her mother only as a money pit.

Grandma cried the whole way back to Canada.

Mary-Jean eventually married three times and had nine children. Maddie continued to shower Mary-Jean and her children with pure motherly love. She gave them every type of support she could. She mailed birthday and Christmas gifts and paid for a washer and dryer when Mary-Jean said her old ones were broken. Yet, according to Mary-Jean's email to her mother later in life, Maddie was still a shit mum.

Mary-Jean visited Canada five times to spend vacations with Maddie, who paid for Mary-Jean's travel and the cost of excess baggage fees; Mary-Jean always returned to England with luggage crammed full of goodies for Maddie's' nine grandchildren.

How much can one woman take?

Maddie's greatest weakness was having a big heart.

One day, after Mary-Jean assaulted Maddie with manipulative pleading, Maddie paid for Javier, Jr., now sixteen, to stay with her. "Please, Mum, help me. Can Javier come and stay with you. He's out of control, heavily into drugs, and I can't handle him anymore."

Against her husband's wishes, Maddie agreed to help "fix" the Canadian-born teenager she had rescued and still loved dearly. She ended up paying for Javier's British passport renewal and his international flight to Kelowna, BC. She bought him winter clothing (he arrived with two pairs of socks, one pair of jeans, a couple of short-sleeved shirts, and a pair of sneakers). She broke down in tears when the six-foot, handsome, Hispanic-looking Javier, accompanied by Hernando who had picked him up at midnight from the airport, flung his arms around his short-term substitute mother. "I love you, Nana. I'm so happy you let me come to stay with you," he enthused.

A few weeks into his stay, Maddie discovered Javier had more serious problems than smoking too much dope. After finding blood-stained tissues in a wastebasket, she discovered he was deliberately cutting himself. Maddie knew she had to hold it together, even though she was shocked. She pulled off a bluff. "Are you still having those nose bleeds you had when you were little?"

Javier started to cry. That did it! She flung her arms around him and said, "There must never be any secrets between us if I'm to help you. Please, my special grandson, talk to me."

Inner trauma was etched deeply on Javier's brown face. He sat on his bed and unburdened his raw inner pain to the one person he trusted, his loving grandmother.

He told her that when he was about nine years old and swimming lessons were part of the high school's curriculum, his classmates made fun of his dark, Hispanic nipples. "Hey, you breast-feeding, mate?"

Later that same day, when Javier told his mother what had happened at the swimming pool, she just laughed at him, and a deep, underlying neurosis began. That night Javier began to self-mutilate his left nipple.

When Maddie discovered Javier's dark secret, she went on her computer and researched the reasons behind self-mutilation.

Armed with studies, she took Javier to see her doctor, whom she had to pay privately because Javier had no BC Health Insurance. Maddie agreed with her doctor that a cosmetic surgeon could correct the mangled nipple skin and decrease the dark tone by using lighter skin from his buttocks. Her doctor agreed to contact a surgeon and refer Javier on Maddie's behalf. Maddie was surprised to learn that the surgeon was from South Africa, where she was born!

Meanwhile, Maddie sought the help of the psychologist at Slocan Valley High School, where Javier had been enrolled one week after he arrived.

Meanwhile, Maddie made an error in judgement. In a moment of emotional weakness, she had confided in her daughter, Mara, who had failed thus far to befriend her nephew. Javier detested his aunt when he learned from Hernando that she had physically abused his grandmother.

The following day Maddie received a nightmare phone call. Javier had been in a fight with the son of one of Mara's friends. Javier beat the teenager and was suspended from school. Why had he done this?

Mara had wickedly betrayed her mother's confidence about Javier's cutting. There, for all to see, Mara posted on her Facebook page: "What a sick F*ck! My nephew Javier tried to cut his nipple off!"

Javier had no idea Mara had posted this deplorable message until he arrived at school and became the target of disgusting and vulgar baiting by other students.

Maddie collected an angry and shamed Javier from school. "I'm so sorry this has happened to you. It's my fault. What was I thinking telling your evil aunt about your pain? Please forgive me!"

"There's nothing to forgive, Nana. *You* didn't post it."

In the weeks that followed, Mara's hate-filled heart continued its vengeful campaign against Javier. She was angry at him for ignoring her as if she didn't exist.

One afternoon, when Javier was walking with some school buddies on the town's main street, he became, once more, the victim of Mara's bullying. She hurled foul language at him through her truck window. "You can't get away from me A-hole. This is a small town."

Javier underwent cosmetic surgery and psychological therapy. In the days that followed he became a new person, prepared to face the world with strength. He was doing well at school until ...

Mara sent an email to her sister, Mary-Jean: "Mum is poisoning your son against you. She told him that you didn't want him and Carlito. She said that's why the boys were left behind when you went to England. And the best, Mum told Javier that you were a stripper when you lived in Canada."

Following that email, Maddie was bombarded with dreadful telephone calls and emails from Mary-Jean, her new husband, Joanne, her husband, and from a stranger she didn't even know. The contents were so vile that Maddie felt impelled to reveal them to Hernando.

Mara had succeeded in alienating her loved ones with un-founded, vicious lies. The hatred became too much for Maddie. She was rushed to a hospital following a mini stroke. Hernando put his foot down.

Sadly, Maddie knew what had to be done.

Javier was returned to England at Maddie's expense. He got a job in the hotel industry and eventually climbed the ladder to become Hotel Duty Manager at The Plaza. He married, had two children, and never forgot his grandmother.

Before leaving her home for England, Javier delivered a parting comment: "I don't give a flying fig what your bitch daughters have said about you, or about my mother's foul accusations. You were the best thing that happened to me when I was young, and I'll love you forever. One day I will come and see you and repay every cent you spent on me."

Maddie paid nearly $9,000 for Javier's surgery and his return flight to England She never regretted spending this money on a child who needed rescuing from himself. At least *he* was grateful to her.

The same year Javier returned to England, Maddie grew so tired of being a punching bag for her dysfunctional offspring, of being so unappreciated and lied about, that she considered legally disowning her grown children in a court of law.

Now childless, Hernando and Maddie tried to pick up the pieces of their abused lives, but the mentally ill Mara had other plans. She became Maddie's worst nightmare.

Mara was beyond redemption.

But Maddie never stopped loving her.

CHAPTER TWENTY-FIVE

"Sometimes you just need someone to tell you that you're not as terrible as you think you are."

M ara completed high school with respectable grades. She took a year off before deciding what to do with the rest of her life.

Hernando was more than happy to drive her to Edmonton in Alberta, where she was going to share an apartment with a class-mate. Maddie felt sad seeing her last child fly the nest. God only knows why. This child had harbored hate in her heart from the day she was born toward the woman who had always supported her. But pretending to be joyful when she really was in pain was a measure of Maddie's strength.

A few months after Mara's departure, Maddie sold her B & B for health reasons. Her cancer gremlins were back. The sale of her home and business relieved Maddie of the huge debt she had accumulated from the loans she had taken out to help her children and grandson.

While understanding that the grass is not always greener on the other side of the fence, Maddie yearned once more to make a fresh start. After doing some homework, she chose Point Roberts, a U.S border territory, an American exclave 328 yards from the Canadian border. It was a rustic, serene area with cedar forests and driftwood strewn beaches, just what she needed to heal her body and mind. She described it as "Almost heaven, almost Canada; nowhere, surrounded by somewhere." She discovered through a Google search that Point Roberts happened by chance when, in 1846, the U.S. and Great Britain finally agreed to separate their western possessions at the 49th parallel. What she most appreciated was that the crime rate was close to zero in her gated community.

Obtaining a Nexus access card, Maddie and Hernando bought a modest ranch house. They learned from a friendly café owner that St. Josephs' hospital in Bellingham, a seventy-minute drive, had some of the best cancer doctors in the U.S.

Maddie began a private experimental blood transfusion treatment: her rare blood type, AB rhesus positive, was replaced with the common O-positive, the universal donor blood group.

Miracles do happen!

After two months of this radical procedure, Maddie became an outpatient. Her gremlins were finally annihilated, or so she hoped.

Now, a heathy but discontented Maddie was homesick for the place she loved most, the Slocan Valley. They didn't have any trouble selling the ranch house and relocating back to the Valley.

Their tiny two-bedroom, one-bath log cabin sitting adjacent to the Slocan River was peaceful. It was a wonderful way for Maddie and Hernando to start their new life, that is until the phone began ringing off the hook. Maddie wished telephones had never been invented.

"Mum, you have got to help me."

Maddie, still wearing maternal blinders, paid for Mara's huge veterinary bill for a cat she had taken with her to Alberta. When the cat subsequently died, Maddie paid for the cremation. She also paid Mara's outstanding rent and paid off, then cancelled, the secondary credit card she had given Mara for emergencies. Mara had decided that fancy swimwear and Japanese takeout were more important than paying her rent. Later, when Mara lost her job at Tim Horton's and was being evicted from her apartment, compassionate Maddie brought her daughter back to BC, where she moved to White Rock. Maddie's soft heart prompted her to buy furniture and pay for rent and groceries so that Mara could get on her feet.

Hernando was furious, but he stood by his manipulated wife.

The extortion continued as the years passed. "Help me, Mum," Mara pleaded. "I'm living out of a vending machine. I need tools, a computer, and a cell phone. I want to get a horse trainer certificate."

The list went on and on.

Suffering under Mara's insatiable demands, Maddie still believed that Mara intended to turn her life around and pay her mother back. No such luck!

Finally, Maddie opened her home when Mara announced she was pregnant by a man who had left her. She insisted she couldn't work. This request almost brought Maddie and Hernando's marriage to a breaking point.

"If you let her come here, I'm leaving," he threatened.

Maddie was so torn. She went to her bedroom and cried for days.

Mara returned home not only with a baby in her belly, but also with a horse to care for. Relenting, Hernando supported his devastated wife and never blamed her for being so stupid! He even built a stable for the horse, as winter was approaching. Hernando added an extra room to the side of the cabin, and his hard-earned money provided Mara with the necessaries her baby needed. He tried to get along with Mara, whom he detested, as he had Mary-Jean.

One day, when Maddie was out of the house at the grocery store, Mara casually remarked to Hernando, "You know, I've always been looking for another mother, as my mother never took me to Disneyland."

The anger overwhelming Hernando's face communicated his reaction, but he didn't mention Mara's ruthless comment to Maddie until many years later.

Maddie penned in her journal:

I have the Right to say *no*,
The Right to be free from abuse,
The Right to be guilt free,
The Right to have peace of mind,
The Right to have reasonable expectations,
The Right to be imperfect,
The Right to determine what to do with my own money
and without being obligated to others,
The Right to retirement,
The parental Right to reap the benefits of a lifetime of care,
which no adult child is automatically owed (bailouts).
This may be the most crucial right of all because it is a
prerequisite for all other rights. Parents must be able to
say *no* so they can stop and prevent abuse, claim peace
of mind, and control their finances.

These rights, so carefully penned by Maddie, did not seem to exist for her because she yearned to belong to the children whose heartbeats she had held inside her. Of all her three children, Mara had the most twisted mind and the greatest lust for revenge. She was addicted to hatred for what she deemed past wrongs, whether they were real or not. Her lust for vengeance consumed her, and she took it out on the one person who would never dream of hurting her.

Nobody knew about the physical abuse. It always happened when Maddie was alone with Mara.

Mara lacked remorse and denied the physical abuse—breaking one of Maddie's ribs in a bear-hold, inflicting bruises, and threatening to end her mother's life with a snap of her neck. Maddie lived in a dark tunnel of shame. She never told a soul. Shame prevented her from divulging this abuse even to Hernando. She kept her dreadful secret until her doctor noticed several bruises on her back. "Maddie, I hope this is not Hernando's doing?" he inquired in a regretful tone. "I will have to report this to the police, Maddie."

But Maddie understood her doctor-patient confidentiality rights. "No. It was not Hernando!" After identifying the aggressor, she added, "This must remain between us. I will never allow my pain to be the cause of Mara's child being taken away from her. For all her viciousness, her child needs her, so my injuries must remain confidential. Okay?"

Mara loved to hate. She used hatred as a defense to protect herself. She relished her odious state of mind and received pleasure from inflicting hurt on others, especially her mother. Maddie was convinced Mara had surrendered herself to a cold, burning hatred of her mother and that she planned to nourish it the rest of her life. Even so, Maddie still couldn't grasp the sad reality that a daughter who had once proclaimed love for her could hurt her without conscience.

In public Maddie put on a cheerful face, but privately her reality confined her to demoralized hiding, a slow death by deep, raw internalized pain.

Maddie suffered several minor heart attacks, and became paralyzed from the waist down after a rare spinal-cord infarction in 2006. When Hernando notified Mara that her mother was critically ill, literally at death's door, Mara's responded, "I have no transportation or money to come see her. I might be able to borrow some money from my employer, but you will have to pay me back."

Hernando forked out $300 in cash!

Mara, the narcissistic bully, was the last person Maddie wanted to see when she awoke from unconsciousness. She stared at the child she had loved unconditionally and thought, *One day you will fall short, like all parents do, and you too will suffer the unbearable pain you inflicted upon me.*

Maddie defied medical odds, stood up out of her wheelchair, and walked.

"I waddle like a Canada goose now, but at least I don't feel so crippled," she told those who inquired after her health.

Following a visit to a ninety-year old spiritual man in Haida

Gwaii of British Columbia, in 2018 Maddie reclaimed her life. She finally, with sadness, closed the door on her children, grandchildren, and two great-grandchildren:

Joanne-Jean had three children. The oldest gave Maddie a great-grandchild.

Mary-Jean had nine children. Javier, Jr., gave her a great-grandchild.

Mara had three children.

Maddie refused to be baited anymore by the abominable fallacies posted about her on Facebook, and she did not respond to Mara's threat to take her to court for slander! That would have been amusing. Her children had no idea who she was officially, or that she had Her Majesty's Secret Service to back her up.

Maddie's life with her beloved husband grew more loving and wonderful. And she renewed her friendship with Alwyn, who had responded to an ad Maddie placed in a Welsh newspaper. Maddie had always felt grateful for the woman who had shared her clothing in the Italian hostel in Milan.

Maddie reminded herself ... *Alwyn is a precious soul! And so am I!*

CHAPTER TWENTY-SIX

"Death must be so beautiful. To lie in the soft brown earth,
with grasses waving above one's head, and listen to silence.
To have no yesterday, and no tomorrow.
To forget time, to forget life, to be at peace."
—OSCAR WILDE

O ne summer afternoon Maddie had a sudden and strong premonition that she was about to die. Having already experienced several near-death ordeals and numerous medical scares, she wasn't afraid. She knew it wasn't as frightening as other mortals imagined. However, she didn't want to worry Hernando with her suspicions.

In the early morning hours of the following day, Maddie snapped wide awake. With an unsettled feeling, she reached toward Hernando and gently placed a hand on his forehead. It was moist with perspiration. "Darling, wake up," she cried, placing her hand over his heart. As far as she knew, Hernando was in good health, but that day her beloved partner succumbed to cardiac arrhythmia in his sleep. Maddie didn't cry out. Instead, she whispered in his ear. "Don't you dare depart without me, Hassam El Din! I'm not going to wait thousands of years for us to reunite."

Being clairaudient, she knew that brain chemistry was separate from consciousness, and she sensed that Hernando had heard her.

Maddie reached out toward the bedside table. Unzipping a pouch that she kept there, she removed a syringe. She stood up, opened the bedroom window wide, and climbed back into bed. Carefully, drawing the syringe back, she filled it with air, pushed the needle into her carotid artery, and depressed the plunger. The air bubble traveled through her vein and lodged in her heart. Her breath became progressively shallow as imminent death approached.

Ageless, Lela's and Hassam's astral cords were tightly intertwined. Their spirits ascended and departed through the open window.

The two lovers returned to the Western Desert, where life had begun for them, never to be separated again.

Click, click, click.

"I'M GOING TO MARRY YOU ONE DAY, LELA, DAUGHTER OF CHAIM."

The shutters of Maddie's camera closed forever. She finally ran out of film. At last Maddie was at peace. She was free of *hate*!

~ The End ~

NOTES FROM
Shaman Nana'Eek-Chechowa,
Haida Gwaii, BC, 2018

Joanne-Jean, Firstborn Daughter

S leeping with this picture, I had many short dreams. Some were exciting, and some sad. Joanne chose you, and she could not wait for her spirit to jump in. Three months into the pregnancy, her soul displaced that of the son who had originally chosen you as its vessel. He did not want to leave, and would eventually return as your second daughter, with female traits.

1. Joanne came through you to get to her male parent. Today she is unhappy with her decision, which did not work out the way it was originally planned. Now she realizes that her choice was mistaken, and she has reluctantly decided to live out this life and delay the return to the other side for a period.

2. I tried to explain to you about the school that exists with the Universe, where there are doors to enter and exist in this temporal plane.

3. When you pass to the other side, you review your previous life and the lessons you were to learn. If some lessons remain

unlearned and you have to return, the soul transfers to a place where you are helped to understand your past incarnation and what you have yet to achieve. Some souls reenter a new life prematurely, before they are ready. The child spirit should have remained in this place of understanding and completed her teaching and contemplation with help from the higher authority.

4. In Joanne's current incarnation, her spirit lives in something of a dream and travels within her own mind believing everything told to her.

5. She will choose more wisely in her next incarnation.

6. Your last-born daughter will successfully alienate this first-born from you with evil lies.

Nana'Eek-Chechowa

Haida Gwaii, BC, 2018

Mary-Jean, Second-born Daughter

When I first started to sleep with this picture, all that I could see and hear was the word "manipulation." As I continued the process, further aspects of her current life came through.

1. Mary-Jean is very manipulative, especially towards men. She uses her children to obtain monies on which to live. Though she possesses many skills that could help her to obtain employment of various kinds, she prefers to obtain financial support by her devious use of her children for emotional blackmail. When she chooses to go out into the world, it is generally to have fun and enjoy herself, rather than attempting to obtain gainful employment.

2. Her younger sister, Mara, fabricates stories about you and relates these to Mary-Jean: that you are wealthy but refuse to help support her and her children; that you attempted to take her children away from her in order to obtain their child support money and prevent them from seeing her; and other untrue statements.

3. Mary-Jean is a very confused woman and has been so for much of her life. As the lies and derogatory statements about you are repeated, they gather force in her mind and begin to assume reality. This is delusional behavior and has no existence in fact.

4. It is better for her to remain in England surrounded by her own untrue, but believed, stories about her mother, and away from Mara, who would dominate her and lead her fur-

ther astray. If allowed, Mara would assume the role of paid child minder. When finances became tight and Mary-Jean could not pay Mara, violence would ensue between the two sisters, possibly of a severe nature.

5. Life has not been easy for Mary-Jean, but she chose this path prior to her current incarnation. As a child she was very defiant towards her mother and caused much sadness and strife. She too will be alienated from you at the evil hand of the third-born.

Nana'Eek-Chechowa

Haida Gwaii, BC, 2018

Mara, Last-born Daughter

I have been sleeping with the picture of your last, third-born, daughter, Mara, and the following information has been revealed: The original soul of your daughter was displaced by that of another entity, with her permission. The soul that came into her body during conception has departed and has now been reincarnated in another developing embryo. The current soul is a troubled one and has spent eons jumping into and out of numerous incarnations. When life becomes too demanding, this spirit departs and tries again.

Some event appears to have occurred between your sixth and seventh month of pregnancy, which is when the switch may have been made. Were you ill or over-stressed to the point of no return, as if your life force was leaving you?

1. The substitute soul is very mean, and masculine, and is outraged by the confinement of the womb.

2. In its fruitless reincarnations this soul has become an Earth-bound entity. Originally, this spirit was a wonderful and beautiful entity, but on passing over found that the revelation of its shortcomings, and the corrective lessons to be learned, were too hard a burden to bear, and, fearing this, chose to become Earth-bound to avoid such future encounters. From that point onward, it became increasingly vindictive.

3. Thus, in accumulated Earth-bound existences, the level of its negativity progressively increased and was not cleansed by passages over to the other side. This was a choice that the soul actively made.

4. The soul is a relative from Maddie's Jewish past, from many thousands of years ago, and experienced some form of detrimental confinement for an extended period of time, at the mercy of humans of evil intent, but eventually escaped.

5. This soul's last earthly incarnation was as a man who helped to deliver his own people into the German Gas Chambers during the war.

6. Mara will be this soul's last permitted incarnation, until its lessons are learned. It will no longer be allowed to continue fleeing its spiritual development, but will be placed, instead, in captive bondage until it is prepared to listen and learn from its mistakes. This will be a long and hard confinement.

7. Mara's initially displaced soul has now reincarnated as a boy, which is what she originally wished to be, and he is happy and content in his new life.

Nana'Eek-Chechowa
Haida Gwaii, BC, 2018

Episodic Memory
From Wikipedia, the free encyclopedia

Episodic memory is the memory of autobiographical events (times, places, associated emotions, and other contextual who, what, when, where, why knowledge) that can be explicitly stated or conjured. It is the collection of past personal experiences that occurred at a particular time and place. For example, if one remembers the party on his or her sixth birthday, this is an episodic memory. They allow an individual to figuratively travel back in time to remember the event that took place at that particular time and place.[1]

Semantic and episodic memory together make up the category of declarative memory, which is one of the two major divisions of memory – the other is implicit memory.[2] The term "episodic memory" was coined by Endel Tulving in 1972. He was referring to the distinction between knowing and remembering. Knowing is more factual (semantic) whereas remembering is a feeling that is located in the past (episodic).[3]

Tulving has seminally defined three key properties of episodic memory recollection. These are a subjective sense of time (or mental time travel), connection to the self, and autonoetic consciousness. Autonoetic consciousness refers to a special kind of consciousness that accompanies the act of remembering which enables an individual to be aware of the self in a subjective time. Aside from Tulving, others named the important aspects of recollection which includes visual imagery, narrative structure, retrieval of semantic information and the feelings of familiarity.[4]

Events that are recorded into episodic memory may trigger episodic learning, i.e., a change in behavior that occurs as a result of an event.[5][6] For example, a fear of dogs after being bitten by a dog is a result of episodic learning.

One of the main components of episodic memory is the process of recollection. Recollection is a process that elicits the retrieval of contextual information pertaining to a specific event or experience that has occurred.

ABOUT THE AUTHOR

Lucia Mann, humanitarian and activist, was born in British colonial South Africa in the wake of World War II. She now resides in British Columbia, Canada. After retiring from freelance journalism in 1998, she wrote a four-book African series to give voice to those who have suffered and are suffering brutalities and captivity. The other books in the series are: *Rented Silence*, CBC Book Award; *Africa's Unfinished Symphony*, Indie Excellence Award; *Veil of Blood Hangs over Africa* and *The Silician Veil of Shame*.

Visit www.LuciaMann.com and
www.ReportModernDaySlavery.org
for more information on how you can help
alleviate the scourge of modern-day slavery.

www.ingramcontent.com/pod-product-compliance
Lightning Source LLC
Chambersburg PA
CBHW030929260626
47169CB00002B/417